RUBY'S FIRE

Other books by Catherine Stine

Fireseed One
Dorianna
Refugees

Ruby's Fire
First edition copyright © 2013 by Catherine Stine
New edition © 2015

*For hybrids everywhere: black tulips, blue bunnies, plumcots and
pineberries, eco-friendly blended vehicles, the bionic-limbed and medically
implanted; the biracial and multiracial, pharma crops, chimeras, the
genetically enhanced and all manner of magnificent clones. The future is here!
Come celebrate it.*

Konjur Road Press NYC

Summary: Set on the future earth, seventeen year-old Ruby escapes
from a dangerous desert cult armed only with her handmade Oblivion
powder and her mute brother Thorn. She must negotiate a strange
boarding school, rampaging thugs and frightening physical changes that
threaten the core of her very identity.

Library of Congress Cataloguing-in-Publication Data:
[Fantasy—Fiction, Adventure—Fiction, Dystopian—Fiction,
Thriller—Fiction, Secrets—Fiction, Drugs—Fiction, Runaways—Fiction,
Future on Earth—Fiction, Biotech—Fiction, Hybrids—Fiction, Pharma
Crops—Fiction, Climate Change—Fiction, Cults—Fiction, Science
Fiction—Fiction]

Cover art Copyright © 2015 Najla Qamber
Chapter head and map illustrations Copyright ©2015 Catherine Stine
Black and white map shading by Taili Wu

Paperback: ISBN-13: 978-0-9848282-5-8
For questions about appearances and a free, downloadable study guide
go to: www.catherinestine.com

PRAISE FOR RUBY'S FIRE:

"With an astounding creativity and unique world-building, Catherine Stine creates a futuristic adventure that will keep you turning the pages."

—Books for YA!

"This captivating, heart pounding companion to Fireseed one will leave readers in awe. It's thrilling love story will capture a reader's mind in Catherine Stine's beautiful world."

—[YA] Between the Lines

"Ruby's Fire, returns to the sun-scorched earth of Fireseed One. In this long-awaited companion novel, Stine delivers a thrilling adventure led by a new and exciting cast of characters. Ruby, Armonk, Thorn and Blane are memorable, and the romance is really well handled. Favorite quote: " It feels wrong to lean on Armonk right now with Blane staring at me, a hungry, lonely look in his eye. It's as if he's never been hugged, never been fed, never been loved..."

—YAs the Word

"Gripping and addictive, Ruby has imagination packed into every page and scene. Unexpected and original."

—M. Pax, author of The Backworlds series

"Ruby's Fire unfolds layer by layer, like a Fireseed plant reaching out and calling you to figure out the mystery, mystery. What's revealed is even creepier than expected in a world already steeped in exotic technology and bioengineered strangeness. Great science fiction imaginatively told, this a wonderfully crafted story will make you think – and be glad for a cold drink of water ready at your fingertips.

— Susan Kaye Quinn, indie bestselling author of
The Mindjack Trilogy

"A heart-pounding tale of deception and danger set in a futuristic world teetering perilously between metamorphosis and destruction."

—Ciara Knight, author of Amazon bestsellers
Weighted and Escapement

"Action, emotion and incredible world building—Ruby's Fire will have you hooked from the very first page."

—Kelly Hashway, author of Touch of Death

***

AWARDS FOR RUBY'S FIRE AND
ITS COMPANION NOVEL FIRESEED ONE:

Ruby's Fire was a YA finalist in the Next Generation Indie Awards. Its companion novel Fireseed One was a YA and sci-fi finalist in the USA News International Book Awards. It also won an Indie Reader Approved notable seal.

RUBY'S FIRE
A FIRESEED NOVEL

CATHERINE STINE

KONJUR ROAD PRESS
NYC

1

I slide under the red-tinged leaves in the cave garden and wait. Try not to flinch as their warm, scalloped fronds brush my cheeks.

A streak of yellow flits across the edge of my vision, and is followed by a tiny fin. When I see the mottled tail my hand darts out and pinches it tight. The Dragon Lizard arches back and hisses at me. Its golden-ringed eyes glare fear and hatred.

"Save your venom, little one," I whisper as I throw a cloth bag over its head and gingerly pack in the rest of its tail.

Sliding back from under leaf cover, I try not to catch my hair on any Fireagar thorns. Instead, one snags the bag's drawstring. I curse as I unhitch it. This lizard's a fighter, flipping the bag left to right on my hip as I rise. "I'll take you back as soon as I extract your medicine. Promise."

A whoosh of scorched air catches me as I near the cave front. I slide my burn mask over my face and inch out into the searing air toward the compound. Today, it's hot as ever— a rousing 165 degrees, yet life is timidly returning. It's only been a few years since these Dragon Lizards peered out from the caves. "A sign from Fireseed that the desert is slowly coming alive again," pronounce the elders. Fireseed is the mythical red crop that Professor Teitur planted all those years ago to feed the desert folks. The flower with a five-pointed star, and a five-foot stalk. The flower we never found, except as a god in the sky.

Everything is a supposed sign from Fireseed.

For me, Dragons Lizards are for one thing—sleep.

I've learned how to squeeze the golden elixir from their cheeks and mix it with flakes from the sand caves. Leave it to dry and then pound it into powder. This Oblivion Powder is how I attack my sleepless nights and the waking nightmares that come—always the same. A dark man comes for me under the new moon, the same moon that will creep up the walls of the sky tonight.

I need to make extra strong powder and bring it along.

For someone's long, long sleep.

～

Tonight the moon is a blood orange that oozed over the horizon even before the setting sun. All day I dreaded its rise, because tonight is my initiation into the Founders' Ceremony.

Three girls every month.

I see the man who will lead me away with him from the Fireseed alter to our gazebo. He's the head of the Initiation committee. Stiles. He has a bristly beard and a back like a dried, curled up beetle. His eyes are sunken yet glinting out with an oily sheen as if he's peering into my private pool of emotions. He's hideously old—forty-one—a full twenty-four years older than me. I won't survive his spongy lips on mine, or his bony arms pinning me down.

But I didn't come unarmed.

The men tip their torches to the fire columns, and it explodes upward, crackling and popping from three giant pillars in the shape of Fireseed stalks. I sneak a peek at the two other girls down the row, friends of mine—tall, lovely Freeblossom who tirelessly reads to the young ones, and chubby, rosy Petal who always has a kind word. Like mine, their crimson cloaks have been freshly pressed. Under their hoods, their long hair has been freed of their braids and washed. Under their heat masks, their eyes are wild and fearful. I press three fingers of my good hand to my heart in a secret message of support. They do the same to me and then quickly look away.

The head of the ceremony clears his throat and speaks through the amplifiers set in his heat mask. "The Founders will take their maidens to their private gazebos now, while the chorus sings the Founding song. It is a sacred duty and gift that we bestow on our Fireseed God.

Not my Fireseed God. My god would shelter me, wrap me up in its winding, red branches and hide me from Stiles.

As if Stiles can sense my silent criticism, he lurches for my hand and grips with fingers that are cold paper and flint.

The group begins the song about the original planting day, and how Professor Teitur, the founding saint, planted the first crop to save the world. Never mind that we still don't have Fireseed. At least we have a hybrid to feed us—the red-tinged Fireagar sent from up north that now grows in our caves. My own pounding heart, and Stiles' low, husky voice drown out the rest of the song.

"Move along, sweet Ruby," he urges as he tugs me along the path freshly raked for us. I imagine drool sliding down his lower lip as he says it.

Since I was little, I've seen his sneaky side-glances at me as if he was picturing what I was wearing under my red tunic, even before my flat chest blossomed into buds. I shudder. Over the years, Stiles wasn't the only man to do that. I've often cursed my huge brown eyes and soft skin. Beauty's a liability. I've even tried to chop off my hair that flies around me like an electric halo and the frizz of curlicue bangs that float above my forehead. The elders gave me the third degree for cutting it.

"Our girls should take pride in their hair," Stiles said to me then. As though he already had dibs on my every breath. He did, sad to say. One of the powerful elders, he claimed me early, when I was a child. If only I could choose my own partner I might choose Sage, who I built sandcastles with and who teaches me math. He's too loud and always has a strong opinion but at least he's seventeen, my own age. I look over to where Sage is standing with the other seventeens, in the crowd pressed into a five-pronged star shape. Each prong stands for an oath: faith, family, fire-in-the-heart, fidelity and ferocity. Sage is talking to his friend, Dusty. They look over at me with a mixed expression of pride yet sadness—I'm not sure if they wish they were in Stiles' shoes, or it's more they feel bad for me. Either way, even Dusty would be a better partner than Stiles. He has a fetching smile and he's good with running games, which is how he got his nickname. He left everyone in the sandy dust when he ran.

I have no choice in the matter though. Not as long as I remain here. And where would I go in this vast desert? The elders always told us there is little but chaos and death outside of our compound. They swear that roaming nomads would eat me if they were hungry enough. That desert nomads have no god and live only by their thieving, bloodthirsty hands.

Besides, I could never leave my brother Thorn here. They used to think my brother was a saint, because his birth was auspicious. He was born two years to the day that the raging sandstorm blew in Professor Teitur's son, Varik. The elders at first thought Varik was the second coming, but when they realized that he was a false prophet who only wanted to escape, they decided to make my own infant brother a saint instead.

To mark the day.

They worshipped Thorn until he reached four and he still wasn't speaking. The elders scratched their heads at that, and called him slow. Two years later, they were beating him and searching the skies for the next saint that never came. Even yesterday, they gave him a fresh burn on his already-scarred forehead for being too slow at numbers.

They'd surely kill my brother if I left without him.

"Daydreamer, hurry up," Stiles grumbles as he tugs on my arm. I've heard stories of what happens to young women on Founder's day. I'd keep him waiting forever if it were up to me.

Reluctantly, I shadow him as we wind past the torches, to the dark sandy dunes behind the podiums, and further, into the warm desert blackness. To keep from shaking I focus on the steadying thrum of beetles, as they settle into their creviced hideaways for the night. My hand goes to the bulk on my hip, under my red cloak. I take a deep breath inside my steely mask.

"Want a little drink?" I ask, as I move close to Stiles. Pat my hip to show him I have a hidden treat. "To get you in a celebratory mood," I add, swallowing my repulsion at the idea.

"Oh?" His greedy eyes follow my hand down. "What is it?"

I giggle. "Only the best of my father's elixir for my... partner."

At the word partner he grins, raises his mask and licks his lips.

We are almost to our gazebo, shrouded by red heat fabric, to allow us privacy.

Privacy that I dread.

He pauses at the curtained doorway. "Show it to me," he says greedily.

With my good hand, I swill the liquid around. Before my father passed on, he brewed many bottles of hard liquor from beetles and sea-barley pellets he bought from a black marketeer trekking south. Called it the Cure. His secret recipe was burned along with his body. My mother saw to that; no elders would copy it. Since it's so rare, the liquor is still prized among them. My mother doles it out slowly, only on special days to stay in good graces with the leaders of the camp. Even so, she's not been able to loosen Stiles' claim on me for a precious carton.

I imagine the Oblivion Powder swimming in the Cure as I place my hand on Stile's chin and tip it up suggestively. To make sure he swallows it all.

"You clever tart." He sticks out his tongue, allowing the foul mix to slide so fast down his gullet that my job is made easy.

But not so easy after all! Once we're behind the curtains, he grabs my arms and pins them behind my back so swiftly I have no ability to fend him off. "I've waited so long for this," he murmurs and plants his lips on mine. They're every bit as horrid as I imagined them—like gluey, smelly dish sponges.

Fear seeps through me. Will the Oblivion mix work fast enough? Maybe I didn't put enough in to knock him out. Will it work at all? I clench my jaw to swallow a scream. Forcing a smile of devious warmth I whisper, "Let my arms free and I'll stroke your head."

He ignores my obvious ploy. Instead, he again presses his disgusting sponge lips to mine. A second shriek presses against my throat, and I break away from the kiss. "Not so fast," I coo. "Let's take some time."

Finally he eases his grip. My arms throb. I'm sure there are bruises wherever his palms have dug in. Why isn't he sleeping? I gave him five times the dose I give myself when I need Oblivion. Stiles lowers me toward the mattress and one of his hands goes to untie the red curtain. It billows down around us, to the rhythm of the wind. I tense up, every muscle flexed to run. The powder's not working!

But wait, Stiles sways on his knees as he turns. I attempt to sit up, but he flops down on me before I can. His weight is stifling. He fumbles with the ties on my cloak.

Reaching for his hands to stop him, I say, "Slowly please, I'm new at this, teach me slowly." I *am* new to this, but the last thing I want is for him to be my teacher.

"Oh, Ruby, I've waited, and waited and I'm very impatient." At this, he tears open my cloak and puts his paws on my breasts.

It's not working fast enough. I have to get away from him some other way, but how? My breath seizes. The air is too thin. I wriggle out from under him.

His dark stare is furious. His mouth is open and pursed in a way that looks like he's going to spit on me. "How dare you—" His eyelids flicker open, closed, and then his body slops over to the edge of the gazebo. Catching himself just before he falls off, he rolls back toward me at frightening speed. I swerve away. "You coldhearted bitch, you… tricked…" His eyes orbit up to their whites, and his head sags like a limp plant stalk. Frothy phlegm bubbles out of his mouth.

It worked! Holy fire, but for how long? I bolt to my feet. Peek out of the curtains, and cringe when I hear the high whimpers of my two unlucky friends. I wish I could save them too. But that would be an impossible task.

At least for now.

Tiptoeing out, I see the old Founders, even older than Stiles, the ones who can no longer be active participants. They are sitting in a row by the burning stage pyres, and closer to me, are the guards, each armed with a spear, whose handle is a carved Fireseed flower.

I decide that the only way out is to slither on the sand like a Dragon Lizard, use no light at all. My cloak makes a dragging sound, so I ditch it. All I have under it is my under-cami so the sand immediately scrapes and sears my flesh. Even at night, it holds in heat. It's worth any amount of blisters to get away from here.

Back in the compound, I streak to my room and throw on a spare cloak. I toss my stash of Dragon Powder in my hip purse, a few bars of beetle loaf that I've been hoarding and some Cure Mead. A change of clothing too. Then I sneak to my brother's room, on the boy's wing, off limits to us girls. Luckily, the lazy night watchman is asleep, his head cranked to one side, eyeglasses dangling from his nose.

I was a child on the night that Professor Teitur's son, Varik showed up, and talked the Founders out of seeing him as the Second Coming of Fireseed. But I'll never forget the look on his face as he glanced over at me, and how his eyes moved over my three missing fingers as I waved. He looked pained, surely at wondering how I lost those fingers and at seeing how thin I was, how thin we all were. In contrast he filled out the space.

I wanted to tell him how I lost those fingers, but I was too loyal then to talk. It's a strange world, with few answers. Maybe one day, I'll figure out the why and where of things.

That night, ten years ago, when Varik took off, with his

beautiful redheaded mistress, Marisa by his side, I was relieved for them. That's why I waved. They brought me hope. Hope that Varik, and maybe his mistress from the north would tell people the story of the starving people down in the desert, and bring us help. Before then, and after, the elders taught us that people everywhere are mad heathens, who want to kill us, eat us for food. What am I to believe?

Varik called us a cult. He told Stiles this when he came that night and argued with him. I was small, but I'll never forget it. Is that what we are?

So, two years later the elders crowned my newborn brother as the Second Coming, a sign that Fireseed had listened to us on that terrible night of destruction, when our compound was torn apart in the sandstorm like a child's pile of twigs.

Thorn talks to no one. I understand him though. Once in a while he'll say a word, but only to me. His eyes tell me entire sentences. His shudders convey fearful omens. I know he senses things, future things. He's my weathervane.

"Thorn, we need to leave," I whisper now in his ear as I gently shake him.

He stirs, scratches his head, and then looks at me, wide-eyed. His brown eyes scan my face, and then he's up, fumbling for the dragon toy I made him from petrified sand. No crying, no one-word questions, as if he knows how unspeakable this really is—a choice between being devoured by Stiles or having our flesh eaten by nomads in the desert.

In my imagination I've planned for this moment dozens of times. Run to the back exit, where the workers bury the trash. Where it reeks so no late nighters would want to hang around, sipping hard mead. We dare not take a light, but the full moon's burgundy glow is some help. We streak to the line of gliders that the men take to the runners' depot, where they pick up the monthly supply of food from up north. Our gliders' engines are solar powered, engines sent from the north years ago. It's not often that we get new parts, so mostly our boys from eighteen section patch the vehicles with abandoned machine parts to keep them running.

Thorn keeps up with me. He's still sleepy but he almost looks eager. This makes me less guilty, and more hopeful that we'll get out before Stiles wakes.

But the line of gliders is gone. What was I thinking? Of course, the men have flown them all to the Founders' ceremony! And the celebration runs all night and into the dawn. Dread crashes through me. I look down at Thorn. "They're gone. We've just got to run." I take off into the desert, with Thorn at my side. This is crazy. We'll never survive. Thorn must know that. He tugs on my arm to stop.

His eyes throw off a dim, hopeful light. He nods his round face back from where we came from.

"Thorn, we already looked. There's nothing back there."

He nods again, more decisively toward the side of the compound.

I take his hand, and we pad back with caution, my every nerve pricked for footsteps that don't belong to us. Once back at the building, I still see nothing—no gliders, and not even a trash wagon with clumsy wheels. "Thorn, come on. Please talk!" Sometimes I wish he would speak to me—even a hushed whisper would do.

But all of his words have been beaten and burned out of him. I know this.

He scrambles around the corner of the building and disappears. I imagine Stiles there. To come back here was a bad mistake. When I follow, though, I see Thorn's genius. There's one battered glider that someone junked here. Its treads are bent in, and it's missing its right handlebar but my good hand's the left one so as long as the things runs...

I hop on and reach for the key. Nowhere. "Thorn, there's—"

He's scrambling around by another dirty refuse pile edged up against the compound. He leans over a crooked sign that we used in one of the classrooms to hang cloaks on. It has nails on it. Whirling around, he holds a key up triumphantly.

I wave him over. "Hurry! Get on."

Sweeping him up, I warn him to hold tight as I fire up the glider. It's making rumbling, farting noises, which I fear will wake the guard. But in fits and starts it rises a few inches and begins to glide unsteadily over the sand. I steer it south, the opposite direction of the Founding Ceremony. We'll cut a wide swath around, even if it takes us out of the way.

Thorn's hands press into my sides as we pick up speed. His touch fills me with relief. He's the one person I truly love on this earth aside from my mother. Oh, I wish I could take her; she'll worry so much. I'll try to send word soon. I also love my father, who graduated to the sky.

And the Fireseed God.

I disagree with how the leaders worship Fireseed, but that doesn't mean I don't believe. I whisper a prayer to its invisible five pointed red petals as I gaze into its home in the sky. "Help speed us away. Guide us to a safer place."

The Fireseed God only grants part of my prayer. The feeble glider makes it fifty miles to a building labeled Depot. And then, just after we escape its smoky chamber, in a firework of explosions, it dies one last death.

2

Dread courses through my veins. The proprietor is jogging toward us at an awkward, gamboling clip. Must've heard the loud death rattle of the glider. A grizzled man with leathery skin, he also has a pendulous belly—from eating the arms of unlucky nomads? I gulp. Thorn and I are perfect fodder for his night kitchen. Plus, it occurs to me that he'll naturally tell the founders where we are. Why wouldn't he? Why didn't I think of this before? He depends on them to pay for our Fireagar and clothing. He needs to remain on good terms. I consider running.

Thorn grips my cloak. Now he's tugging on it. A warning? Too late! The man is only twenty paces away, and growing closer by the second.

"Who goes there?" he bellows, cupping his eyes with his hand, as if that will help him see us more clearly under the bleeding moon.

I know what I must do—perform in a similar way as I did with Stiles. My theatrical, seductive charm is the only tool I know against these men. I shudder. "Wait here, Thorn."

Thorn doesn't obey, but comes scrambling after me, still clutching my cloak. So be it. He'll have to witness my shameful acts.

I saunter over to the man, seeing up close that he's at least a tiny bit younger than Stiles. But still, his face is a craterland of pocks and burn marks from working in the sun. A scarf around his neck must've been white once, but now, is smeared with brown sweat streaks.

"What brings you out?" He studies me, and then my small brother. A knife gleams from his side holster. I'm sure he has to deal with all kinds of shady folk coming to rob him—or eat him—under the shroud of night.

Raising my mask, I force my mouth into an alluring grin. "I came out for air and—"

"Air out here, eh? It's bad tonight—dangerous carbon dioxide reading. You like breathing fumes?"

I swallow my disgust and add, "That and … some fun."

"Fun, ha!" The man grins back. So, I've amused him. Good. "Aren't you cult people all supposed to be at your Founding Ceremony tonight?"

Cult, that word again. For a second, this catches me off-guard. He's not a member of our Fireseed group, so how would he know what night the ceremony is? But I can't look unnerved. I widen my smile. "It ended a little early." I wink. "Men, you know." With this I let out a girlish giggle. As if I know all about men and what they do.

I can improvise, if they're anything like Stiles.

"Missy, you look pretty sweet yourself," the depot man says. "You sure you weren't in that ceremony—one of them *special full moon* girls?"

I shudder. Too accurate a guess for comfort. Thorn is hanging behind me, using my cloak as cover. I need to get out of here. Fast, and I need my brother to go too.

"If you give us a lift," I start, "I'll give you something too."

"Oh?" His eyes move over me the way Stiles' did, clearly taking in everything he can see and imagining the rest. "Well, now," he says, "where would you want to go on a night like this?"

My mind is foggy from fear. I warn myself to think fast. Returning is not an option. "How about taking me and my brother west?" I suggest.

"*Where* west, Missy?"

"Anywhere west, the further, the better."

"You don't care where? What kind of crazy is that?" he asks. "There's nothing much from here to hell except for miles of Skull's Wrath Desert. What say we take a short spin to uh, get acquainted and… leave your brother right here? I'll feed him a real nice treat. Depot Man has the goods." He chuckles. "Meat? Sugared Fireagar? Kids like treats, right kid?"

My mouth is watering at the mention of food, and probably Thorn's too. But Thorn's mask is down and he's scowling at the guy. He knows better. I give Thorn a warning look to keep his feelings buttoned up and raise the mask. We walk to the depot where I see shelves and shelves of goods. The guy must be fat from skimming the food allotments.

I can play a hard bargain. I'm used to smiling and flirting with the elders to get extra helpings of cake or avoid a lecture when I score a C on a test. I'm also used to swerving around a groping hand. I touch Depot Man's plump arm. "I like adventures. Skull's Wrath sounds exciting! Why not take my brother along? Feed him in your vehicle. He's quiet. He won't, um... interfere." These words have their price. I'll need an extra dose of Oblivion Powder tonight to drown out a new set of repulsive memories.

"Okay, Missy, okay. But I don't know how far I can carry you. I can only leave the depot for so long before—"

"Take us to the next settlement?" I have no idea where the next one is, or even if there *is* one down here at all.

He doesn't answer, but hurries to shut the depot's heavy corrugated screens and lock them with padlocks. Then he loads us in. Larger than our glider, this one is crafted from old plane parts and other machine bits I can't identify. It's messy inside, with food wrappers and a jumble of wrinkled, grease-dotted clothes. All I care about now is that it has wings and flies.

Thorn settles into the backseat with a generous hunk of something that actually looks and smells like meat. I've only had meat a couple of times this year, and my stomach screams for it. Thorn hands me a chunk of it between the two seats.

Chewing deliriously, I gaze out in wonder at the sights— tall stone formations and cracked earth, dunes that rise and fall the way I imagine ocean waves must. I saw a photograph once. That's how it looked but blue, the bluest ever. I wonder if there still is an ocean, and if so, if it's still as blue. I wonder if I'll ever find out. It would be such a beautiful living dream.

The man sets the dials to autopilot, and leans over to me. I need to honor my side of the deal, while stalling as much as I can. I allow him a light peck on my cheek. He does this softly and with more respect than old Stiles. But when his hands reach for the front of my cloak, I clear my throat loudly, and swerve away. "Not so fast," I mirror from earlier, with Stiles. "We have time to... enjoy."

My toes curl in their boots as we pass over skeleton-shaped formations of Skull's Wrath desert. Under the full moon, and even with Depot Man's glider lights, I can only see the eerie caps of the skulls glowing red.

He shifts over toward me, his big belly grazing the steering wheel. Beyond his shoulder, I see a sign of a life on the ground. Hope bubbles up cautiously.

Outlines of a large, rundown compound flicker in the burgundy shadows and a smattering of vehicles parked at all angles, next to uneven sections of a pliable, sagging roof.

"Let's land now, please," I beg.

"But we haven't even started," he protests. His hand moves to the fold in my cloak.

"Let's explore outside!" I bray, "There's a settlement there. Can't you see it?"

"That place? Some crazy ex-cult lady runs that."

"A member of my… Fireseed group?" I venture.

"No, the ZWC—Zone Warrior Collective. They did a bunch of breaks across the northern border. The head of it was the one who killed Professor Teitur."

"What?" *The* professor Teitur? Varik's father? The original Founder who planted the first crop in the desert? "The man we worship and pray to bring us back our Fireseed, down from the sky, to feed our people? That one?"

"Lady, you're even nuttier than the woman I'm talking about. What is it with you cult people?"

"I don't even know what a cult is!" I explode.

He looks at me sideways. "It's a bunch of crazies who make up a fairy tale and get a loony guru to lead them and keep the fairytale going. Especially you Fireseed people who worship a flipping flower."

I gape at him. The creep takes advantage by clamping his bumpy lips on mine. I try to wriggle away but he weighs a ton.

From the corner of my eye, I see my brother's arm thrust forward, dragon toy in hand. He stabs the man in the neck with its pointy tail. I release a yelp of shocked laughter.

"You sunnofa…" Depot man rubs the wound, but then grabs me, smearing his blood on my cloak.

I yank back my head and fake a gag. "Let me out or I'll be sick all over you. I'm serious, please let me—" I don't even have to fake it this time, because this whole experience on top of Stiles is truly nauseating.

"You freak, why'd I let you talk me into this?"

When I gag again the guy makes a sudden, lurching landing that makes me temporarily forget my heaving stomach.

He opens the door. I stumble out just in time and retch onto the sand. It could be that meat. God knows what that actually was—month-old boar from Restavik? My brother follows and slams the door behind him.

The guy hovers for a few terrifying minutes, probably weighing his options. There's no way we can outrun his glider and if he decides to come get us, he'll be much less friendly this time. He swerves down. "Get in!" he yells. "You can't stay here in this desert."

"I told you, I'm sick. And I need to visit this settlement, I need to talk to these folks."

An out-and-out lie.

He looks doubtful, and I realize that he's not all bad after all, worried about leaving us here. "Suit yourself," he mutters and slams the door. Finally, his glider begins to whir and he's off, dumping his troublesome cargo.

I wipe my mouth, and peer through the murky darkness ahead. Thorn is already running ahead. I clamber after him.

3

The compound is ramshackle but any shelter is better than none. Hurrying toward it, I see a clutter of melded structures, some side-by-side, and some built atop each other, like a child's crude sandcastles. The compound itself is smaller than ours at home, but there's a huge, oblong tent-like extension on the front about four times the length of the complex. Flags flutter in the dark, attached to the top of what I see now is a series of clumsily attached tarps. We're walking toward it, but I can't see what's under this makeshift tent. Could it be something the people here want to protect? Or hide? Like cannibal's cauldrons?

I've caught up to Thorn and taken his hand. We move closer with caution. I figure the desert folk don't get many unannounced visitors. They're surely armed. I only hope they've been fed. If I think about it any more I will die from fear, so I turn off my mind as best I can.

From about fifteen feet away, I see a rip in the side tarp that hangs down. We pull it open and peer into the dim space. "Looks like a field of plants in there," I mutter to Thorn. "I thought plants only survived in sand caves," I add. Anything else would perish under this heat. Thorn and I exchange glances. His eyes, even in this murky light, burn with something indefinable.

Already, he's sliding under the tarp. Following him I reach over to a plant beyond the inner, more formidable barbed wire barricade and rub a leaf between my fingers. It's Fireagar, a whole crop of wrinkly green leaves branching into ruddy rust. Before I can stop him, Thorn has bent up a section of barbed wire with his boot and wriggled under that too.

I lie on my back and shimmy under that same section. I try not to catch my red cloak on one of its many barbed hooks, but I nick the fabric more than once.

Thorn starts to run into the thicket leading to the compound. Losing sight of him, I panic. Depot Man described these folks out here as violent. The desert seems to bring out the scary in people. "Stop! It's not safe," I yell. Thorn must hear me yet he keeps going. Does he see something I don't?

"Thorn!" I yell. "Where are you?" The Fireagar's bunchy leaves crunch underfoot as I run, straining my eyes through the leaves for a blur of movement. I hate to crush them, but I need to find Thorn. In a couple of minutes I reach a line of sandy dirt where the Fireagar ends. It's too murky to see much, so I fire up one of the precious mini-torches I brought. Hopefully, it'll last an hour or so. Under its glow, I see narrow tubing set along the line—an embedded water system? Pretty fancy, if so.

Beyond that, I see impossibilities.

Aiming the flickering light on a taller crop beyond the line, I study a field of red plants as tall as me, and tightly packed. Topped by star-shaped flowers, their branches wind down gracefully the same way they do on our compound's sandstone statues at home. Fireseed? This must be a poison mirage. That's it. Depot Man told me that tonight's air is especially toxic. My brain is feasting on carbon dioxide and other poison vapors. My heart stuttering, I shine the torch on another section.

Wonders! It's all still there, and ten paces ahead Thorn is on his knees, bowing to one of the plants.

"Fireseed! The gods are alive, Thorn," I exclaim. He looks up just for a moment and grins. Or are we already up in the clouds with the Fireseed? "Are we dead?" I whisper under my breath so Thorn can't hear. Did we crash in that glider? I touch my arms and reach out for the firm red stalk in front of me. The stalk and my arms are solid, not spirit.

Dropping to my knees near my brother, I hug the plant's trunk and place my forehead on it. Cool to the touch, how is that possible in this desert heat? Swaying to an unseen wind, it arches down and brushes me with its tendrils, reaching for my shoulder almost in a gesture of affection, like my mother used to do when I was little. My mother, she would wonder over what I see here.

"You're here, starflower," I murmur, overcome with hot tears that spill onto the sand. "How can I serve you? Will you protect us from hungry nomads?" I glance to my left, at Thorn, who's rocking back and forth, head to the roots.

Something moves in the corner of my right eye. I angle the torch up. This desert is eerie, especially under this crackled, sagging tarp that slumps down like an old lizard's belly.

A rustle. Startling up, I squint into the jungle of red, and search for a repeat movement. Another sound of brushing against leaves, again to my upper right. Every nerve in me alerts. Is a Dragon Lizard skittering along the branches of a Fireseed plant? No, it sounds like something bigger, from about four feet up. I'm sure of it. I sniff the air. Only the heat of the sand and the mineral-sweet liqueur of veined leaves fill me.

Thorn isn't visibly upset. He glanced up once, with mild curiosity, only to return to his rocking. My muscles relax as I lower my own head again to the pliable roots. If those sounds signaled something dangerous, Thorn would've known. He senses things my eyes can't see.

Hard crunches explode by my right ear—a wild beast charging? I snap upright. And see it. A large human in an iguana skin suit with an arrow pointed straight at my heart.

"Hey!" I cry. No!"

The owner of the arrow steps forward. He grazes the sharp tip against my forehead above my molded burn mask. The guy's dark eyes blaze out at me from his own mask. The little I see of his exposed skin is bronze and his long black hair gleams even under this dank tarp. Despite his fierce gaze, he doesn't shoot the arrow. "Lift your mask," he orders.

Thorn is up and clutching at my cloak. Am I this man's dinner now, my brother his dessert? Why didn't Thorn give me a sign earlier? My heart pounds through my ribs.

When the man sees my face and my electric haze of hair, his eyes soften. That spark of wonder that men get whenever they gaze at me is in his eyes. That spark I almost always hate.

Somehow with this stranger, it fills me with unexpected lightening. "You're from that desert cult," he remarks, as if he knows everything about anything.

"How do you know?" The lightening fades.

He says, "Those flower brands on your wrists. There's talk about your people, down in Chihuahua. How you think the flower is god, think it lives in the sky."

"It does."

"Does the flower god sit on a throne like a king?" Laughter escapes him.

"Fireseed *is* god. And god is right here. Fireseed saved us." I give the red plant beside me a loving stroke.

Thorn frowns at the guy and aims his toy dragon tail out like a sword.

"That's Fireseed?" The bronzed guy's eyes widen as he examines it—its winding red branches that sway, its artful sprinkle of thorns, its curving tendrils that look like dancing cacti. He lowers his bow, slides the arrow back in its quiver and loops the bow over one shoulder.

Thorn, wordless as always, packs his toy away in his latch bag.

"Why don't you take off *your* mask?" I ask.

The young man shrugs and pulls down the mask to rest it on his neck. A brand marks each high cheekbone with a leaf. A matching leaf earring dangles from one ear. Twine around his neck has a shiny, curlicue gem on it. His face is deeply tanned, chiseled, with a faraway glint in his eyes. I see now that he's not a man, but a boy about my age. He's dressed in the strangest clothes, a suit resembling lizard skin that clings to every muscle and slope. I try not to gape but it's hard not to. The guys at home wear loose capes that hide these things. My sly gaze follows his slim hips that arc up to broad shoulders. He's perfectly built except for one odd-shaped leg. Wait… where that flesh and blood leg would be, his is molded from a smooth, cream-colored substance. It's thin at the ankle and then swells out, mimicking the natural curve of his other calf. The device is badly bowed and nicked, as if it's seen better days.

Like most things here in the desert.

When the boy sees me studying his leg, his dark brows knit. He tilts his head down and his long bangs shroud his eyes.

"I'm Ruby," I tell him, "and this is my brother, Thorn. Do you live here?"

"No. I'm from Black Hills Sector, up north. I'm Armonk."

Most people I know are named after desert things, like Sage, or aspects of Fireseed, like Freeblossom, Crimson and Thorn. Armonk's an odd name but I don't say so. "What brought you to Skull's Wrath?"

"Private business."

"Here? At this compound?" I ask.

"It's The Greening."

Now it's my turn to laugh. "The Greening? I see *red* Fireseed plants and a *sand*-colored compound. Not a smidgen of green! The guy at the depot said a crazy lady lives here, says she belonged to a bizarre group of killers."

"You have no right to talk about bizarre," Armonk snaps. And then, as if he knows he's veered too far into mean, he continues in a milder tone. "The lady's an old friend of my mother's."

"Oh." She couldn't be evil then, could she? "Well, then, I'm going to see her too."

"Suit yourself." He gives me a hard glance as if I'm the eccentric one for changing, rapid-fire, from one extreme position to another. "Need a hand?" Offering his, in a surprising gesture that gives me gooseflesh, he helps me up, while my brother scrambles up on his own, an odd calm still etched on his face.

We weave our way through the Fireseed field. Every leaf that brushes my face is a caress and every thorn prick is a pleasant nudge. My god is here on earth!

Armonk looks down at Thorn. "You're awfully quiet, what do you think of this?"

Thorn only stares back at him.

"He doesn't really talk," I explain.

"Why is that?" Armonk addresses his question to Thorn.

"No reason," I answer for him. How can I explain when *I* don't totally know?

We're almost to the front porch of the compound, where the tarp is seamlessly attached to its roof when we hear a war whoop and a loud crashing of branches.

I yell, "Who's stomping on Fireseed? Stop it now!" I'm bold with the miracle of being surrounded by the star-faced beauties; also, from the way Armonk is looking at me, and his quiver full of sharp arrows.

His mask is back on but I can tell by his quaking shoulders that he's laughing. "Brazen one," he says.

His laughter stops when we come face-to face with three burly guys who tower over even Armonk. They're wielding clubs. For a third time tonight, my heart is up in my throat. Will they club us and boil us for stew? Could everything Armonk said about his mother knowing the owner of this place be a lie? He certainly doesn't know these guys. This may have been a huge, huge mistake, but it's way too late to turn back now.

4

G et off our property," the biggest one snarls. I can't see his face under his burn mask but his shoulders are massive.

Thorn hides behind me.

"Why are you trespassing?" says the guy's sidekick, whose orange hair explodes over his mask like a lit pyre. His voice is a higher, more tentative. These guys are huge but judging by their voices, they may only be a couple of years older than me. Hard to tell under their suits.

Armonk steps forward and past them, onto the tarp-covered porch. "I'm here to see Nevada Pilgrim."

A moment of surprised silence hangs in the air as the three guys pause to consider this. I guess they weren't expecting Armonk to know the proprietress' name.

The biggest guy's mouth settles into in a sneer as he hops onto the porch and swings around to face Armonk. His burn suit is stretched tightly over his meaty torso and his square jaw underscores unfriendly hazel eyes set far apart. He sways his club in front of him. "No further. What do you need to see Ms. Pilgrim about?"

"I don't have to answer any questions," Armonk hisses.

"She's not expecting visitors. You answer to me."

Armonk starts walking toward the inside door.

"Hold it right there!" orders a third guy, tall and wearing a nose ring, the same green burn suit, with his blond hair cut short. Armonk continues walking.

To which the meaty guy smacks Armonk hard on the shoulder with the club. Armonk flinches though he manages another step. The guy whacks him harder this time, on the back.

"Stop that, you creep!" I yell, to which the blond, nose-ringed guy clamps a wide hand over my mouth and holds me there.

Armonk draws an arrow so fast I don't see it coming from the quiver. He aims for the guy's veined neck. The arrow tip pulses in mid-air to his heartbeat. "Let me pass," he says slowly, determined.

The phalanx of guys lets him by, but Armonk only gets four more steps toward the front door before the brute with the club jumps on him, tearing the bow and arrow from Armonk's hands and hurling it to the ground. Then he proceeds to box Armonk's head like it's a flimsy practice dummy. The red-haired guy is the only one who doesn't participate. He has a pained look on his face, as he watches blood spray from Armonk's nose. Even so, this guy is body-blocking Armonk's entrance to the compound.

I wriggle free of the tall cretin and yell, "What is wrong with you people?" I'm ready to jump in the fray, but the font door opens and a woman bursts past the guy who's playing blockade. She has wispy hair the color of morning sun. It's tinged with green ends and she has the same leaf patterns on her cheeks as Armonk. Are they from the same tribe or what?

"Blane, stop right now!" she commands. She's older than us, but not by a whole lot—maybe twenty-seven? Her safari style pants and shirt are all made from the same honeycombed iguana cloth as Armonk's suit. Do they get it from the same fabricator? From her high-cuffed boots to the flimsy scarf around her neck, she's coated in fine dust.

Blane, the overgrown bully, sneaks one more punch to Armonk's already bloodied face. Armonk careens backwards. Behind me, Thorn clutches my cloak even harder. Poor kid, he's terrified.

"They trespassed," Blane claims. "They refuse to say what their business is."

"Liar!" Armonk lowers his mask, leans over the porch edge and spits blood into the sand.

Nevada—I guess that's who this is—helps Armonk to his feet, because his leg prosthetic has slipped and is hanging sideways. I see now, it's way too short for him, and he's tried to compensate by gluing a mismatched extension to the top of the leg.

He straightens it and clamps it back on as if he's used to doing this. I feel so badly for him, even though he's a stranger. Even though he had an arrow aimed at my face not even fifteen minutes ago.

The woman stares at Armonk with curious green eyes. "Do I know you?"

"I'm Armonk, from Black Hills Sector," he rasps. His

tongue makes bulges in his cheek as it works inside his mouth, probably exploring for cuts.

"Armonk, from Black Hills Sector," mimics one of the overgrown louts behind Nevada. She whirls around.

"Another word from any of you and it'll be three times the chores." That does the trick. Impressive, a woman calling the shots even though these guys tower over her! This would never happen back at our compound where the women obey the men, or else. Nevada's attention turns back to Armonk. "*Who* are you again?"

"Rain's son," he says simply, as if that's enough.

Nevada lets out a cry. She rushes forward and hugs Armonk. His blood smears onto her chameleon-fabric shirt but she either doesn't notice or doesn't care. She holds him out at arm's length to look at him again, this time grinning. "Rain's son, wow. You've grown into a handsome man."

At this, Blane and the redheaded guy exchange smirks. If Nevada notices she chooses to ignore it. "How's your mama these days?" she asks.

"Worn out." Armonk nods wearily at the image in his head. "The sector, it's not so good. The trial gardens didn't really take. Could be all of the rock, or the iron in the soil, or…" He trails off.

"Sorry to hear that." Nevada says in sympathy. "What brings you down our way? It's not as if we have a superhighway to Skull's Wrath. Must've taken you weeks to get here or… did you catch a ride? I hope you did!" Nevada giggles like a girl. She's hard to get a grasp on. One moment she's a sympathetic mom type, the next, she's waifish, fashioned from mere air and dust.

"I got a ride, part way and then…" Armonk lowers his head and his black bangs fall over his eyes. "I've heard that Dr. Varik is headed here." At this, Nevada draws a sharp breath. "I've heard he's a doctor now, and wants to help people down around here." Armonk lifts his head and stares at Nevada. "Have you heard any news?"

"I hear things here and there." This answer seems cagey, and when I look at Thorn, he's studying her the way he does when he's trying to eke out a lie. "What do you need with Varik?" she asks Armonk. "Are you sick?"

Armonk taps on his fake leg. "This was amazing so many years ago when Dr. Varik sent it after his trip our way. He made it himself." Armonk's voice lowers. "But now, it's battered, too small."

Nevada lays a gentle hand on Armonk's shoulder. "You must stay."

"How soon did they say he'd be coming?" Armonk asks. "I heard he was building a facility. Has construction begun? I was going to wait just until I saw him and—"

"Nonsense, stay as long as you want. Study here."

"Wait a minute!" Blane bursts out.

What about me? My brother? Nevada hasn't even noticed us. Would I want to stay, if we even could? These boys frighten me, but something about Nevada is drawing me in. A school, a chance to learn! For Thorn too; maybe she could teach him how to really talk. I step up. "Do you think we can *all* stay? For a while?"

"Oh!" Nevada looks at me startled, as if she hasn't ever seen me in the background all of this time with my brother. "Do you have family? Your brother is so young."

"My brother's eight," I tell her. "He's quite smart." Behind me, I hear titters of barely suppressed laughter, but I don't care. He's surely smarter than all of them, if you count his inner sight.

"Eight." She nods vaguely. "That would be third grade. I run a high school. Do you have family near here? Did you say?"

"Nowhere near here," I lie.

"As for me," Armonk says, "I'm not planning to stay. I need to get back. This is a school for, um, stranded kids and I have my mother back at home." Is he rubbing in the fact that Blane, Radius and the others are all alone, or is he trying to be fair and acknowledge their more legitimate claim to the shelter of The Greening?

"Yeah, you already have a home," pipes up the redheaded boy. "You must too, flyaway girl. Where's yours? He stares at my frizzled, honey-hued hair with his steely blue eyes.

"Radius, I wasn't discussing this with you," Nevada warns.

I need to fight for this. We can't exactly go back now, and on the way here we saw no other compounds. "I'm Ruby and this is Thorn," I say as I fold my brother in close.

Unease shadows Nevada's elfin face. "Well, Armonk, Ruby, Thorn, you're—"

"Don't bother applying. It's a complicated process," says the tall, nose-ringed guy as he lopes over. You have to be good at science, or something." The heat of a new intense energy drips off him like oil as his eyes linger on my hair, and travel slowly down to my chest. I shudder. Does that mean favors like Stiles would have demanded back at home? Where are all the girls? Is this an all-boys school?

Nevada gives him a threatening look. "Jan, back off, that's up to me—"

"What he's saying is that you have to qualify," Blane pipes up from where he stands. "You have to bring something to the equation."

"What does he mean?" I ask Nevada.

Blane answers for her. "You have to take an academic test—test in. You also have to offer a payment. I had two fat stacks of old hundred dollar bills, from before the Border Wars," he says proudly.

"And I had these clubs from a museum." Jan thwacks one against his calloused palm.

"I had four cartons of dried food. I hauled that stuff hundreds of miles over frying sand dunes," Radius brags.

I think about my Oblivion powder. It's worth a lot. But I could never part with it. I need it too badly.

Armonk collects his bow and quiver. He dusts them off. "I'm an expert marksman. Not that I'm staying… just until Dr. Varik—"

"What's there to hunt in the desert?" Jan sniggers. 'There aren't even any dried up lizards to eat."

Wrong, I'm thinking. There must be Dragon Lizards here too, hiding in the sand caves. Maybe even one or two out in the elements, among the Fireseed, the Fireagar. I'm thinking that if Jan isn't more careful with his caveman clubs, Armonk can hunt him and hang him up by his stupid nose-ring. My ruthless dreaming makes me grin. Thorn senses my amusement; he must because his own sudden grin is as glorious as a new moon.

"Shush! All of you. I run this place. I'll make the final decision." With that proclamation Nevada ushers us inside.

Blane, Jan and Radius shove their way past. Nevada might run this place, but she hasn't taught her students any manners. If this is a school, I'm still not sure what kind. At least we're inside, out of the heat.

Everyone scrambles out of masks and burn suits. I face away from the group and take mine off slowly, cautiously. I know what happens when people see my face, my body. I'm even slower taking off my cloak. As I do, my back crawls with the squirrely feeling of eyes on it. I'm wearing a long skirt and jersey top, old but in nice blue colors. Blue's my favorite color, like the sea I dream of seeing someday. Finally I gather the nerve to turn around.

Blane openly stares, as does Jan. Blane mumbles something to Jan like "Holy Fire, that girl has curves." Jan chuckles as he takes off his boots and throws them under a long bench. Radius, the redheaded boy takes a long, furtive look before shuffling off to sit. Armonk looks at me, and then away, in a distant, distracted manner that confuses me because I seem to have no effect on him.

Blane might be ugly inside, but outside he's handsome—they all are, really. The guys at this school have that look of being well fed and well bred, like in that ancient college brochure from before the Border Wars my dad had. In one of those photos, a group of athletes were sweating and laughing, dressed in shorts and shirts that revealed firm arm and leg muscles. Imagine! If you showed that much skin now, you'd be crisped out in the desert. Under their burn suits these guys have on pants and shirts from that strange iguana skin, yet much more worn and faded than the fancy outerwear. Maybe this place isn't so grand after all.

I catch myself staring back at Blane. His head and torso seem designed by a great sculptor who wanted to create that perfect threatening persona. His brow is hard, and his mouth is set in a permanent frown, but his hazel eyes are golden flecked and his cheeks have a light sprinkle of honey freckles. He catches me staring and there's a momentary grin in his eyes before he spins around to talk to Radius. Radius is the shortest, but not by much. He's slim, but solid, seemingly carved out of pink gypsum. What do these guys eat, Gila monsters? I doubt Nevada can keep her larders stocked with them around. In their fortunate youths, were they fed so generously that they ate enough to last a whole lifetime? This has me weirdly jealous, but I have more important things to dwell on.

I look away, and attend to my brother, in faded, patched pants. He's gripping his toy dragon as if it's the one solid thing in a desert of mirages. "Thorn, are you okay?" I whisper, not expecting him to answer, especially in front of these guys. He doesn't. But he holds himself looser, as if he's relieved to be inside, to have me pay some heed to him. I ruffle his hair.

Nevada raises her brows at me. "So, welcome, Ruby and Thorn. I'm Nevada Pilgrim, the owner and principal of The Greening." She makes everyone introduce himself. So, this is it—no girls after all. Wistfully, I think of Freeblossom and Petal.

"Guys, I'd like you to go and warm up dinner," says Nevada. "Jan, please set a table."

"Can't the girl do it?" he asks with a frown.

"No, she's still a guest," says Nevada firmly. Then, she smiles at me and at Thorn. "Vesper and Bea are upstairs, they should be down soon. In the meantime, have a seat in the parlor with your brother. I need a minute with Armonk."

So, there *are* girls here! They might be quite an improvement from the reception we've received so far. She waves her hand toward the room in question and I choose a wide, saggy chair smelling of dust and dried shale. The room is lit with wall torches and an ancient hurricane lantern, and furnished with various cast-off chairs and side tables. I see one poster of a sparkling sea with a hovercraft zipping across its waves, and the word AXIOM COASTAL splashed across the bottom edge in bold red letters. What's Axiom?

Nevada unlocks a door inside the parlor and ferries Armonk through it, closing it firmly behind her. Thorn weasels his way in beside me and rests his head on my shoulder. I sink into the chair, letting my muscles relax. It's a slow process. They've been locked up so tightly. Being here, with Thorn and feeling safe at least for now, has me pleasantly groggy. A delicious unnamed scent wafts out from the kitchen. My stomach growls; I'm starving.

Thorn taps me on the hand. "Fireseed," he whispers. My ears prick. He never speaks to others and rarely speaks to me, so this is momentous.

I lift my weighted lids halfway, look over at him. "What about Fireseed?"

"Weak."

"Fireseed is weak?" He nods.

Worry cramps my empty stomach, which emits another low growl. "What's wrong with the Fireseed? Tell me, Thorn!"

His brown eyes are guarded. He rests his head back on my shoulder, and links his soft arm around mine.

"Thorn? Please, please tell me?" I press him once more, but he's done talking.

I should hold him right in front of me, shake him gently and force him to speak. Knowing Thorn, he may not speak another word for weeks. But exhaustion overcomes worry and my eyes close again.

5

I startle awake to the sound of a girl's shrill voice. "Dinner," is all she says.

Sitting upright, two girls stare down at me. One is tall with ebony skin and wide-set green eyes. She looks about my age and has a perfectly proportioned face. Her combination of green eyes and dark skin is shocking and beautiful. But she's not smiling, not even close.

The other one looks younger—by about two years. She has blond hair like Nevada but thicker and lustrous, and her slim figure is curvy in all the right places, as if she's a perfect china doll. She's not looking too friendly either.

"Hey," says the blond girl. "Get up."

"It's rude to be late for dinner," the other one adds.

I scramble to my feet and follow them into a dining area off the parlor.

Armonk is already in there, and there's an empty chair next to him, so I take it. At least he doesn't look at me like he wants to burn me with a torch. What's wrong with these people?

Blane serves some steaming round vegetable with crinkly skin that I've never seen before, and the slinky, surly Jan comes around the table, doling out a slice of beetle loaf to each plate. I'm familiar with beetle loaf, which I like. And I'm so famished I'll even try that bulbous thing next to it.

Nevada, sitting at the head of the table passes around a beaker of water. I pour myself some and practically inhale it, but I don't dare pour more. She asks if I've met Bea and Vesper.

"Not exactly."

Nevada sighs and makes them tell me which one is which. The tall darkly tanned one is Vesper. The shorter blond girl is Bea. They glower at me disapprovingly.

Kids back at home would never get away with rudeness. Up until eighteen years old the elders would flog them for that behavior. I don't understand, is there not enough food to go around or what? I recall Blane saying that we had to pay, and test in. Is all of this hostility because we're getting a free pass?

Everyone digs into the food. The crusty oblong thing turns out to be quite tasty. It's soft and white inside and it sticks to my ribs in a way the beetle loaf doesn't. My stomach's so empty I worry it'll never be full.

After a time of gulping down food, Nevada pipes up. "Bea and Vesper, I want you to all welcome your new classmates, Armonk and Ruby. And Thorn is going to live here too."

"They're staying here for good?" Bea exclaims.

"No," Armonk says, "I'm only here until Varik—"

"Shush, I won't hear of it. You need a good education," Nevada insists.

"They need to test in and pay up," says Blane. "Did they pay up?"

"That's my business," Nevada remarks.

Armonk is stony. I don't blame him; his face is swelled from being bashed in, and the bloody evidence is hardening in uneven splotches on his suit.

"I can cook," I offer. "I'm good with, um, mixing things."

Bea is studying me. "Where are you from?" she asks in a voice as cool as midnight stone. I didn't answer Nevada before but maybe I should answer Bea, because at least it's a civil question.

"Over in Chihuahua," I say.

Blane points to my arms. "So, that's what those flower brands are!" Now that my cloak is off, there's no hiding the line of flower brands that we girls get every year, starting at the wrist and growing up our shoulders like living vines.

Jan says, "I hear that at the full moon, they dance around a bunch of torches and rape their girls."

My face flames up. I'm not sure what a rape is but it sounds terrible. Is that what Stiles was going to do to me?

"Enough rumors!" says Nevada. "Yes, they are staying and yes, you will welcome them, and yes, they have paid up in one way or another."

Everyone is silenced. Though Nevada seems not that much older than the guys, and definitely not as robust, I suppose she's got some psychological power over them. It's her place. Her authority may hold for now, but for how much longer? In Thorn's fearful expression and in the tightening knot in my gut, I sense this is not the end of our grilling by the others, not by a long shot.

I'm installed in Bea's room on a cot. Just like at the compound at home, the girls all share a bathroom. Bea's room is on the left wing of the second floor, with a heat-sealed window overlooking part of the Fireseed crop, or rather the tarp.

She's tried to make her space cheery, with drawings she's done of rock formations. They're not regular ones, but fairytale rock shapes with wings, and female beings in flowing gowns. I rather like them and I tell her so.

"Thanks." She rolls over toward the wall. "But don't try to butter me up. You and that guy with the bow and arrow are cons. You conned Nevada into staying here."

"How do you know?" I ask as sweetly as possible under a newly simmering anger.

"He used connections. Said his mother knew her. That's a lie, that's cheating."

The possibility that Armonk was lying about who his mother is never occurred to me. Who would do that? Maybe someone as desperate as me to gain asylum I conclude with a shiver. I want to ask Bea why it matters so much, and why it's any of her business. But I know from my own experience that I get more information from playing a charm game and holding back from putting my cards on the table. If that makes me a con, so be it. It's helped me survive. "His skill might come in handy," I reason, and then change the subject entirely. "How did Nevada come upon the Fireseed plants?"

"Wouldn't you like to know." Bea laughs. "That's your god, right? I guess your god flew down from the sky and planted itself right in our garden. It favored us, not your people. Now, please, no more talking, I need my sleep."

Turning onto my back, I gaze out at the bowl of stars and the blood moon, finally waning. It seems like years since I ran from Stiles, yet it's only been hours. In so short a time so much can change.

I wonder how Thorn is, in Radius' room? Radius seems the mildest of the three guys, and all I can hope is that he's not torturing Thorn like Blane did Armonk. Blinking away mist from my eyes, I think of my mother back home. She must be frantic with worry for me, for Thorn. Mist spills over into tears as I think about how I miss my friends, Freeblossom and Petal who I'll never see again. I imagine what they went through on Founders' Day, with their partners, too old to be any good match.

Rape.

Jan's ugly word swills around in me like toxic liquor, making me queasy. I need to get Freeblossom and Petal away from there too, but how?

Despite my worry, my eyelids flutter lower, and I slip into a waking stupor. I'm back at the ceremony, with Stiles holding me down. I'm screaming for help, seeing his eyes bulge out. Like a toad's tongue his eyes lick my cheeks. Suddenly, it is no longer Stiles' pinning me down. It's Blane and then Jan and then a giant, monstrous toad whose tongue wraps around me and sucks me into his warty mouth. He swallows me in one drooling motion and hacks my bones onto the hot sand.

I bolt upright. Looking over at Bea, I listen for her steady breaths. She's asleep. I wish I could sleep, even rest without my dangerous visions. Tiptoeing out of bed, I check on Thorn. He and Radius have both nodded off, thankfully. I creep back to my room, and reach for my hip bag, which I hid in my folded cloak. Pull out the vial of Oblivion Powder. Visions of Depot Man's leer and Stile's greedy stare still plague my mind. The other elders too; how they pinched and tickled me on their way by, how they gave me secret, unwelcome winks. And now, the handsome bullies here who used their clubs and fists on Armonk; what might they do to me next? I shake a generous dose onto the top of my hand, and snuffle it in. Inhale hard until the pile is gone.

Immediately, its treacherous medicine streaks into my nerves, soothing them to a mindless lull.

Oblivion. I'll need it to survive this mean place, is my last thought before I wilt down to the cot.

6

My bleary eyes open to a wall drawing of a glorious being with sandy wings and a long, flowing skirt. Where am I, still in the Founders' Day gazebo? If so, this drawing wasn't there before. I look below the drawing to an empty bed and its wrinkled bedclothes. Bea. I'm sharing Bea's room, this is her wall drawing and she's already up. The sun is afire outside the window. It takes up the whole zenith in its fury.

In a jumble of cascading images, yesterday's events crash along the ridges of my memory. Stiles, the escape on the broken glider, the depot man's clumsy groping, the crash landing, Armonk's arrow glancing my forehead, Blane beating him up, the other mean kids, Thorn warning me that the Fireseed plants are sick.

The Fireseed plants! The crop. The Greening!

When I stand up my head pounds. The Oblivion Powder, *ack*, I took way too much last night. Fighting off a wave of dizziness I reach in my cloak for my flask and take a gulp of restorative water. There are only a few dribbles left. I remember the pitcher of water we had at dinner, and make a mental note to replenish my own flask the first chance I get. Who knows how long I'll be able to stay here, or even if I dare, among these horrid people? At least I'm protected from the elements.

As best I can, I freshen up in the tiny bathroom. It's cluttered with the towels and discarded clothes of the other girls. Their chatter filters upstairs, so they must be already down for the morning meal. My eyes move back to a shirt made with that sheer, iguana fabric, worn, but still shiny, with curious octagonal patterns, like cells. Gathering a section of a sleeve in my fingers, I rub it to determine more closely what it's made of. No clue, but it changes color with every glint of light. Uneven footsteps in the hall startle me, so I quickly drop the shirt back on its hook.

It's Armonk. His cheeks are so swelled and darkened from yesterday's punches I hardly recognize him, and he's limping badly. My first thought is that Blane and company landed extra punishment after lights went out. I have no time to ask him because Jan blazes past us.

"Class started," he warns. "Peg Leg and Cult Girl, you're late."

I'm not in a mood to protest the stupid names right now. What class and where? I don't even bother to ask. It'll only give Jan another chance to put us down.

~

It turns out that a real teacher has flown in from somewhere to give us lessons in math and astronomy. She's older than Nevada, with gray hair but the same leaf tattoos on her cheeks that Nevada has. Her name is Irina. I have no clue as to what calculus is, but I understand astronomy—the sky, the stars, the swirling purples and blood oranges of the heavens. Except that Irina insists there's no Fireseed God up there. Not even one lousy Fireseed star. Really? We learned that Fireseed exists in our hearts, but also up on its own star, a reddish, five-pointed one like the blossom. Irina's fairly convincing with all of her charts and calculations, but wrong. Our teachers at home couldn't have been that off the mark, I'm sure.

After Irina's class, Nevada teaches us history. She talks about the Border Wars at the middle of the 21st century, and how the northerners built a robotic wall to keep us desert folk from crowding out their great, advanced cities—northern cities like Restavik in Land Dominion and Vostok Station in Ocean Dominion. I've heard of these. Land Dominion is where we get our food shipments. But how advanced could they be? The elders taught us that the fiends in these cities would think nothing of killing us. Eating us even. But this class has got me wondering, why would a dominion that ships us food be out to kill us? My head reels with confusion.

Nevada pauses at the mention of Vostok, as if it hurts her heart, and she and Armonk exchange knowing glances. What all did they discuss behind the locked doors of her study? I make a note to ask Armonk as soon as the time is right.

Why didn't my own teachers ever speak more of science, of the politics behind the Border Wars? I search Nevada's face for lies, and study how her blond brow raises when she makes a point; the way her voice takes on speed when she's dropping a gem of obsidian at our feet. She seems too genuinely impassioned to be spinning lies. Or is this whole Greening Institute a place of lies? Myths? The images of Bea's mythical beast drawings flit into mind. I wish I could simply turn to Thorn to get his reaction. He would sense the truth. But he's too young for these classes, and has been set up in the parlor with some ancient jigsaw puzzles. I won't be able to ask him later about this either, because he's the kind of sensitive who has to feel it in the moment.

At lunch, in the dining room, Nevada serves a spicy-sour juice of some kind, and steamed Fireagar. I've already eaten two big meals and it's not even dinner. Back home, we ate only once a day. My belly feels like an overblown balloon.

Again, I sit with Armonk on one side, Thorn on my other. Blane, Jan and Radius keep to themselves and I hear more than one giggle and mention of Cult Girl and Peg Leg. Bea and Vesper join them, followed by more loud whispers. Armonk sends them occasional scowls and I worry that he'll incite another brawl. If this happens, his swelled up face will break wide open.

"So, what did Nevada talk with you about?" I ask, as we help clean up from lunch. It's our turn. The others have wandered to the parlor and are busy playing some card game.

"She spoke about Dr. Varik." Armonk puts a dried food pack on the shelf. "How she met him a long time ago and helped save him. He'd crashed through a rock formation—a mimetolith shaped like a cup—and was almost dead. He…" Armonk stops there and lowers his head until his black bangs curtain his face. I guess he's not sure how much he wants to tell me.

I need to break through Armonk's hesitation. He's the only friendly one around, so as soon as he looks up I send him a winning smile. That's always worked before. "What happened after she rescued him?" I ask. "And did you ever meet his father, the professor?"

Armonk looks surprised that I don't know the story. He explains that Varik's father was murdered up north by terrorists who wanted access to his research on Fireseed. He tells me how Varik found the Fireseed plants inside the cup-shaped rock formation, all those years ago where he crashed in the desert, and that he dug a few of them up north to breed with the last known agar seeds. He says that the last three Fireseed plants died when he got them up north, but a few days before they withered, they bred like crazy with the last agar seedlings.

And that's how Varik saved the world with the new hybrid, Fireagar.

My jaw hangs open. This is such a different story than the elders told us. They said Varik was a false prophet, a good-for-nothing who didn't deserve to be called a Teitur. And no word was ever uttered about the Professor being murdered, or how Fireagar came into being. We still worship by that cup mimetolith! And all of that time, Fireseed was hiding inside it? The world as I know is becoming a weak, faded fabric that first the teachers, and now Armonk are shredding into irreparable rags. It makes me shake with anger.

"But Fireseed is here, at The Greening!" I exclaim. "How did it get here then?"

Armonk peers around to see if anyone else has come in.

I check outside the door to make sure no one's in the adjoining room. "Coast is clear, come on, you can tell me," I wheedle.

He looks unconvinced, but continues in a hushed voice. "Nevada went back to the cup mimetolith and dug up the rest of those plants. Kept them hidden. No one knew."

"That's impossible!" I hiss. "That rock face is near our

compound. Our elders would've known it. They would've gone down inside and dug up every last plant." I pause. "Besides, *Fireseed* would've told us."

Armonk studies me with that sad pity as before. I don't need to hear him say it. It's clear that he doesn't believe in a Fireseed god. No one does around here, except for Thorn and me.

I don't want Armonk's pity. I want information. I offer another melting smile that shrouds my anger and confusion. It's the only reliable way I know to keep a guy talking. "But why would Varik want to come down here again, when he has everything he needs up north?"

Armonk doesn't return the smile, yet he goes on. "He doesn't have everything he needs up north. He needs us."

"Why?"

"He wants to be a doctor down here. Help the desert people."

"Is that what you were talking about with Nevada?"

"Partly." He reaches down and touches his alien leg. "He made this for me when he stayed with us in Black Hills Sector, on his way south."

I nod wistfully. "I never spoke to him but I waved to him, at our compound." I slowly raise my right hand with its three missing fingers. "He saw this. Maybe he can fix me too."

"What happened to you?" Armonk's voice shows his alarm.

Now it's my turn to be silent. It happened soon after Stiles first picked me. I was little then, but I already hated his burning eyes, his smelly breath, the way he'd come up to me at mealtimes and tell me that I was his special girl. The second or third time he said this, my mother told me that I spat a wad of my chewed up food on his boot. That he lost his temper and took his knife to me, catching my three middle fingers and slicing them half off. I ran to my mother, screaming, and she hurried me to the nurse. The nurse sewed them on, but infection set in, and they had to be removed. My father pleaded with the elders to have me paired with someone, *anyone* else. But things like that are set—set from way back. The elders threatened to put my father out. My parents had seen others put out. Found their curled up corpses in the shadow of the mimetoliths, like newborns exposed to the sun's wrath. But I can't tell Armonk this. The words catch in my throat and my eyes glaze over. I yearn for a lengthy draw of Oblivion Powder to deaden the humiliation my father must've felt. I've never thought about that much before but I feel its rawness now—a father unable to defend his own daughter.

"S'okay," says Armonk, and I focus again on his dark, understanding eyes. "Don't tell me if you don't want to." Something in his voice makes my arms erupt in gooseflesh so I hug them to my chest. He says, "I'm sure Dr. Varik could fix them."

7

Fix what?" In stampede of feet, Blane suddenly crowds into the dining room with his troop. They're loud and sweaty and handsome.

"His jacked up face," laughs Jan.

"We're going to play soccer," Radius claps Armonk on the back. "You be our goalie."

"I don't play," says Armonk.

"Me neither," I add.

"It's mandatory," Blane states.

"Chop, chop, we don't have much time." Vesper ferries us down to the basement with her long, waving arms.

I exchange uneasy glances with Armonk, as we head downstairs. His fake leg catches on a steep step but he reaches out for the wall and rebalances.

It's a large space, cooler than the rest of the compound, and full of sports equipment. I see weights and a hoop set up high, for some kind of ball game. The court also has goal nets on each end. My heart aches for my friends back home, what fun we could've had here! We could've used a gym to stretch and play in. We had nothing like this. Even it its battered state, this array of equipment floors me.

Blane, Jan and Radius begin to boot the scuffed ball into the goal nets, while trying to steal the ball away from each other. Bea and Vesper join in, with giggles and light pushing.

After a few minutes of this, Blane approaches. "Okay, Peg-Leg and Cult Girl are on one team. The little kid sits on the sidelines." Thorn looks at him blankly, goes over to the side but refuses to sit. "Bea, you join the gimps," Blane adds with a flick of his hand in our direction.

"Armonk and Ruby," Armonk corrects.

Bea's annoyed. "*You* join their team, Blane."

Blane's square brow bristles into a flush. "I'm the head coach. Follow my rules." He wags his head at Radius. "You be on their side too. Otherwise, it'll be too easy."

Radius mutters something under his breath but stalks over. He gathers us around him and, in a voice dry with resentment, explains the rules. Armonk nods as if he knows already. Does everyone in the desert know how to play soccer but me?

Even with Bea and Radius on our team we're no match for the rest. Vesper is a natural athlete, tall and lean with coiled muscles that spring easily into attack. She keeps pace with the boys, and I picture her on a real, varsity team, like in that old college catalog of my father's. Jan, all angles and elbows, streaks by me time after time and slams the ball in the net. Blane is a beast, and a dirty cheater. He holds out his foot when Armonk runs by and snags his artificial leg. Armonk goes flying, face first.

I hurry over and lend a hand. Armonk must not want to look weak in front of all of these hardheads. He doesn't take it.

Our next task is to pick Fireseed leaves. We suit up and put on our burn masks, because it's hot enough to see mirages of sparkling water, even under the tarp. Back at my compound we never went out until nightfall, even under a canopy.

Nevada tells us to pick the leaves and press them under wide rocks she's set on a shelf so they flatten. It goes against everything I've been taught to pluck Fireseed limbs from their stalks, but I do what I'm told, because Blane is keeping a close watch over us. As he said before, he's clearly Nevada's henchman. At one point Armonk disappears and Blane asks me where he went. I tell him I have no idea. I have enough trouble trying to keep an eye on Thorn.

Thorn seems as disturbed as I am, to pluck off leaves, and, with a sad grimace, he points out more than a few blotches. The blotches are white and fuzzy. The leaf around each blotch puckers and wilts. It hurts to see it, and I ask Thorn what's wrong with them. He's my radar after all. His eyes pool with hurt but he stays silent. No one-word hints this afternoon. Instead, he wanders off and disappears behind a clutch of red leaves. Maybe he needs time alone, I think, as I head off in a different direction.

I'm absorbed in collecting more leaves when heavy footsteps crunch up ahead, and I hear fast, labored breathing. Blane appears through the crimson foliage in front of me with an armful of Fireseed leaves.

He puts them down and brushes off his hands. "So, what's your story, your real story?"

"I don't know what you mean."

"Why did you leave your compound for this place?" he asks.

I shrug. There's no way I'd tell him about Stiles, or any other details of my life. Would he tell me his? "Why did you leave *your* home?"

"That was a long time ago," he declares.

"Where was it?"

"East Coast Sector, near New York. I went to a reputable school, where the kids had money, good families." Blane kicks at a stone. When he looks back at me, his gaze radiates the pain of people and things long gone. "You wouldn't know that kind of thing."

"Sure I would. I love my folks back at home."

An unspoken message simmers between us that no matter where we're from we're all the same. Or did I misread that because Blane's voice is suddenly shrill. "Why are you here then?"

"Why are *you* here, if your family is so perfect?" I challenge.

He snorts, rubs his hands on his burn suit. "I saw my parents drown, if you must know. I saw my brother, Percy drown, and our dog, Cloud. They went under in a cold, black wave of death that washed over the sector, if you really need to know. I clung to a roof for two days, watching bloated bodies float by—dead dogs, cats, little children, their mouths still open, as if they were ready to scream. What do *you* bring to this equation, girl?" Blane's voice is hardboiled, bitter. I imagine tears spilling down underneath his mask.

"I'm sorry to hear that. No one should see those things." I think of the tiny ones at the branding ceremonies back home, how they screamed when the brands crackled and bubbled star-shapes into their flesh. But that was for the cause. Blane saw meaningless death. "Is that why you're so tough on people?" I make the mistake of asking. Because Blane's face immediately snaps closed.

A mask of armor over a jaded soldier. "Where's Peg-leg?" he growls.

"I have no idea, and that's not his name." Here we are, back to battle. And I thought we'd made some human progress.

"Find him, Cult Girl." Through the slits in his mask, Blane's cold eyes fix on me like crosshairs on a rifle. He treads closer. His breath on my face is as hot as the scorching air. A heavy bodily threat presses in on me. I know it from Stiles, and the other men. It's hate and sex and power, all mixed together like snakes circling my waist, their sharp scales scraping my flesh.

"I'll do my best." I turn away to dislodge his gaze.

Blane spins around to the front of me, even closer, demanding my attention. "Do your best at what?" he teases.

"At ignoring you," I say, backing up. I'm scared, more for Armonk than myself.

Blane lunges for my arm. At that moment, a high whiz and burst of wind flies by.

With a dull ripping sound Armonk's arrow tears through Blane's pack that sits between his muscled shoulder blades.

"You…" Blane is temporarily speechless, and then madly sprinting after Armonk, who has miraculously melted into the red jungle. Armonk reminds me of an ancient savage from a myth, with sticks through his earlobes and a fusty spear in hand; one who knows the crests of rock, the sheltering caves, and every cliff switchback.

I gather up Blane's pile of red leaves and add them to mine. Then I go find Thorn.

At dinner, I see that Armonk's face is no worse off. The mottled purple of his bruise seems a shade lighter. Blane must not yet have caught up to him. I smile inside. Never mind that Armonk's leg is two or three sizes to short for him. The supposed gimp has found a way to humiliate Blane. And protect me. I'm grateful for that. Armonk will pay for it though. He might need my help after all.

That night, I crawl into bed exhausted in a good way. I've eaten, I've gotten exercise, and I've managed to fend off Blane. I've checked on Thorn and Radius seems to be leaving him alone. Bea hasn't said anything truly nasty to me today, though she's rolled toward the wall again without a word. Now she's breathing steadily with a soft snore.

Progress, I may not even need Oblivion tonight.

But as I lay there, staring out at the orange-streaked sky and the distant, blinking stars, my mind sinks to a dreadful reverie. I'm standing in front of the garden shelf where the red leaves are trapped under those wide stones. The Fireseed seems to be emitting a high-pitched wail. Blane is there too and he's pressing his face into mine, his lips biting at my own lips. His meaty arms trap me. He shoves me down on top of Fireseed stalks that crack and split, sending out more high-pitched *whees*. As Blane's weight pushes hard against my chest, his face becomes Stiles'—the flared nostrils, bloodshot eyes and accusing stare. "You are mine," Stiles says. "How dare you…"

I bolt upright, sending such a flurry of fearful energy into the air that Bea chokes in her sleep. Coughing, she turns my way and returns to her steady breathing.

Her eyes could snap open at any second. She could steal my bag of Oblivion or knock it from my hands, scattering the powder over the floor. It would be lost forever. I hold my breath as I pad across the room, reach for the velvety sack in my cloak and feel the reassuring give of the powder. It's diminishing with every dose, and I won't be able to make more here. I need to ration it carefully. My heart hammering, I flutter into the bathroom, inch open the drawstring and shake a line onto my wrist. I inhale greedily, desperately.

Stumbling back to bed, there's only enough time to thrust the precious bag inside my pillowcase before sweat erupts on my upper lip and my eyes roll up.

Then I bump off swollen ridges of pain as I fall deeply into never.

8

"lass, we have a very special visitor today," Nevada announces after breakfast. "He's multitalented: the governor of Vegas-by-the-Sea, a businessman and a philanthropist, helping many in the sectors. He has an exciting offer for all of you, and for The Greening," she adds with evident pride. Nevada shakes out her hair, freshly adorned with an array of tiny braids. Her leaf earrings are carved from a stunning green stone and her matching green chameleon suit clings to her lean curves. High beige boots with a brushed finish show off her coltish legs. I'm curious about this man she seems dressed to impress.

Blane, Jan, Radius, Bea and Vesper push their way into the parlor and grab the best seats. Thorn has managed to scramble in too, but he's saved me half a seat in the stuffed armchair that we fell asleep in together on that first day here. I offer Armonk a magnetic grin. His eyes dart quickly away. It hurts that he's immune to my charms. I'm confused too; I thought that his shooting that arrow at Blane meant that Armonk liked me, at least as a friend. I need an ally here, and how else can I get close, but to smile and play coy? That's how it worked at home. Guys, bah. I don't get them. The pleasant memory of talking with Freeblossom and Petal tugs at me. Of us fixing each other's hair and making gemstone necklaces. Of us piling up pots and spoons in my mother's kitchen when we cooked a special beetle cake on Petal's birthday, of us scribbling goofy desert critters on each other's notebooks.

I consider offering Armonk my seat, but Nevada offers her first. More points against him I worry, as I glance over at Blane's jealous stare. Blane might be Nevada's henchman but Armonk is clearly her pet.

As I'm wondering how long it will take for our guest to arrive, a deeply tanned man emerges from Nevada's private study and steps up to a podium. He looks like no man I've ever set eyes on. Running a hand through his teased up platinum hair, he beams out at us with a perfect row of teeth and a diamond earring that winks. With his spotless white shoes, gossamer white shirt and gleaming shell buttons running down its front it's almost as if he rocketed down from an entirely alien planet. He's spotless and breathes wealth, enough to buy all the feasts he needs to last a lifetime.

"I'm George Axiom," he starts, "of Axiom Coastal." My classmates gasp. Should I know about Axiom? Sounds vaguely familiar. Is he famous around here? I feel a surge of resentment toward the elders for keeping so many things from us. Was there a reason?

And then I remember the poster. I turn to it on the far wall. It's still there, except that a hovercraft levitating over pretty turquoise waves still doesn't explain much of anything. I turn back to Mr. Axiom.

"Call me George," he's saying. "I hail from a long line of Texas drillers, who drilled for oil before the Border Wars. I studied geology too, I know these desert buttes and mesas like the lines in my palm," he brags.

What does this have to do with The Greening, or us?

"We built up Vegas after the mega-quakes destroyed California, may she rest in peace. Now, since I've taken on the role of governor, Vegas-by-the-Sea has become the most prosperous sector ever. We have new agar skyscrapers and hovercraft, new bridges and tunnels." My classmates shift restlessly. Sounds like one of the elders back home, bragging. Clearly they're also wondering what this has to do with them.

"In the last five years, we've acquired Stream embed technology from the north. We're fast developing new genetic reorg, and ways to change this desert into a Mecca that will far overshadow Ocean and Land Dominion's progress. This is where you kids come in."

At this, Blane and the others' snouts prick up like hungry lizards at a plump spider.

"As you know, we've secured Fireagar from the north, and it's feeding our people as never before." Everyone nods, and he pauses to let this sink in.

Does this mean there are no more hungry people—no more starving beggars who would trap a lost soul for food down here, I wonder. If so, there goes another warped myth that my elders need to answer to if I ever set eyes on them again.

From his case, George extracts and opens out a magical glimmer screen that hovers in midair—at least it's magical to me. On it is a revolving 3D image of tall, red Fireseed stalks on the left. In the center are the scrunched, scalloped leaves of olive-green Fireagar bleeding crimson, and a tube of emerald-bright agar spins alluringly on the right. How does this guy, George do this?

He points to the middle plants. "Everyone knows that Fireagar is a hybrid of Fireseed and agar. Then he points to the Fireseed. "You all know that Nevada has a special, secret crop of the original Fireseed growing inside the protective border of the Fireagar." He waves a generous hand her way as if she herself is an enticing product. She tips her head, setting her leaf earrings to jingling. "Now we need to discover what Fireseed can *really* do," he says, "above and beyond just feeding us as Fireagar does. Because Fireseed is destined for greater things than food."

Well, duh, Fireseed is a god.

What's Nevada doing then, with all the pressed leaves we gather each day? Funny, I didn't think to ask. The Fireseed won't be secret for long if George is flashing this video around the sectors.

In one long, liquid motion, Vesper leans forward. "Why are you telling us this?"

George Axiom reaches for his case and dumps a pile of shiny packets on the podium. He clicks the screen into another 3D image. Its blinking headline spells out Axiom Student Innovation Competition. "Nevada tells me that you students at The Greening are some of the brightest minds of the Hotzone." This gets a lively response. "I believe in good old competition, so I've started the first ever Axiom Contest to study and develop Fireseed!"

Blane booms out, "What does the winner get?"

"I'm getting to that." Geo Man threads a tanned hand through his poufy hair and beams. "There's a huge cash prize, 7,000 Dominions, and a bonus prize for The Greening, should one of you win." Cheers erupt. Even Armonk's face lights up. I wonder what he'd use the money for.

"How many schools are participating?" asks Radius. He's the smartest guy here from what I've seen in history and math classes.

"The Greening, Vegas Central High, Spokane Way and one up near the border, Baronland South—"

"That border school doesn't count!" Jan bellows. "Those rich kids came down from the north. They're not climate refugees."

Climate refugees? Is that what we are?

George's mouth opens as if he's about to scold Jan, but he stops himself. "If I have my way," he starts, "We, in this dominion will never again call ourselves refugees! *We* never ran from anything. The northerners did. We are proud to live where we do. In fact, if I absolutely have my way, we'll rename our land Axiom Dominion, and never again refer to this rugged, beautiful land as the Hotzone." He snips off the last word with extreme distaste.

The room breaks into enthusiastic clamor. Armonk looks over at me and we nod vaguely. Something we both can agree on. I'm not sure about naming the *whole* dominion after this George guy, but anything would be better than the north's condescending name for us.

"So, with only four schools vying for the grand prize that gives you a darn good chance of winning." George reassures.

"That and plenty of hard work," adds Nevada in her teacherly way.

"Do we get anything else?" Only Blane would be so rude to ask.

"As a matter of fact, yes." George nods. "The finalists fly into Vegas-by-the-Sea for a whirlwind tour of the city, a Skye Ride over the Pacific Fury Ocean and a fancy banquet."

This does it! See the ocean for real? I'm wobbly with excitement. Does the sea look like blue jewels all gleaming at once? Surely no flesh-eaters live in Vegas-by-the-Sea if everyone walks around dressed like George Axiom in white shoes and pricy shirts with shell buttons.

George Axiom's holo-screen switches to an image of a spinning beige lozenge. There's a tiny pastel blue pearl-shaped logo on its widest part. "As part of welcoming you all to our Axiom contest community I'm passing out Stream implants. Northerners have had them for years. In fact, they get them stapled in at birth. It will be a great way to keep you pumped and for us all to stay in touch during the contest dates." He picks up a bunch of shiny packets filled with beige lozenges and what looks like a staple gun.

Radius peers at the gadget with suspicion. "How do they work?"

"You'll hear the latest contest details, inspirational chats and news from Vegas-by-the-Sea." George winks. "And the daily surf report."

I'd love to hear any report about the sea!

Bea recoils into a doubtful cringe. "Where do you staple them?"

George approaches Bea and opens a packet. "Everyone, gather 'round," he says as he inserts the capsule in the staple-gun. The implant reminds me of Armonk's fake leg, with its line of round sensors and smooth beige surface.

"May I?" He gathers Bea's lustrous blonde hair in his other hand and gently lifts it up to expose the nape of her downy neck. "We inject them here. No unsightly scar or protrusion. Just a quick pinch."

Bea flinches and lets out a high squeak of surprise more than pain as he pushes down on the stapler. Funny, as much Oblivion Powder as I inhale, the idea of injecting an implant, however tiny, has me feeling faint. I can't help but notice that Armonk's gone from hanging back to the head of the line. The prospect of winning a contest, and money does tempt me to get past my distaste at an implant. Has the contest money changed his mind about staying here? I'm not sure how to get him to talk more, but I'll find a way.

Thorn is the one hanging back. "Want to do this?" I whisper to him. He doesn't answer, only bites on his fingernails. "It's worth a ride on a hovercraft," I say. At that, he follows me.

The stapling feels like a spider bite then it's over. Immediately a blast of news literally explodes in my head.

Congratulations, Axiom Contest Entrants! You're now part of the vibrant community we're building together in Vegas-by-the-Sea and beyond. Onward to Axiom Dominion. This first step, of developing Fireseed is exciting and will usher in new ways to thrive. We're counting on you, bright students of the future.

Brought to you by Axiom Water Pellets, where thirst is quenched in bursts of color.

At this, an animation of pellets rolls across my mind's eye in candy yellows, blues and oranges. Axiom makes our blue water pellets! Who knew there were so many different ones to choose from? And wow, you can watch films with this amazing implant. Looking around at the others, I see they're grinning and rubbing their necks. They must hear it too. I glance over at Thorn. His face is lit up for the first time here. It warms me. If he's happy, I'm happy.

That night, Nevada calls us into the parlor. She fields questions about what the Axiom Contest is all about because at dinner a few of us confessed we were confused.

"We know it's about applications for Fireseed, but that's very general," Blane complains. "Can you give us specific ideas?"

I have to admit, I agree.

Nevada toys with one of her green-tinged braids. "It was originally bred for food, but as George said, now that we cultivate the less exotic Fireagar, we all feel that Fire*seed's* destined for greater things." She giggles. "We're just not sure what."

Bea pipes up. "Can I design clothes with it? They'd be heat resistant. Our own cellular burn fabric's getting really old."

"Perfect!" Nevada sounds relieved that someone's figured something out. "You're already good at that." Nevada wags her head at Bea's outfit. "You made your shirt, didn't you?" Bea beams as others turn to jealously admire it—a ruffled purple design with wide, flowing sleeves. Clearly pleased to have a plan of action, Bea relaxes into her chair.

"How about using it in some form of transport?" asks Radius.

"Certainly!" This loosens Nevada's tongue. "What about medical applications, household products, or totally, completely surprise us."

By the end of the session, most everyone's come up with a rough idea, though unlike Bea, most are keeping it tightly guarded.

As I circle the room, extinguishing the storm lanterns— my evening chore—I startle when an unfamiliar news report blasts inside my head.

Huzzah, Fireseeders! I trust you've come up with great contest ideas. Axiom Inc. will begin delivery tomorrow of advanced tools to use in developing your projects.

Remember, colossal ideas win colossal prizes.

Brought to you by Vegas Beach—for all of your water-sport needs—whether for hovercraft, air surf or Skye Ride. It's all good and all Vegas Beach.

I'll have to get used to this, because it's not going away any time soon. It's such a new thing to be so connected to the outside world.

9

The next day George Axiom returns in an equally cheery sky blue suit with coral buttons and his hair blown-out in an even higher platinum up-do. "How are my Fireseeders today, hmm?" We smile vaguely. "That won't do," he insists. "Give a loud, enthusiastic cheer!" We cheer on cue.

"What exactly are the rules?" Blane asks. "I mean, can we do *anything* with Fireseed?" He's obviously not trusting Nevada's word alone.

"Anything colossal, anything stupendous, anything revolutionary!" George says with an extravagant waving of his hands. Blane nods, arching his brows in a look of bemusement.

Axiom's people—in a caravan of seven white gliders—drop off rolling containers of lab equipment brimming with the latest in holo tablets and software, testing chambers and micro-tools for performing experimental surgery on tiny particles of the Fireseed plants. The new equipment crowds out the old-fangled beakers and test strips that Nevada has scavenged over the years in what she's now calling The Project Room, a spacious but sparely furnished room on third tier. With Blane and Radius' help, she's moved in four long tables that she had in her storage barn. They are all bowed in the middle as if the heat of the sun has melted their cores.

Nevada's beaming and buzzing about, coordinating the delivery. It makes me realize how determined she must've been to start a school on nothing, really. Nothing more than a big heart and wanting to give a bunch of wandering teenagers a better life than she had.

It makes me intensely curious as to how she fell into the grip of the so-called terrorist group that Armonk mentioned. He called it the Zone Warrior Collective, and went on to tell of the time they bombed the border wall up north, and poisoned Varik's father's crops to protest the starving folks down here. I make a mental note to ask Armonk more about her past. He must be aware of it if his mom was a friend of hers. When we start to sort though the supplies Nevada looks on like a proud mother. If she can love these mean kids, maybe I can try harder.

I glance over at Blane, his overgrown muscles clenching up out of hardwired habit, and Jan's defensive stoop as he hoards his picks, and I decide to give them a second chance. They've had a horrendous time of it—I know Blane has—wandering around in the desert, lost, parentless. Thorn and I were only exposed one night and it seemed like forever.

But they are nothing if not fast on claiming what's theirs.

While I am surreptitiously studying them, Blane, Radius, Vesper and Bea have already put dibs on their equipment. Only Jan seems at loose ends, pawing around in the jumble of leftover items and restlessly moving them into and out of his pile.

Armonk rubs his still-swollen cheek with its ragged cut as he chooses some random storage containers. He puts them next to Thorn's pile of smaller containers and micro-scissors. "How are you, little guy?" he asks Thorn, who of course doesn't answer in words, only with a slight nod of the head. I see him angle up one of his tiny boxes for Armonk to see, and I smile inside when Armonk answers, "That's quite the box, Mr. Thorn. I can't wait to see what you put in there."

Thorn goes to officiously organizing the boxes in rows with the cutting tools at neat right angles. He's always been precise that way.

Nevada enters the room and she and Armonk exchange quiet words. Armonk settles a square of cloth over his selection of goods and they exit together.

At this, Blane lets out an irritated, "Phss." He and Jan exchange comments about how Peg Leg needs his nursery mom to bottle-feed him.

"She better not be angling to share the grand prize with that con," grumbles Vesper. After that she keeps a close watch on the project room door for Armonk's return.

"Peg-leg isn't smart enough to invent anything," Jan says darkly. Jan doesn't look so smart either, pacing around aimlessly. His work materials are scattershot: some paper, a scissors, a mirror and a vessel of glue. Good for a third grade art project.

Brushing off my urge to defend Armonk, I concentrate instead on my final choices of Axiom equipment. I decide on a pair of tiny pinchers, red threads, sample syringes, matches, test containers, spinning devices, a box of beakers and tiny collection jars. A holo tablet too. There's one for each of us! I've never had access to one at home, and I'm not even sure how to use it. Last, I choose an array of oils of unknown contents. I'll figure out what these are and why Axiom thought to deliver them. It shouldn't take long. My specialty is mixing compounds, and most do need some type of lubricant base. Who knows exactly what kind I'll get from Fireseed, but my set of tools look professional, lined up on the table in front of me with my nametag claiming them.

Bea and Vesper are sharing a table, Blane and Jan, Armonk and Thorn. I'm stuck with Radius, who moves as far from me as he can. As Radius and I organize our materials we shoot off wary side-glances as if to say, don't even think about figuring out my angle.

With a pronounced click, the project room door opens, and Armonk walks back in. His expression's determined, and he says nothing more about returning home empty-handed.

Jan raises his hands in a pantomime of a baby at a bottle and makes sucking noises. Only Vesper laughs.

~

By the time we don our burn suits and enter the Fireseed plot everyone is rushing forward as if the field is a fully stocked candy store. As if everyone's salivating at what they could do with the sweet prize money. I know I am.

I could buy a new glider and go back for my mom and my friends. Move them in with Thorn and me in the giant wave-colored house we'll buy in Vegas-by-the-Sea. We'll enroll in high school there, and I'll find Thorn a specialist who can teach him how to talk in real sentences. We'll eat succulent fish and fly trendy hovercrafts and I'll make clothes with pretty shell appliqués for my family and friends.

Everyone scatters in a different direction, including Thorn. I'm less worried about one of my classmates messing with him out here, because people are preoccupied with their projects. So, I head deep into the west field as the Fireseed sways around me. It's as if the plants are talking, the way they bristle with a sense of expectation as I pass and bend to wave me on by. I imagine them saying, "Walk in here, spend time with us!"

This time, in addition to gathering the leaves and flattening them under the wide stones, we'll get to keep samples to experiment with. I can't wait to get started making concoctions like my dad and I used to do.

From the time I turned four, my father and I would creep into the caves, and then slither, belly-first as the rock ceiling lowered, and the cooler air floated lazily though the brushy Fireagar. We'd lay still, our eyes silently laughing together as we waited for the switch of a Dragon Lizard tail. He taught me to pitch my hand out, as swift as any arrow. He taught me to ask the beast for permission, and promise it a safe return after we milked out the elixir. Then, with our wide, flat blades, we'd scrape the cave walls for moss, for schist, for minerals.

"Put each in its own treasure box," he'd whisper, "my little desert fairy, collecting your gold and gems."

Oh, how I'd giggle at that.

And then, in the kitchen, we'd get every pan and spoon out, and simmer shale powder with moss to perfection, eke out the Dragon Elixir and make a salve with it for rashes. Or we'd mix it with Fireagar for a special healing tea. Best thing for headaches or fever.

"We're making a magic drink, king of the desert," I'd tell him as I stirred.

"And you, my fairy princess, are the best potion-maker in the land of dunes and sky!"

My mom would come in and fuss about all of the pans we'd dirtied, and how she'd have to scrub them for an hour with sandpaper. But pretty soon, my dad would be swinging her around the room on his arm, to a tune we'd all make up. And we'd scrub the pots and spoons clean together.

Here, in the field, I come close to a star-shaped blossom. "Fireseed, hah, you're the most magic of all, aren't you?" When I break off one of its leaves, the branches around rustle as if they're murmuring, "Use us, but don't take too much. Don't tear too hard."

"I won't," I promise, "just enough."

White patches have puckered some of the leaves, and spots mar the trunks. Thorn was right. Whatever it is has spread.

"Tell me," I whisper, "what's ailing you?" But I hear no spoken answers.

The massive tarp overhead casts a dreary blue sheen on the crop, and with the heat of the day, a sour, synthetic odor wafts down. I wonder if whatever chemical is in the fabric could be affecting the plants. As I think this, I could swear the plants around me quiver. I'll mention it to Nevada later.

Creeping further and further into the red jungle, I sink down toward the cooler root beds. Lower my head to one of the stalks and pray. Prayer is still my currency here. Fireseed is still my god, and nothing has proven otherwise. "Please, let me take pieces of you, only to help the people down here. I'll repay you—somehow."

In response, one of the star-shaped flowers arcs down. I gasp as it lightly strokes my back—a signal to proceed? Taking the crimson flower head between my thumb and index fingers, I nick it off. Then I bend to the lowest set of leaves and cut a few more samples. Place them carefully them into my latchbag.

Something scoots by my right hip. I startle and look over. Another skitter and dash—of dark speckles like an artist flicked his loaded brush of soil-colored paint onto the beast's leathery back. My arms dart out to catch a wriggling tail. Lizards are here too! Not Dragon Lizards, but… It whips its tail in protest as its conical irises study me, the monstrous human subject.

I'm flooded with joy. The desert truly is springing to new life! A lizard would be unheard of outside the protective caves back at home, even under a thick tarp.

What else breathes inside this mysterious garden?

By the time we head back, I'm astonished by my haul. I've collected four of the lizards that I've coined Spatters for their patterns and five purple beetles. I've never seen this type of lizard or beetle before. Each beetle has a set of curved antlers as big as my thumbs, each with scalloped ridges along the underside! I inaugurate the breed as Antlered Purples after their shade. I've also collected two Fireseed flower heads, four leaves, and a brimming bag of crimson pollen I've coaxed from the stamens.

As I head back, I see Vesper and Bea up ahead. Their arms are full of bagged samples, and their angular burn masks glimmer as they laugh and talk. Jan, Radius and Blane are right by them, jostling each other. "Have you seen Thorn?" I ask them.

Only Bea answers me. "Not since we first came out. Why?"

"Oh, nothing, thanks," I say.

Has he already gone inside with Armonk? I'll worry about that later. Right now, I need to find somewhere private to squeeze out the venom from the lizards' jaws and release them back to the field before they get sluggish and sickly. Lizards are hardy creatures, but sensitive to human touch—too much of it and they wilt.

I wonder if these Spatters produce anything close to Oblivion. I'm running out, which makes me quite anxious though I'd really like to stop this constant need. I hate being tied to anything not of my choosing, especially after being tied to Stiles for so very long. But my night terrors... I can't quit... not quite yet.

The only room with a lock is the bathroom. I'll have to do the deed in there. Bad idea; Bea starts knocking impatiently. "Don't be a hog, we all live here," she complains.

Normally I can milk venom in a few expert moves, but I'm rattled because now Vesper's knocking too—hard raps on the worn door. "Turn's up, Cult Girl, we're late for dinner."

Tiny jar in one hand, I squeeze the jawbones of the last lizard with the other hand, and shoot a strong line of chartreuse venom into the jar. I breathe in through my mouth in order not to smell the pungent vapor wafting up as I secure the top. Its odor is stronger than the Dragon Elixir, does that mean it's poisonous? Hard to say.

I pop the Spatter Lizard back into my latchbag, where he slithers in among the others. This feat is not easy with three missing fingers but I've learned to compensate. The moment I unlock the door Vesper pushes her way in. "This place stinks," she snorts. "Your idea of perfume?"

It's true; the Spatter venom is a nose-bristling mix of rotten moss and armpit sweat.

Now, what to do with the Antlered Purples? Most everyone is down for dinner, so the project room should be empty. I dash up to tier three. As gently as I can, steady a beetle by its cycling legs and examine it under the magnifier. I'm supposed to be examining Fireseed but it's these creatures living in their garden that have snagged my imagination. Ah! As it rubs its antennae together it secretes a powdery toxin, which falls like fine spice onto the lab glass I've put under it. I repeat this with each beetle.

I think of Dad and his Cure Mead. How popular it was with our people, still is. I remember our family, in the kitchen helping him stir steamy vats of the stuff. And before that, asking the beetles' permission before adding them to the mix. This time, it looks like I'll be able to release them back to the garden.

My father taught me how to make other concoctions: wing powder for seasoning Fireagar stew; mica salt and Spidersoothe fashioned from spider legs and northern tea, used as a poultice for the nasty burn of Fireseed brands. My mother would help me package it.

With a sharp pang, I picture her back at home, fending off questions about my and Thorn's whereabouts. She must be so worried. I'm a terrible daughter for running off. But then, in an unexpected surge of frustrated anger I wonder why she didn't protect me from Stiles? Couldn't she have? Somehow? She could've made me ugly or told him I had a strange, catching illness, or have wheedled him so much he figured that I wouldn't be worth the trouble. I sigh. My parents did try, and if they'd pursued it more, they would've paid a terrible price. Lord only knows what the elders might be doing to my mother now. Ripples of fear pass through me when I think of Stiles searching for me. I was pledged to him so young. How far would he go to get me back? It's all too dreadful to picture.

"Ruby, are you up there? You're late for dinner," Bea calls up.

She's called me by name! A bubble of happiness rises in me as I plop the last beetle into my small collection jar and secure that to my hip pouch. They'll ride with me tonight. Perhaps I can slip out to the field and return them after dinner. Downstairs, on second tier hallway I peer into the room Thorn shares with Radius. The beds are made, school notes are in a neat pile on the desks and burn suits are hung on pegs. No Thorn though. And Radius must already be downstairs.

Downstairs, Thorn's not in the parlor or the dining room. The hair on my neck stands up when I think of him lost and I'm just about to run out into the fields when he slips through the kitchen door and peels off his burn suit. He glances over at me and away. His liquid brown eyes, usually full of silent messages, are mysteriously veiled.

Dinner is quiet. Everyone seems intent on eating, as if they're still keeping secret about their project—if they even have one yet. As soon as dinner's over, Blane invites us down to play soccer, and when I try to bow out, he insists.

"Come on, show us what you can do, fighter," he says with the hint of a smile. I'm pulled in by his hint of warmth against my own will.

Blane assigns Armonk to Jan and Vesper's team, and Bea, Radius plus me to his team. I should be flattered, but every time I look at Armonk's swelled up face with its cut, I'm reminded that Blane is one mean guy no matter how much he suffered, no matter if he's given me one lopsided grin. Armonk doesn't protest the team choice though. He seems content for the moment anyway, that his message for Blane to show respect hit the mark. Blane gives Armonk his space now, and he hasn't gotten physical with me again.

Thorn refuses to play. He sits on the sidelines, nibbling his fingernails and pocketing the half-moon shards. He's compulsive in a few ways, but I've not yet seen this one. It worries me. If only there were someone closer to his age to play with. Not that he had many friends back at home. How does a kid play with someone who won't talk?

Radius scores our first goal. I manage to kick the ball once to him for his second score. "Nice assist," Bea admits.

I feel badly for Armonk, limping around on that too-short leg, and I hope, for his sake that Dr. Varik makes an appearance in Skull's Wrath soon. But Armonk is adept at kicking with his other leg. He also performs a spectacular head slam, which lands the ball straight into the goal. According to Blane, head-butts are an official part of soccer. Sure is a strange rule, and I worry when I see that Armonk's cut is reopened from the indirect impact though it does get him a begrudging compliment from Vesper.

Jan, on the other team is the best player, hands down. He swivels past us like an oiled snake to score goal after goal. Jan's team ends up with a score of thirty, to our dismal three.

"You didn't bring much to the equation," Blane mutters as we trudge upstairs. I resent how he's making me feel like I'm the one who's disappointed him, and I rethink my decision to give them all a second chance. Sometimes trauma just makes you hardcore mean.

As I'm in the bathroom that night getting ready for bed, the manic Stream blasts in my head, scaring me so badly I squeeze toothpaste all over the sink.

Huzzah, Fireseeders! George Axiom here. We in Vegas-by-the-Sea are putting finishing touches on our new convention center and Axiom Skye Ryde so your contest finalists will be feted in complete luxury. So, craft those projects with special care.

Brought to you by NanoPearl, a proud sponsor of the Axiom Contest,
Where nanogear is as priceless as rare Orient pearl.

Who knows what the heck they're talking about in these crazy blasts and ads? All I know is that I thought I'd love to be connected but all I feel is startled.

Later, I toss in bed, trying to avoid taking the Oblivion powder. I have half of what I came here with and should save it for emergencies. I could try to make Oblivion from the Spatters, but who knows what I'd end up with. The moon glows a bloody red as my mind reeks with rancid images of Stiles' hairy face and luring words. "Come here, my child," he coaxed the time he cut my fingers. "It won't hurt, not that much." I throw off my covers. I'm hot, claustrophobic.

The sound of Bea's voice startles me. I thought that her soft, steady breathing signaled she was asleep. I'll have to take that into account in my nighttime forays. "Do you have insomnia?" she asks.

"Nightmares," I tell her, swinging my feet over the bedside.

"About what? Your cult?"

I'm tired of hearing that word, but this is the first time she's ever cared to ask me anything. "Someone in it," I say.

"That's too bad," she says. "Did you find anything today?"

I'm not sure I should reveal my incredible finds. This is a competition, after all. I don't trust these people. Why should I? Though Bea seems friendlier now. She called me Ruby earlier. I won't tell her about the lizards, it's too big a find. "One thing, want to see?"

"Okay." She pads over to my side of the room in a long sheer nightgown, her blond hair flowing in waves. I unbind the collection box from my suit belt, open the top just enough for her to peek in. "Whoa, I've never seen those guys! Such sculptural antennae." She's referring to the Antlered Purples.

"Sculptural," I mirror. "You see them that way since you're an artist, right?"

"That's true." Her face lights up. "Hey, I could draw them."

I nod as I pop the top back on. It would be one thing to have these amazing beetles all sprawled out on a table for her to sketch. But another thing if everyone sees them. I have to be careful though. I don't want to snap at Bea and discourage her from talking to me. "You could. Sometime," I add vaguely.

"What do *you* intend to do with them? And how does that relate to Fireseed?" Her voice tightens. She must sense my hesitancy.

I'm proud of my skills. But I only dare reveal a tidbit. "I make potions."

"Like that stuff you sniff up when you think I'm asleep?" Her warm blue eyes turn to chilly cat slits, which frighten me.

"Don't know what you're talking about."

"I think you do," she retorts, but softens inexplicably. "We all have our vices."

I'm too shocked to protest. "Um, really, what's yours?"

She releases a musical giggle. "Radius," she admits, and pads back to her bed. She pulls the covers up to her chin, gives a dainty yawn. "Look, I need to go to sleep, Ruby," she says. "So keep those beetles caged and be quiet when you snort that junk."

My ears flame up. A defensive retort is ready on the tip of my tongue. I bite it down. What good would that be? It would only be a lie.

So I stay as still as a butte until I hear her snore. I sneak downstairs, out the door, and release all of the lizards and beetles. Then, back upstairs in bed, I snatch the pouch and sprinkle out a stingy dose. I sniff it up hungrily with barely time to close the pouch before I slump onto my covers.

10

The next morning, over beetle loaf and Fireagar juice, Nevada declares a house meeting. She wastes no time with small talk. "The Fireseed fields have been breached," she starts.

"Have any plants been stolen?" I ask, my gut jumping.

"I can't be sure," says Nevada. "I haven't checked the entire field." Her eyes are underscored with sallow arcs and she's thrown on a plain, colorless outfit, not her style.

"How do you know someone was in there?" Blane asks as he serves himself a large section of beetle loaf. He seems suspiciously unconcerned.

"Someone slashed three large holes in the tarp. I only checked part of the field. There may be more damage." She gives us each a lingering stare. "This exposes the crop to overhead surveillance and detection, and to further breaches. To theft or destruction of the entire field."

We all stop eating and the room grows heavy with worry. Nevada has taken on so much with this valuable crop. Now that Axiom has announced the contest, many people may know about us, this very special field. No doubt, it's worth a ton of money. Who knows how many thieves and black market profiteers are hovering out there?

"Why would anyone do something as stupid as ripping the tarp?" Vesper asks. Her accusing eyes look directly at me. Automatically, I feel guilty. Did I lead the elders to my whereabouts? Oh, horrors, that hadn't occurred to me until now.

"We have to fix the problem," Nevada says. "But the repair will be expensive. I'm out of tarps. Even that one was hard to come by." Her pale eyes widen inside the smoky kohl she lines them with, and I picture how she might've looked as a younger girl, living in the wild, always alert for danger, planning out missions with the Zone Warrior Collective. Not so far removed from this apparent mission to breach the Fireseed crop. If it were someone who followed me from my old compound, I'd be indirectly at fault, for putting my spiritual gods in harm's way.

"Thieves," Blane stabs his fork into the beetle loaf.

"Crazies," Jan echoes.

"Hooligans," hisses Vesper.

Even though they're accusing with words they look frightened; all except Thorn, who's absorbed again in chewing on his fingernails. Why isn't he registering upset? Is he still too young to appreciate the gravity? Or perhaps his brain really *is* damaged. Perhaps the elders were right. I refuse to accept this, but I can't help my doubts from seeping in.

"We can't afford to lose the crop," Nevada remarks as she stirs her tea.

Looking around, I notice the threadbare curtains, a chair missing an armrest, the chipped bowls and mismatched silverware. I notice the dull patches in her shirt where the iguana-cell fabric has rubbed away with wear.

"We can't afford to lose any of it," she repeats, "or The Greening will go bankrupt."

"We'd be out in the desert, on our own again," says Blane.

"Sucking moss from inside rock crevices," Bea whispers.

"Sticking up folks for food," says Jan.

And kissing toady men for rotten hunks of meat and a wrinkled bed to pass out in.

Nevada instructs us to work in teams of three, and to sew up the three jagged tarp rips nearest the compound, with worn rolls of twine she hands us. I get stuck with Vesper and Bea.

Nevada deems Thorn too short to help. He runs off with an odd grin on his face. What's so funny, I'd like to ask? But I'm forbidden to run off after him. Sometimes I wonder if he's more spoiled than brain addled, and then I silently scold myself for having the thought. He has been through more hell than most.

The tarp is so dry from sun damage that it may have cracked on its own. I suspect this until I see that it's the clumsy cuts of an amateur using a very dull blade. Which makes it all the harder for Bea and me to pull the two sides together while Vesper tries to sew. Vesper has quite a mouth on her and Bea and I are subjected to every rotten curse in Vesper's rotten vernacular. It gives me perverse satisfaction to see Bea roll her eyes at Vesper.

"How will you use the Fireseed leaves for clothes?" Vesper asks Bea in a lighter moment.

"I make my own patterns," says Bea. "Leaves for flat parts, parts of the stalk for belts."

"Where did Nevada get that incredible cellular fabric that you all wear?" I ask.

"Don't know," Bea admits. "But it's worn out. We need something new. We get burns through it now, in the faded parts."

"I'd be a model for you, if you need fittings," I offer.

"Who asked you, Cult Girl?" Vesper scowls at me.

I look to Bea to vouch that I'm okay to talk to since we've shared a word last night. But Bea's eyes are impassive and she's not saying anything. "No one asked me, Vesper, I believe I asked Bea," I retort. Bea stifles a snort of laughter. I may not be able to see Bea's true expression under her mask, but I surely hear it, and it gives me great satisfaction.

Radius and Jan saunter by on their way out. "Hey, Beehive, how's the repair job going?" asks Radius as he brushes against Bea. She lets out a delighted laugh and gives him a playful shove. Blane gives me a long look, but doesn't say anything obnoxious. "You girls need to work harder," Jan remarks before they all thunder off into the crimson jungle.

We do work hard. We manage to fix one massive tear before lunch.

Exhausted from the effort of clutching the heavy tarp above our heads, the sweat pours off of us as we remove our suits. Vesper and Bea talk about going up to sponge off before lunch. As soon a Bea leaves the room, Vesper turns to me. "Drug addict," she hisses. "We all know it." Has Bea told her? They don't get it. Oblivion powder is not to get high on. It is for deleting.

Rattled by this latest comment, I wait to clean up, and

instead, look for Thorn. When I last saw him, he was headed to the parlor.

He's not there. Not in the project room, or his room, or in the bathroom, or anywhere. I feel a hard spasm of panic. Why is he biting his fingernails day and night? Why was he grinning when the Fireseed crop is in jeopardy? I need to find him and get something out of him, even it if involves no words.

I head to the big chair in the parlor, ease into its friendly squash and smell its dusty essence. Let me rest here, take a break from all of the stress, Bea's mixed messages, Vesper's petty jealousy, the worry of where Thorn could be.

Armonk wanders in. "Mind if I sit in here?" he asks.

"'Course not." I raise my heavy lids to glance over at him, in the seat under the Axiom poster. "Your face!" I hurry over to him. "The cut opened when you were playing soccer. It's infected."

"It's nothing. Just needs time to heal," he says but doesn't sound so sure.

"Do you mind if I take a look?" I examine it closer. It's an angry, swelled up mess with edges that are turning almost blackish-green. Gangrene? My belly curdles.

"What's your verdict?" he asks, studying my face for clues.

"You need something, fast. I'll be back," I say and dash up to tier three.

The project room is blessedly empty. I get out the Spatter venom and mix it with a peck of the Fireseed and Antler Powder. Determining that one of the Axiom oils is a simple fixer, I add in a few drops, blend the ingredients and carry the jar downstairs. It will heal him, do nothing, or make it much worse. There's no way to predict, not even my dad could've called this one. All I can hope is that Spatter is similar to Dragon Elixir. After all, they are from the same lizard genus.

Drawing in an uneasy breath I say, "Settle back on the headrest."

I smooth his long, shiny hair from his swollen forehead and cheeks. He gazes up at me with his deepset eyes before shutting them. I so admire his trust. Would I do the same with a relative stranger? Doubtful. "Let me know if it hurts," I say, as I apply the mix and gently rub it in with the index finger of my good hand. With my other hand, I keep strands of hair from the gooey mix. When I apply it to the pus-filled gaps in the cut Armonk groans but claims it's not so bad. He's lying. A wound that badly infected stings even when nothing touches it.

"What are you doing?" Blane treads in with heavy boots, his weight and presence sucking up the free air in his wake.

"Armonk's face is infected," I snap. After all, it's Blane's fault! Blane slinks out, knowing better than to encourage another arrow in his back. But not before he throws me one of his shrouded, troubled stares. What does he want from me?

After the salve is smeared over the expanse of Armonk's once-chiseled features, I slip back into the sagging easy chair to wait—for signs of allergic swelling, or toxicity from poisoning. And I wonder what I'll do, with no doctor for miles, if that happens. The only one that I know of is back at my old compound. Would I risk going back to save Armonk, a boy I hardly know? I hope I never have to make that decision. My eyes sink lower. Sleeping is safer in the afternoon when the sun still hovers on the horizon.

Waking with a shudder, I jump up to look at Armonk's injury. He's not in the chair, and the sky outside is purple night. Good god, how long was I sleeping? Why didn't he wake me? I scramble into the dining room. "Anyone see Armonk?" I call out.

Armonk himself emerges from the kitchen carrying a steaming plate of potatoes. For a moment, his face is covered with hot vapor, so I rush forward, impatiently swerving around the plate to examine him up close. Will it be bad?

Sweet baby Fireseed! The swelling is entirely gone. And the black-edged cut is now a pink, rheumy zigzag traversing his facial planes like a spirited river. My dad's voice plays in my mind. "Fairy princess of mine, poof! Your magic has worked."

Armonk places the potatoes on a hotplate in the middle of the table. He faces me, with his eyes alight. "Great job, Ruby, It's not throbbing anymore. I don't know how you did it."

Bea comes out with a bowl of sautéed Fireagar. She sees me gaping at Armonk's face. "*You* fixed that?" she asks. I nod.

Thorn slips in through the kitchen door as the last of the dinner is carried to the dining room. He peels off his burn suit, avoiding my stare. "Where were you?" I ask him when the rest of the crowd is in the dining room. He shrugs. "You can't just go out anytime, anywhere you like. Speak up!" I demand before realizing that in my reflexive command, I've ordered him to do something he absolutely can't. I sigh. "At least show me a sign that you get what I'm saying."

He pats his pockets and takes out his fingernail clippings. Holds them up proudly.

"What in the world? Thorn, really! You've been outside chewing your fingernails? Stop it! You'll eat your fingers to the bone with your obsessive nibbling." I hate that I'm so exasperated by him these days, but isn't it a guardian's duty to apply a firm hand when necessary? Surely Nevada must keep a tight leash on her rowdy male students—on Vesper too.

Radius opens the door to the kitchen and peeks in. "You coming to dinner? We're all waiting."

"Be right in," I tell him.

Thorn's moon face grows dull with disappointment, which fills me, in turn, with terrible guilt. He sticks the fingernails back in his pocket. God only knows what he's collecting them for. I put a hand on his shoulder as I ferry him to dinner.

When we sit down, people are already buzzing about

Armonk's miraculous healing. But they don't all believe it had anything to do with me.

"I did see her messing around with his face," Blane reports before he stuffs in almost half of a potato.

"What did you put on it, Ruby?" asks Bea. She's freshly sponged off and her hair's in a long ponytail. Radius, sitting next to her, glances at her admiringly.

"One of my special elixirs," I say as I look around the table. "That's what *I* bring to the equation. I can heal people who are burned, who have bad infections."

"That's a very handy skill, Ruby," says Nevada. "Pass the greens," she tells Jan, as she hands him the bowlful.

"Heal them with your *drugs?*" A sinister smile spreads across Vesper's face.

Bea's mouth opens as if she wants to come to my defense, but she's silent. Is she so controlled by Vesper that she's afraid to speak? Why?

"They're elixirs," I correct Vesper.

"Whatever they are, the infection's gone," Armonk insists. Indeed, his face is glowing with an ebony sheen, and once again, his high, elegant cheekbones are evident above his jaw.

"I call them drugs when you sniff them up and pass out," says Jan.

"That's enough!" shouts Nevada. She looks at Armonk and smiles. "I'm just glad you're face is healed, however it got that way," she adds, as if she can't quite believe me either.

I sigh. This will still be an uphill battle. I guess I'll have to prove myself again; although I hope no one gets sick enough to need it.

11

We're still in our beds the next morning when Nevada's voice explodes up the stairs and into my eardrums. "Everyone up! Another emergency repair. More cuts in the tarp. Someone was here during the night."

People scramble out of their beds and grab the first thing they find to wear. I throw on my old red cloak. Bea hurriedly tucks her nightgown into her pants. Blane's shirt is on inside out. Armonk has on his faded lizard-cell pants. Only Vesper has chosen her outfit with care: a pair of her best shimmery Harem pants and solar-cell shirt. She shoots me an evil stare as we assemble in the parlor.

"This is the second breach," Nevada announces. "Clearly someone's out to steal the plants, or destroy us." She's the worse for wear, in a patched shirt and sand boots badly cracked at the toes and ankles.

"One of the schools is trying to ruin our chances of winning the competition," Jan guesses. He sounds paranoid. But who knows? The stakes are certainly high enough.

Bea says, "It could've been cut by someone who was starving, or needed shelter."

"They didn't cut any stalks down though," reasons Nevada.

"Plus for shelter, why would they cut from the top to get in?" Armonk asks.

Blane rubs his chin. "Jan's point makes the most sense. Mr. Axiom should never have announced that we have our own crop."

"We don't know that he did," says Armonk.

"We don't know that he didn't," says Vesper.

"Axiom Inc. is bringing us fortified fencing, and… other means of protection," Nevada says ominously. "But for now, we must repair the cuts, before the sun destroys everything."

She assigns us to work in pairs. This time, Radius works with Bea and Vesper with Jan. Nevada herself chooses Armonk, which wins him more bottle-sucking noises and snorts. Again, he ignores this, but sooner or later, if it doesn't stop, another arrow will fly.

I'm paired with Blane. I'd ask to switch partners, but Nevada's too stressed to ask. She had no way of knowing that Blane got aggressive with me the other day, because I'm no snitch. I'll try to make the best of it, and stay far from his clutches.

There's a clamor of activity—boots scraping against the floor, the *thwap* of suit closures, and clunk of masks pinging off of surfaces—as we all gear up at once. Something isn't quite right, but I can't put my finger on what. Then it hits me. In the chaos of the moment, I hadn't noticed that Thorn wasn't among us. My pulse speeds up. Where is he? Did whoever ripped the tarp take Thorn?

I ask the person standing next to me. "Radius, have you seen Thorn?"

"I don't keep track of your brother. Ask Bea."

"Has Thorn gone outside?" I ask her while she's attaching her mask.

"I think I saw him earlier, putting on his suit," she offers. At this, I sigh with relief. He does like to be first in the field. He's probably beaten us there.

Dashing out, I call his name. No answer, but the field is huge, and Fireseed's wide, plush leaves absorb sound. I will myself not to panic.

Once I'm out from under the porch, I see that the tarp is a mess! Someone's ripped three new gashes in the section near the porch alone. Uneven pieces droop down like torn tent flaps after a sandstorm. Already these gaping wounds in the structure have raised the temperature enough to heat up my suit.

Blane and I are assigned to scout the far western quadrant. This field is twice the square footage of my old compound that housed hundreds, and more oblong. I follow Blane as he parts the Fireseed leaves, their profuse growth forcing us to bushwhack our way through. More than a few times I have to remind him not to crush the plants underfoot in his emphatic push forward. He grumbles at this, yet seems almost chummy when he says, "Impressive show with that elixir you gave Armonk. What did you put in there, Cult Girl? A witch potion?"

"Wouldn't you like to know? Name's *Ruby,* by the way."

He pulls back a thorny section of plant so I can pass. "So, it's true you take drugs."

"No!"

"Someone saw you. Do you like getting high?"
"I take nothing to get high, or for entertainment either." This much is true. "What vice do *you* have?" I add, in an echo of Bea's sentiment from the other night.

He laughs as he presses forward, crushing more Fireseed saplings. "Being too good at playing bodyguard."

"What's that mean?" That he's more violent than I've already witnessed?

"It means I take my job very seriously." He raises his brows in a way that chills me.

~

I'm tempted to ask him if he's ever killed anyone, but I'm not sure I could handle the answer. With his massive biceps, trunk-like limbs and giant's hands he could squeeze the life out of someone without even trying.

By the time we travel almost the whole quadrant I'm thirsty and my belly's growling because Nevada had us work before breakfast. I'm sweating hard under my suit. I hate to admit that the flex and release of Blane's substantial shoulders under his burn suit is mesmerizing me. So much so, that when he stops in mid-step I hurtle right into him. With a half-grin, he steadies me, while at the same time raising an ear and tapping a finger to his lips. What?

Why didn't I hear it before? A distinct sawing reverberates off of the tarp and echoes dully through the leaf cover. Then it stops. Blane gives me one of his brooding stares, and then mouths Stay Here.

Before I know it, he's forging madly ahead, destroying leaves and stalks as he goes. I almost scold him again, but he's warned me to stay quiet, and something about him warrants attention, no matter how off-putting he is.

Huzzah, Fireseeders! booms the Stream implant in my head. It scares the living day out of me. I forgot all about that implant. It blares on.

The Axiom contest is heating up! A high schooler from Baronland South has already finished his project. He's keeping it under wraps but suffice it to say that colossal projects win colossal prizes. So keep those projects moving along. Only two weeks before we pick the finalists who will travel to Vegas-by-the-Sea.

Brought to you by Crab House Delights, where a Faux-Crab feast is only a melted butter dish away. Children eat half-price on Fridays.

It's daunting enough hanging out in this dense jungle alone without being startled by the darn Stream. In vain, I peer through the leaf canopy for a glimpse of Blane. All I see are star-shaped flower heads and arching stalks, like a forest of red mirrors, until I'm disoriented. What if Blane runs off and leaves me here? Would I find my way back through this rustling labyrinth? Reaching in my pocket, I palm my compass, thankful for small, simple things.

It's been a long ten minutes, when out of the morass, Blane shouts in great, accusing blasts, "I caught you, crazy! You're in for it." My heart thunders with a terrible sense of dread. "Ruby, get over here now," Blane commands. Shocking, he's used my actual name. I bound toward him blindly.

Coming to a small clearing, I witness a horrifying sight. My brother Thorn has climbed high in the branches of a thick Fireseed stalk. He's brandishing one of Nevada's carving knives, and the shards of another clumsy gash in the tarp dangle down from above, clearly and utterly Thorn's own handiwork. Blane has trapped him by the ankles, and is keeping him there.

I'm as speechless as Thorn ever was. I wish we'd never come to The Greening. Clearly, it's driven my brother insane.

"Thorn, what are you doing up there?" I ask stupidly.

"Speak up, bastard!" Blane yanks on Thorn's legs. Still Thorn makes no sound, but I see from his contorted red face and mouth pressed flat that he's in pain, yet stubbornly and determinedly holding his own. Why is he cutting these holes in the tarp? He's always had a reason for his various irrational behaviors before, like the time he stayed out in the Fireagar caves until sundown. Using one word—"guard" he explained that he needed to protect them. It made no sense until the next day when a poacher tried to steal half an acre.

"Stop pulling at my brother," I yell. Blane doesn't listen. Instead, he wrenches Thorn from the branches and grips him tightly around the waist. "You're ruining our chances of winning the contest," Blane shouts at him. "Destroying our livelihood. I should strangle your—"

"Don't. Don't you dare!" Running over, I try my best to pry Blane's monstrous hands from Thorn's waist. Blane's eyes are distant, bulging, frightening. "Let him go. Stop!" My face is up against his, no doubt I'm spitting on him in my fury.

Blane snaps into focus long enough to loosen his grip. Thorn falls to the ground, wheezing.

Now that I know my brother is safe, my own rage is released. "Thorn, you're ruining things!" I exclaim. Rushing forward, I kneel down next to him. "Why are you doing this? Tell me, right now. Give me a signal." His eyes are shut and he's rolling back and forth the way that he does to comfort himself.

"Give you a signal?" Blane bellows. "Give you a flipping signal? What kind of nuts are you people? I'll force the destructive cretin to talk." With that, he scoops Thorn up like an oversized sports ball, and plunges him headfirst through the field, with me struggling to keep up.

The punishment is swift and clear. Thorn is no longer allowed out in the Fireseed field. He is under house arrest, quarantined on second tier until we head up to class in the morning, which was when he apparently made his slashing forays. Not only that, Nevada is planning to boot us out of here.

"We can't afford chaos at The Greening," she threatens. "I always suspected your brother was too young to fit in here, and I was right."

"Sleep on it, please," I plead. "We'll be good. I'll talk sense into him. I'll watch him more carefully." Not so sure I can, if Thorn's gone off the deep end, but I'll try.

"No promises," she warns. "I'll give it a day or two." Nevada only allows me to speak to Thorn for a few minutes. It's clear by the way he hugs himself as he rocks that beneath his determination he's terrified. He's only a kid, but clearly Nevada doesn't trust me now, as if she thinks we're plotting like she used to do in her ZWC group. Why we would plot this type of destruction when we're in dire need of shelter is a mystery to me. Obviously we need the contest money as much as the next person here.

I sit on the floor next to Thorn, in the room he shares with Radius. He's still rocking. His hair is matted with sweat, and I can tell by his dirt-striped face that he's been crying.

Nevada is stationed in the hall, so any correspondence with Thorn must be full of stealth. It's a self-fulfilling prophecy about Thorn and I plotting. Now undercover communication will be a necessity.

"Why? Tell me why?" I whisper, so close to his ear that strands of his hair tickle my mouth. "One sign so I know you're not…" I catch myself about to say 'mental'. He'll clam up worse if he feels criticized. "One clue, that's all. Please, Thorn?"

He pauses in his movements. That's how I sense he's registered my desperate words.

Nevada peeks in. "You done in there?" This prompts him into rocking again.

"A few more seconds, please." I try again, more urgently. "Thorn, tell me! I won't be able to talk with you again for a while."

He stops rocking, and presses his damp, round head against my ear. "Food," he murmurs.

Miracles! I guide his chin up gently until he's looking at me, and pantomime bringing something to my mouth. He nods solemnly and then looks away. I know it makes him uncomfortable to look at someone for long. It's painful to him. Food. He said food! My faith in his sanity's restored, but what does he mean? I dare not ask because Nevada's walking in.

"Time to go downstairs, Ruby," she says.

I feel the prick of tears.

"*Now*, Ruby."

I press Thorn close, inhale his little boy scent of dirty hair and something irrepressibly sweet. That's how I imagine the ocean waves too—blue, buoyant, briny yet sweet. I rise to my feet and reluctantly leave. Looking back over my shoulder I see him already swaying again behind the closing door.

Now, he'll be trapped in his shut-in world even more than he already was.

Food—food for what? Food for us, for the Fireseed? Food for the Fireseed. That seems right. Don't know why but it does.

What kind of food for the Fireseed? I thought it survived on basically nothing.

It takes all day to repair the rips nearest the perimeter, which are most vulnerable to invasion and theft. My arms throb from the effort of holding the tarp steady above my head, as I sew with my other hand. At least Blane is respectful. He doesn't tease me or even make obnoxious comments about Armonk. I'm more grateful than it makes sense to be.

At dinner, though, hatred pours out as fast as water from the pitcher.

"We should toss your brother out to the lizards," Vesper spits.

"Hurl him through one of his own holes in the tarp," Jan suggests.

"Send him to a loony bin in Vegas-by-the-Sea," Vesper adds, as she spears a hunk of beetle loaf, and drops it on her plate.

"Make *him* sew up all of the rest of the holes," says Radius. "Why should we slave away at fixing them if we didn't even cut them?"

"Better yet," Vesper's eyes narrow at me, "get his sister for what he's done."

"She told him to give her a signal," Blane tells his comrades as if I'm not even there. "Why would she do that?" He gazes at me. "Are you two working as a team to trip us up?"

"Well, *are* you?" Bea leans over the table and stares at me with her chalk blue eyes. It hurts most that she would question me.

"Of course not," I insist. "I'm trying to get answers, just like you."

"That kid can talk, he's faking being mute," Jan claims. "He'd talk if I shook him."

"No," I say. "That was the problem in the first place. He's had the voice beaten out of him."

"I'll beat it out more," warns Jan.

"The hell you will," says Armonk.

"Defending the loon?" Jan sneers.

"Enough!" Nevada finally demands order. Though I get the distinct impression that her sentiments lie at least in part with the others.

~

The image of Thorn with Radius scares me. Normally he's the mildest of the guys, but tonight he's surely angry at Thorn. I dare not pass by their room though. So that night, I toss under the covers, worrying. My various stash bags are attached to my belt because I don't trust anything to the Project Room right now. In her bed across from mine, Bea is already snoring lightly. I'm thoroughly exhausted too, from all of that fieldwork. As disturbed as I am by Thorn's actions I might even be able to sleep on my own tonight. I need to try. I've got to stop taking Oblivion powder, deal with my nightmares some other way.

Sinking gratefully into my pillow, I brush my flyaway hair behind me and curl up into a comfy ball. My eyes drift lower, lower, and I fall into a dark reverie.

I'm back under the tarp. Through the holes that Thorn cut, sneak men in pearl blue ships. They hover in the Fireseed fields, waiting, waiting for someone to steal. They don't say this, but somehow I know. Dozens of them hover in great ships that drone—

Someone grabs me and clamps a firm hand over my mouth. Presses down to the point where I choke. "Rggh!" I gargle, dry-mouthed. "Arghh." I might've been dreaming before but this is as real as it gets. Thrashing around, I try to free myself, but whoever it is, has me in a firm wrestler's hold.

"Get the powder," a guy's voice hisses. "Hurry! What's wrong with you, idiots!"

Just as I start to focus my eyes in the dark, a smaller hand pushes against them, blocking any sight. I gasp for air as the hand widens to cover my nose. My heart is pounding at a breakneck pace.

"Here," says a girl. "Suck on this!" It's Vesper's voice. The fingers over my nose lift as my head is forced upward, and a dry substance is dumped into my nostrils. I choke and struggle for breath. "Sniff it up, Drug Girl, sniff up your red powder. Every last bit."

Red powder? That's not the Oblivion! I'm frantic to tell her she's got the wrong powder. This is the Fireseed pollen for my project. I haven't yet tested it, so I have no idea what it does. It could be toxic, even fatal at this dose. I close up my throat, work hard not to inhale. God only knows what the stuff will do to me. I'm familiar enough with herbs and lichen and varieties of shale to know that what's so-called "natural" when ingested can have very unnatural results. But I need to open my throat to breathe, and my voice is too coated with thick powder to work. I'm choking and gagging and inhaling all at once.

Sparks start to explode in the back of my eyes. A burning sensation hits my throat and spreads wildfire to my lungs and windpipe. Oh, how it stings, it stings!

"Give her more," Vesper's saying. "The whole forsaken pouch."

"No, save some for her brother." Jan's voice.

Oh, lord, not my brother! I raise my arms to fight them off and shove their hands from my face, but someone has clamped my arms at my sides. Blane? Bea? My hope sinks as I struggle to breathe.

More sparks play behind my eyes—exploding ones that leap like hot oil in a pan. The hovercraft from my nightmares lowers itself down and down, and a horde of hairy men climb out, their tongues wagging and grinning mouths yelling, "Druggie, get your fix, get it all! High as a hovercraft set for the moon."

My brain, in a cacophony of popping, crackling bubbles, short-circuits to black.

12

Flitting open, my eyes cycle in on a wall drawing with purple lines and curves. What is it? It's hard to focus. My eyes won't work right. They won't steady. I try again to center in, study the paper on the wall. Eddies and swirls—in a whirling pattern of purple. Close my lids once more to stabilize myself from the dizzying sensation. Breathe in, breathe out, heavily, with lungs stinging. They sting so badly I need to scream. Instead I fade out.

A warm rag touches my brow, slides across it, back and forth, up and down, over and over. It feels so fresh. It coaxes me back to the living. I try to open my mouth. It willfully disobeys me by staying closed. I will it to open again, and it creaks open in stages, like the ancient roll-top desk at the Fireseed compound, but no noise comes out.

The Fireseed compound, that was years ago, wasn't it? Whoosh, goes the warm rag, whoosh. With all of my strength I raise my lids to the halfway point, and make out a young man's deeply tanned face with leaf tattoos on high cheekbones, a resolute chin. Ah, yes! It's Armonk. And I'm lying in a bed of wrinkled sheets smelling of sour sweat. I start to raise myself on my elbows. God, the deep ache in my throat and lungs!

With a gentle hand, he guides me back down. "Shh, you've been sick, take it easy, Ruby."

My voice creaks out. "Sick? How long have I been out? Tell me… Armonk."

"A week and a day," he says, as he sweeps across my brow with the warm, damp rag.

My back prickles with fear. "I was really asleep that long?"

He nods, his dark hair and the leaf on his necklace dangling as he leans over me.

The memory of that night returns in sickening waves: a callused palm squeezing out my oxygen, thick, sticky powder coating my throat and scorching the skin inside my nose, my windpipe, my lungs. The hateful, excited voices too—Vesper's and Jan's. "Was I almost dead?" I ask Armonk.

He hesitates, as if he's not sure I can handle the truth.

"Well?"

"You could say that," he admits. "Your pulse was so fast it seemed as if you might explode," he says. "Then it got very slow, and faint and stayed like that almost until today. You only woke enough for us to drip some water down you, but I guess you don't remember." He places the rag on a side table. "The others will want to see you. Here, drink this before I get them." He reaches for a glass and holds it up to my lips.

I take a few tentative sips, and then fat, greedy ones that dribble goop down my chin. It's a mossy, sour brew, but it tastes like rivers of paradise. "Thanks, Armonk. How's Thorn, is he okay?"

"Um, he's fine. Now rest. I'll be back." With this, he pads out. I watch him go—his limping walk, his leather quiver, empty of arrows that he stores in his room, his quiet, sure manner.

I gaze around me in the darkened room, the only light coming in from the half-opened door. I'm no longer in Bea's room. This room is small and windowless, empty except for the bed I'm in, and the side table. And a drawing tacked to the wall by my bed.

I study it. A purple line drawing of the antlered beetle I caught weeks ago! Only this one is made to look like an enchanted queen beetle, with a purple, bejeweled crown and scepter. I giggle. Something like this could look so silly unless it was drawn with grace and spirit, and humor. This is Bea's fantastic drawing.

"Do you like it?" I turn over to see that she's standing in the shadow of the doorway.

"Bea!"

"I drew it for you." She steps closer. "I was worried that you wouldn't wake up, so I… I wanted something magical to watch over you."

My eyes blur with tears. "It's beautiful, Bea! I love it."

"You're not mad at me for drawing your secret? I know you wanted to keep it private, but I hoped it would cheer you up like nothing else."

"It's absolutely fine, Bea. Thank you."

She drifts closer, and sits on the edge of the bed. "Sorry I didn't defend you. It's unforgivable what Vesper did. And Jan," she adds under her breath. "It's just that we've all been through such hard times. It drives some people mad, you know?"

"It hardens people," I say. "But that's no excuse for hurting someone."

"No. Nevada punished them," Bea's quick to add.

"They'll really hate me now. They'll blame me for their punishment."

Bea shrugs. "Maybe so. Stay away from them. You have every right to be here."

"I have a mother I could go back to."

"But you said that you couldn't. You said that a man assaulted you."

"What?" Shame rushes through me. "I never told you that!"

"You were talking in your sleep. Saying all kinds of things."

"Oh, no." My face heats up, inflaming my lungs and throat all over again. "What else did I say? Did it make any sense?"

"You talked about men in ships. Men that had hair all over them, men stealing people."

I grimace. "Those were nightmares, that's all."

"Nightmares come from something real, don't they?" Her shrewd eyes stare into mine, willing out truths. This fledgling friendship is so raw. Dare I trust her?

"I guess they do. I don't know what exactly."

"Maybe something yet to come?" Something in her surety sets my teeth to grind, my worries to creep in. This place feels as unsafe as the old compound ever did. And yet, here I have a new friend, and actually two, with Armonk.

"How's Thorn?" I ask her, remembering Armonk's hesitant tone when I asked him. "Is he really okay?"

Bea's quiet for a moment, wringing her delicate hands.

"What? Tell me."

"He's disobeyed Nevada's quarantine a couple of times now."

I hoist myself up higher. "What do you mean? How?"

"He keeps escaping to the field. Armonk and Blane keep finding him curled up under a Fireseed plant."

"Blane, oh, no. Has Thorn cut any more holes in the tarp?"

"Yes."

I sink as if I'm in a freefall. This is bad, very bad. We'll be kicked out now for sure. "What did Nevada say? What did she do?"

"The funny thing is, well... come out and see for yourself."

Adrenaline pounds into my system, down my spine and into my legs. In one fluid motion that seemed impossible even a half hour ago, I bolt upright, rock my legs over the bed and to the floor and slip on my boots. Holding onto Bea to steady myself, we walk down to tier one and out the garden door.

13

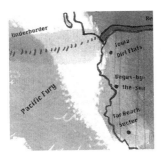

Even before I'm downstairs a humming starts in my head, like string instruments playing all at once. It's nothing like the Axiom Stream messages, not at all. Those are loud and intrusive and overly cheery. This is subtle murmuring, inviting and comforting, and it feels as if it's breathing new life into me. I reach for the door to go out but Bea stops me.

"What're you doing?" she cautions. "You need your suit."

"Oh, that," I say as an afterthought. I shrug myself into it, and with a wave of impatience, reach for my mask. Somehow I don't feel like I need these things any more. Why, I can't say.

My energy returns in great bursts as I plunge into the field. I feel as if I could leap over plants and even people. Is it because I haven't eaten for a week and I've lost weight?

"Be careful," Bea warns, as I falter and catch myself. "Look over here," she says.

But I've already seen it, and I'm halfway over there. Good god! The Fireseed has pushed its way through one of Thorn's intentional holes. "In one week it's grown twice as big as any plant in here."

"See?" Bea states the obvious. "It's shot up like that old fairy tale, Jack and the Beanstalk. How did Thorn know to open up the space for it?"

I brush up against the Fireseed's rustling leaves, as if I'm convinced it will give me the answer. As I do, the droning gets more insistent—a kind of lovely, wild music in my head. *Food*, it sings, *food, food, food.*

That's what Thorn told me! I inspect the leaves. They're clean and red and smooth. Running to another plant, I finger those leaves. "It's gone!" I tell Bea.

"What's gone?" Her brow crosses in confusion.

"The blight Thorn said was on the Fireseed."

"Thorn *talks* to you?" She crosses her arms and gapes at me. "I thought you said that his words were beaten out of him. Did you lie? Why would you do that?"

"I did say that, Bea. Thorn doesn't talk *out loud*. He… he talks with his eyes." Her face is a grimace of disbelief. I don't care about Jan and Vesper, but it's important that at least Bea believes me. "Thorn pointed out the whitish puckering on the leaves. You never noticed it?"

"No." She uncrosses her arms. "What does that have to do with how Thorn knew they'd grow taller if they were exposed to sun? Nevada convinced us they'd burn up and die."

"I don't know," I say truthfully. When I say that, the noise in my head swells. *Sun, sun, sun,* it drones and I have an inexplicable drive to escape the confines of the field and run out toward the dunes.

To hold myself back from running to the fence and ducking under is like trying not to scratch a horrid itch. Bea would surely report me as a danger to myself. I'd be quarantined like Thorn. This I know.

"Where is Thorn?" I ask Bea as I look back toward the school. Suddenly I'm exhausted. Even if I forgot, my throbbing back and quaking knees remember that I was basically in a coma for a week.

"Come on." Bea leads me to the Project Room, where everyone turns to me at once. Blane's mouth drops open as if he's looking at a glowing ghoul from Skull's Wrath. My eyes move to Thorn. He's moved his equipment to the table that Radius and I share where he's standing on a box. It looks from the items in his hands that he's working on a Fireseed project. I run over and hug him. He hugs me back ferociously. Then I hold him at arm's length to examine how he looks. His skin looks tan, he's a little thinner, but he looks amazingly fine.

"You were really disintegrated," Jan blurts out from behind me.

"No thanks to you," I snort, without turning.

"Whatever that stuff was, it was really powerful," says Radius. He's sitting at his end of the long table. "Well, I'm glad you survived."

"Thanks, Radius." That's the first nice thing any of the guys, aside from Armonk, has said to me. Though I did catch a heartening glimmer of relief in Blane's eyes.

Vesper narrows her eyes as I march up to her. "Did you give my brother any of that red powder?" I stare into her striking, dark face, set in a jeer. "Did you?"

"Not me." She wheels away.

I navigate around to her front again, and force her to look at me a second time. "Where's the rest of it?"

She shrugs. "Couldn't tell you."

"Not good enough," I say, though I'm resigned to not finding out. I'll have to collect more for the competition. Besides, it nearly killed me, so I'm not sure it's wise to keep experimenting with it. "Don't you come near me or my brother again, do you understand?"

"Who would want to?" she answers defiantly.

"Then that's settled."

With that, I float downstairs, my brother at my heel. "Did they make you snort up some red powder?" I ask him, when we reach the compound's front door.

He nods, and smiles.

"What's so darn funny?" I ask him. "Didn't it make you sick?"

He shakes his head.

"You must not have taken as much as me then. It made me terribly sick."

He nods, and gives me another puppy-dog hug, clearly happy that I'm awake now. My heart wrenches.

"Shall we go—?" The whispering inside my head finishes it for me. *Outside, outside, outside.*

Thorn answers without speaking, *Outside, outside, outside.*

We slip out the door and tread on light feet to sloping dunes. They look like Bea's drawings of angel wings—curved, graceful, arching over the flatter sands. This is the first time I've been out in the open desert since Depot Man dropped us off, and it feels singular, daring, exciting.

Maskless, we turn our faces to the sun, to the accompaniment of two hundred red plants humming *food, food, food,* just inside the quadrants.

Blane finds us there. We are belly down, our teeth chewing sand, their grains sandpapering our burned, oozing skin. He drags us inside and onto the parlor floor. Now it's not just my windpipe and lungs that sting, it's every part of me that was exposed to the killer sun. I hear him say, "Geez, Ruby, you two must've been out there for a good two hours! What were you thinking?"

I have no idea what I was thinking. None. I don't think that I was. It was more a blind motion—the way the moon follows a sunset. The earlier singing inside my head has transformed into a long yelp of pain. Thorn, too, is rocking and rocking, groaning as tears stream down his red, oozing cheeks.

Nevada stands over us, her expression a combination of horror and anger. "I was just getting ready to tell you that you two could stay on when you do this! Why? Why would you go outside with no mask? Were you trying to kill yourselves?"

Once again, I'm speechless. There's no way to explain my behavior.

"I should take you back to your Fireseed compound," she says. "Clearly, you have no interest in following rules."

In response I emit an agonized moan.

"Is that what you want? You want to go back? Talk to me in English." Her kohl-lined eyes are monstrous with a gray, whirling intensity. They scare me, *I* scare me, Thorn scares me. The burn on my face scares me. I can't take much more.

Where's Armonk? He won't understand either, but at least he's kind.

"And your brother," she continues, "did he learn to break rules from you? First holes in the tarp, then, he disobeys my house laws, and now this. How can I possibly treat your burns? You need to be in a hospital."

This is when I realize Nevada's more afraid than angry. She has no idea what to do and it's clear from the sound of her voice that we are very bad off.

I summon up words. "Tincture."

"What?" She leans over me. "You'll have to do better than that."

"Armonk," I mutter as clearly as I can. "Get Armonk."

Lost in pain as the burns throb to my heartbeat, I clutch my brother who is writhing on the parlor floor next to me. The sting is so bad I feel myself slipping in and out of reality.

I must've lost some minutes, because when I come to, Armonk is whispering in my ear. The airflow from his words pierces the skin around my ear with darts of agony. "What can I do to help?" he asks me.

"Upstairs, in the project room," I gasp. "My elixir. The one I put on your face." I stop talking to suck in the pain, in order not to scream. "Can you get it?" I add.

He's already out the parlor door and I hear the thump of him climbing upstairs. The sheer relief that he's understood me has me floating in another nether zone. When I come to again, he's swabbing goo on my face with fingers that feel like sharp stones. I swallow another scream.

When he's finished with me, he slathers the tincture on Thorn.

After what seems like another half an hour, I can unclench my muscles enough to lie flat and stare numbly at the Axiom poster, at its blue scalloped waves. Thorn too, has stopped whimpering. I take his hand and we lie like that, while Armonk keeps watch over us in the dusty armchair.

A strange, humming peace washes over us as the sun lowers itself behind the dunes.

14

Thorn keeps wandering out to the western quadrant where Blane caught him that first time. I always find him cuddled against a Fireseed stalk and ask him what he's doing. He never tells me. But every time I go out there now, the humming starts. Sometimes it's saying *food, food, food,* and I can actually hear the branches sigh as they stretch out through the new cuts in the tarp. Other times they seem to murmur *come, come, come, come outside.* Those times, it's all I can do to stop myself from ducking under the high fence to stand again in the fevered sun.

Why would my Fireseed gods coax me in this way? Are they turning against me for leaving my home and taking my brother? I choose not to believe that.

More than once, I cheat by standing directly under a cut in the tarp, where the sunlight is streaming down, and where I tilt my head up, hungrily. This fills me. Because otherwise, I'm growing weak, I'm fading in the confines of The Greening.

The last burns were so bad that they formed a permanent pattern of pocked skin—on Thorn's face as well. First our skin blistered, then oozed, then popped, then it peeled and scarred. It was always on the verge of terrible infection. My tincture helped to hasten our healing, but even my good medicine couldn't totally stop the scarring. I feel bad for Thorn. Not so much for myself.

In a way, it's a relief that my face is no longer flawless. My looks often got me unwelcome pinches and leers from the cult men—and always from Stiles. Now the guys here gape at my scars, not at my beauty. It's helped lessen my need for the Oblivion Powder. I only needed it three times this week. My nightmares of Stiles are finally fading.

Today, before I head up to the project room I look in Bea's mirror and examine the line of pocks running down one side of my nose and along my opposite cheek. They're not separate marks and not all identically shaped, more a jumble of scars that form an uneven ridge.

From my side view it's clear that in the span of about two weeks I've become scrawny as well. My appetite's disappeared. It's hard to say whether the red powder or the burns were to blame. But I'm shrinking! My pants hang off me. Bea's been really nice to take them in at the seams, though they're already loose again. Thorn too, has lost any little boy softness he had, and soon Bea will have to take in his clothes, if she's willing. I tie on the apron I wear for mixing elixirs. It's satisfyingly bulky and hides my ribs.

I'm in the middle of revising the concoction made from Antlered Purples that I'm hoping to test today—on my scars, and the Fireseed leaves too, when Thorn runs over to me, and tugs on my arm.

"What?" I say offhandedly. I have patience for Thorn, except when I'm absorbed in experimental work. "I'm kind of busy."

He pulls on my arm again, and nods to the door.

I sigh, and wipe my hands on my smock. "Can it wait?"

He shakes his head.

I follow him downstairs to the garden door. When he starts outside, I call out to him, reminding him about his suit. But then the humming starts. It says *now, now, now*. For once, I give into it. Thorn is moving fast, navigating the thick jungle with ease. These days I find that it's easier for me too. I'm practically flying. Faster, through the shivering, singing leaves.

Thorn is headed for the western quadrant. A couple of weeks ago, it would have taken us a half-hour to hike there. Now, we've gotten there in ten minutes. He shimmies under the first plant where Blane and I found him up in the branches.

"What are you doing, Thorn?" I crouch under the lowest branch canopy and crawl in on hands and knees.

He lifts his palm and holds it under a wide, curling leaf. Then he gazes over at me with a joy that's so pure, so uplifting, it washes over me in fantastic waves. "What, Thorn?" He's always such a puzzle. I'm not expecting the words when they come.

"My. Project!"

"Huh?" I duck further under and crane my neck to peer at the underside of the leaf, examine what his palm is cradling. "That? A leaf bud?" As I focus in closer, I see that it's no regular bud. It's bigger and rounder and the red plant skin is stretched so tight, it seems ready to explode. In fact, now I see a slight movement, a probing from the inside. "What is it? Is an insect caught in there?" I ask Thorn.

He laughs silently, and cups his hand around the swollen bud. There's a harder poke as if something's making a determined effort to get out, and the membrane rips with a sound like fabric tearing. My jaw drops. "The thing has… wings! What the heck is it?"

Its beaklike protrusion roots around in the air, and two eyes, set far apart, blink out at us. It shakes out its leafy wings like some kind of exotic red sun umbrella, and flaps down to the sandy ground by Thorn's knees.

The thing has no real body; it's more just a head with a beaklike snout. And well, a rudimentary body the size of Thorn's fist that seems mainly designed to support the creature's wings. Its eyes are expressive, eerily human, dark like Thorn's. No ears, but tufts of stuff like feathery stamens, some with tiny leaf blossoms.

"What *is* this, Thorn?" As if he would know, as if anyone would know!

"A Red," he answers, and reaches out to pet it. It flutters but doesn't fly off.

"A Red?" I echo. "It's not a Fireseed seedling. It's not a plant. Is it some kind of parasite that crawled into the plant and used it as a chrysalis?" I ask, as much to myself as Thorn. He may be uncannily smart, but he's still a kid.

"Made him. My project." Thorn gazes up at me with his steady brown eyes, and I know, he's telling me the truth—an impossible truth, yes, but an undeniable truth.

"But *how,* Thorn?"

He reaches in his pocket and pulls out a few of his chewed fingernails. Holds them up. It takes me a beat to make the unspoken connections. When I do, I eagerly ask him more. For the exact place that he put his fingernails, for how he knew this would work, for any more information at all. But he's done talking. It's an absolute miracle he's managed to string so many words together at all.

I look back at the creature. "Red," I repeat, and touch it lightly with the fingers on my bad hand. It lets me stroke it only for a moment, before it flaps up to a branch behind Thorn. Its expression, if you can call it that, is one of 'Thorn's my master. Only he can pet me. But you're sort of okay, you ungainly beast.'

I turn to my brother. "You'll need to keep this thing secret so no one finds out until the judging. You're going to win this Axiom competition, hands down! You know that, right?"

Thorn's answer is a wide grin that spreads over his serious face, reflecting the crimson brilliance of the miraculous creature called Red.

15

The next few days are filled with deliveries from George Axiom: new high-tech fencing, and weapons for guarding the perimeter of the field. George's men, gliding along the perimeter in their white vehicles, help lay down the fence, while Blane and the rest of the guys help secure it in the sand with George's amazing self-drilling agar posts.

There are maps—a specialty of Axiom Coastal—also silvery handguns that click open and closed, which you load bullets into. Nevada stores them in the shed behind the kitchen under lock and key. We have target practice every other day.

Jan and the other guys are super excited by this. They take the guns out and polish them, and sneak target practice in the field, shooting holes in the Fireseed leaves, which makes me furious. When they do this, the humming in my head swells into a kind of shriek, and I yell for them to stop, at which they shoot more and faster. They don't know what's playing in my head.

So, I make them clay pigeons out of shale and fixer. The upside is that I'm popular for it. The downside is that I can hardly make them fast enough, and it distracts me from working on my contest project. The Stream announcements seem designed to make us anxious about getting our projects done, and making them the most inventive things ever. They blast into our heads at totally random times:

Huzzah, Fireseeders! George Axiom here. Who's the smartest high-schooler with the most ingenious Fireseed project? We, in Vegas-by-the-Sea can't wait for the Axiom Extravaganza to find out! Only twenty more days for the finalist picks.

Brought to you by the Shark Bar and Grill, in the landmark historic Aquarium Casino from before the Border Wars. Where holo-sharks take a virtual bite out of you only in sim time.

So far, I can't really tell what Blane is doing, other than poring over data on his holo tablet. The Network goes in and out, more out than in. It's all so new to me. I'm impressed he knows how to use it without lessons. They never taught us at the compound.

Radius has drawn wing diagrams that would use Fireseed leaves for some type of fancy vehicle. He's the least secretive, and I take peeks at his sketchbook when he leaves the room. It's a cool and fanciful glider that almost looks like Thorn's

Red but on a grand scale and without a face! Radius spends time flirting with Bea too. They're cute together, his curly red hair and adoring manner, her bubbly, affectionate remarks and pats to his back, his cheek. She's always sketching him, and helping him sharpen the perspective on his own diagrams. He's always coming up behind her and sneaking in hugs while she's working.

Jan is stalling on his project. He paces around with a sour, irritated look on his face while his friends are busy. His tall, reedy frame seems brittle, as if it might crack in pieces should someone call him and he had to turn quickly. I wonder whether he's come up with any project at all. My theory is that he has brain damage, more than my brother ever suffered. I've heard it can make a person unpredictable and violent. Blane told me that Jan stumbled around in the desert longer than anyone else here. He hiked all the way from the deep south—a place that used to be called Alabama—and lived on selling wire he stole from some depot down there. I saw two long scars on Jan's back one time he bent over while he was playing soccer. Blane said it was from a stranger's knife attack.

Nevada has decided Thorn and I can stay. After all, Thorn saved the plants from blight. I pointed out to her the few remaining puckers to prove the point. No doubt she wants to keep him around in case she needs a human weathervane again. She's still incredulous every time she looks at the tallest Fireseed that spirals up and up through the tent to kiss the sun. She even starts petting the stalks in her glee like I do.

As far as George Axiom's deadly arsenal, Armonk says he's not interested. He still uses his bow and arrow, which, inevitably inspires more ridicule. Jan, Vesper and Blane call him Indian and Tomahawk and names that make no sense to me. Bea and Radius stay out of it.

The cache of weapons seems kind of silly anyway, now that we know the real so-called intruder was Thorn.

Nevertheless, Nevada assigns guardsmen to walk the perimeter of the field—Blane in the morning, Radius and Jan alternating afternoons, and Armonk—the most adept at night vision—after dark. The girls are spared, which is fine with me because I hate the cold feel of a gun in my hands and the field is so vast now, it intimidates me to be out there in it.

One late afternoon I'm working alone on my newest elixir up in the project room on third tier. I'm absorbed in my task, my soiled, greasy smock thrown over me, and my hands gooey with fixer oils. I've mixed in a pinch of Spatter venom and a dose of Fireseed's red powder, the first I've collected since the attack. I'm hoping to test it on my scars. I don't really care about fixing mine, but if it works on that, I'll fix Thorn's face.

Nevada's gone with Vesper and Bea to Skull's Wrath Depot, and Jan is on guard duty. Armonk is playing one of Nevada's crusty old card games with Thorn in Armonk's room on second tier. I'm not sure where Blane is. Last time I saw him he was sleeping in the parlor, his head thrown back on my favorite armchair. Seeing him there, I had an odd urge to adjust his head to a less awkward angle. But I left him there, spittle glittering on his lip.

I hear the dull thwack of the front door closing downstairs and figure Nevada's come back. After that, I hear raised voices, men's voices and rough laughter. It's probably Jan and Blane, cracking sleazy jokes so I pay it no mind.

Skimming the extra oil off the surface of my elixir, I wipe it on a rag. Too little oil and it won't sink in. Too much oil and the formula will slide right off a person's face.

The footsteps get louder and I realize that whoever it is, is headed upstairs. So, I hunch over my experiment. That way, prying eyes can't so easily see what I'm making.

"Here she is," says Jan. I swerve around to see a heavyset man who looks incredibly familiar. He's got a saggy potbelly and long stringy hair that needs a vigorous scrub. Oh, hellfire! It's Depot Man from that first night.

"Why are you here?" I blurt. A pit in my belly expands to a doughy, nauseous lump.

Guilty hesitation shadows Depot Man's face. "He made me tell him where I dropped you off."

"You didn't have to tell anyo—"

"He bribed me with money," he adds sheepishly.

"Who?" And then I see.

Right behind him is a grizzled Stiles with a malicious grin slimed over his face at the sight of me. "You wicked, wicked wench!" he bellows, "How dare you try to poison me?"

I forgot how wizened he looked and how whiny his voice was. Like a spoiled child who gets everything he wants. Well, he won't get me. Thankfully, he has no gun, no apparent weapon in his hands.

"You thought you'd get away with escaping? Think again." He steps past Depot Man and lunges for me. Grabbing one of my arms, he twists it, hard. He may look like a crotchety old man and sound like a spoiled child but he's got furious adult strength in his sinewy arms.

"How could you let him up here!" I shout at Jan, who shrugs as he leans against the wall.

Depot Man, on the other hand, has already beaten a hasty exit.

Jan's frown is as bitter as Stiles'. "You brought nothing to the equation," he sneers. "Blane told you that. He warned you. So did Nevada. You never listen. You just give us guys your seductive looks, thinking you can charm any of us to do your bidding. And then you act superior."

Superior? What's Jan talking about? The way he sees me is so warped. But the seductive looks, guilty as charged. That's how I was taught to communicate with men. Must be a better way. Right now though I need to escape Stiles' grip.

Jan is watching Stiles twist my other arm now, and position them both behind my back. "Back stairway's down this way," Jan instructs Stiles. "That's the fastest way out."

I kick Stiles and hear his sharp grunt. Direct hit, my foot arcs off of his rounded kneecap. I'm rewarded with another, more vicious twisting of my arms. If my arms were free I'd take my newest elixir and smear it into right Stile's eyeballs until the cells melt into goo. All I can do is scream and pray someone hears me.

He drags me down the hall past the spare room that I slept in during my coma, and toward the back stairway. I wheel around to screech long and shrill right in his eardrum. I hope it damages his hearing. He veers away, and hauls me down one stair at a time. It hurts, badly. My ankles bump, bump, bump against the sharp corners of the stairs.

Thrashing around to stall his progress and create as much chaos as possible, I trip him. He stumbles but rights himself, then bites down on my hand. With a meaty crunch my flesh gives way. Bump, bump, bump, he bounces me down the last flight of stairs.

I can't let him take me back to the compound; he'll beat me, kill me even.

"Let go!" I thrash against him. We're lost in a struggle of twisted limbs, close to the garden door. Fireseed, hear me! "If I have to go back to that hellhole, I'll demolish everything!" The curtained gazebos where the men pair up with underage partners, the podium where they fill us with unholy lies and false proclamations. Where they singe the small children with brands.

"I'll destroy *you*, Ruby," Stiles hisses in my ear with his putrid turnip breath. "Your face is scarred now, you're not even pretty anymore."

The zing of an arrow misses its mark and thwacks into the sand. Armonk!

Stiles flings open the glider door. He throws me in and secures my arms with agar binding to the seat post. The zing of a second arrow hits Stiles' left shoulder, and Stiles, with a shocked groan, jerks backwards. His hands move upward, fumble with the arrow, but by the look on his face, he can't stand the pain of trying to pull it out. His cloak's already red, but this new liquid, spreads darker red, in pulses. With the arrow still jutting out, he starts the glider.

"Let me go! You don't want me, I don't want you," I shout. I unfasten the door with my foot. He leans over, grabs the handle and slams the door on my ankle. With all of the strength in my other leg, I swivel around and push it open again. Good Fire! Cursing at me, Stiles tries to grab the door handle again. I only have another second or two before I'm airborne.

Then, an enormous body hurls itself on Stiles, all mammoth curled back and rock-hard thighs like some leathery Skull's Wrath monster. I swerve away to avoid being crushed. Looking up, I see Blane's cropped brown hair and wild eyes, mad for the kill.

His potato-fists seize around Stile's neck and squeeze. Stiles burbles and coughs like a clogged pipe.

Armonk sinks his third arrow in Stiles' calf, where Stiles raised it to kick Blane off him. Red spurts onto me, onto Blane, onto the floor. Armonk must've hit an artery.

"Get off me," pleads Stiles. "I'm leaving, get off!"

At this, Blane eases up on Stile's neck. "Leave then!" Blane orders. Stiles struggles to his feet and over to the console while Blane unbinds my arms. "Ruby, go! Quick," Blane exclaims.

I scramble out, taking care not to slide and fall into Stile's bloody mess. Blane gives Stiles a parting punch and then leaps from the vehicle. "Don't even think about coming back," he warns.

From over my shoulder I see Stiles blinking to regain alertness. He fumbles at his wounds in another attempt to dislodge the arrow. Then, he ascends, swerving my way. "Sinful woman," he hollers from the window, "next time, I'll bring an army. And *you…*" He glares down at Blane. "You'll be meat for the flies."

"Coward! I should've shot you when I had the chance," Blane shakes his fist at the departing specter of Stiles in the angry sky.

Already my ankle and wrists are on fire and swollen to ridiculous proportions. My hand smarts where Stiles bit it. Armonk hurries over to help steady me as I limp away.

"That was the man they had you partnered up with?" he asks me.

"Yes," I gasp, and thank him.

"I see why you left. I heard yelling, and had a bad feeling about it," he explains as we shuffle toward the back door. " I told your brother to stay put in his room, and I came running."

"You're a good shot," I say. "Did you see it sticking out from his shoulder?" We both exhale in shaky, relieved laughter.

By this time, Blane has caught up to us. We stop in awkward hesitation as we regard him. Am I the one who feels awkward, or is it Blane? His eye is blackening and the skin under it is torn from where Stiles got in one lousy punch. But it's Blane's expression that tears me up.

"Thanks," I tell him. I loosen myself from Armonk's firm arm and gingerly test my weight on my sore ankle. It feels wrong to lean on Armonk right now with Blane staring at me, a hungry, lonely look in his eye. It's as if he's never been hugged, never been fed, never been loved, as if the sight of Armonk touching me, even just to help me limp along injures him. "Thanks," I tell Blane again. "I really mean that. That man would've killed me if I'd gone back."

Blane only grunts, before forging ahead and beating us into the house.

"What's his problem?" Armonk mumbles. But I know that he knows. Just like I know a lot of other things right now, because now that it's quiet the humming's started up in my head. It knows me, and it reaches out in all directions to tell me things. Tell me that Thorn feels the humming too, and knows something's terribly off kilter.

Stay safe, stay safe it goes as I limp inside and collapse into the dusty armchair.

"Do you want company?" Armonk stands there uncertainly in the doorframe with his long hair all tangled from running, and his bow and half-empty quiver hanging off one shoulder. His leaf necklace rises and falls with each quick breath, and his face glistens nut brown from the effort of chasing down Stiles.

"I'll be okay," I lie. "Just need time alone to catch my breath."

Armonk hesitates. In the pulse behind my shut eyelids, I sense Thorn creeping downstairs and padding across the room. He climbs up in my lap and hugs me. Settles by my side. I know that this hurts Armonk just like I've hurt Blane, because Armonk isn't stupid either. He's smart and patient and kind. I can't help if I'm not ready to be close.

As I sink into the comfort of Thorn's warm, puppy dog presence, I worry that now I have not one, but two men fighting over me. As ugly, pocked and skeletal as I've become, and now swollen with injuries, I'm still a hot commodity. None of that has served to barricade me. Jan's words float into my mind. I mustn't use my seductive charm to get anything anymore. I need to figure out different ways. Honest ways. Upstairs I hear Blane fighting with Jan.

"What the hell were you thinking, leading the depot guy in here with that pervert?"

"Who cares?" Jan's says. "You're sweet on that cult girl. Is that it?"

"That has nothing to do with it, Jan."

"Really? Then what do you care?"

"You're a fool letting *any* stranger in here! Nevada told us to guard this place. I take my job seriously."

With a silent chant, I drown out their voices: *Make it go away, make it all go away.*

Which guy would I pick to be closer to: the gentle spirit that is Armonk or the sweat-scented fighter that is Blane? Must I choose one over the other, ever? Can't we all at least try to be friends?

Thorn rests his head on my shoulder as I sink lower into the cushions and dream of turquoise waves washing over me.

When Nevada returns with Vesper and Bea, Blane blurts out the whole story to her. "Jan's a fool!" he shouts. "He jeopardized the whole school by letting those strangers in here. If I'd had one of the guns, that trespasser would've been blown to hell and back." Blane's voice scares me, even though it's comforting that he protected me. Flattering even. But I can't help recalling what he told me once about being too good at playing guard dog. I'm afraid that it brings out his vicious side. I'm afraid how that weirdly attracts me. It's wrong! All wrong, and I have to keep chanting to myself, *Take it all away.*

I notice a lack of red blood around the bite mark. Or more accurately, the area has a faint greenish tint. Is that what they call gangrene, or is there something else seriously wrong with my blood? It freaks me out so much that I force myself to look away.

Nevada frets over me like a mama bear from that fairy tale, feeding me special tea and oatmeal and giving me a sponge bath with her special sage oil. I'm incredibly grateful to witness this motherly side of her. But I can't help longing for the comfort of my own dear mother. With the memory of her warm hug and understanding voice, tears run down my cheeks.

"You'll be better soon, Ruby," Nevada soothes, misunderstanding the nature of the tears, which she wipes away for me.

I truly can't go back. Stiles would strangle me like Blane did him only Stiles would finish the job. That night, I toss in bed. The night terrors have returned, full of Stiles—his threatening energy, his leering grin, his scornful eyes. I listen to the rise and fall of Bea's breathing. And like the early days, I know that I'm waiting for her to fall sleep so I can sniff up the last of the Oblivion Powder. And I thought I was doing so well, weaning myself bit by bit. My cheeks are already hot with the shame of it.

I reach into my belt pack. Across the room, Bea stirs. "You're having nightmares."

My hands shoot back to my side. "Yes. What's to say he won't be back?"

"You have us. You have Nevada. We'll hide you."

I smile in the dark. "Hide me." Like children's hide and seek, darting from rock to rock. "That's a nice thought, Bea."

"You're a person worth protecting."

My eyes blur. "Thanks. I'll protect you, too. And I'll try my best to sleep without that stuff." She knows what I mean. I sense her nodding.

"You can do it, Ruby. If you can't sleep, wake me up and we'll talk again."

"That's the nicest thing anyone's ever said to me." A tear spills over onto my cheek and I wipe it off.

"Aww," she soothes. Against the moon's purple silhouette, I see her brush back her long hair and settle in.

Curling into a catlike ball, I explore the cool, dry sheets with my toes and drift off softly, fearlessly.

16

E ven Vesper is nice to me for a few days. She picks me for her team in soccer, but I can't exactly play with a swollen ankle. She doesn't whisper any hateful things when I pass by her, and she compliments me on a stew I make.

But it doesn't last. As soon as my ankle heals, and Bea asks me to model her newly designed Fireseed leaf clothes, Vesper turns ugly again.

Bea has designed a Fireseed trench coat and the cutest red hoodie with a built-in mask. They are quite fashionable! I try them on while she pins them up, which I'm happy to do.

"Turn a little to the right," she says, her mouth full of pins. "Now to the left." Finally, she stands back, bobbing her head in satisfaction. "You look great in it." She comes forward and feels my ribs like a worried mom. "Don't get too skinny on me now, or the jacket will be swimming on you."

"She's a scarecrow already," Vesper snipes. "I can model that hoodie for you at the Axiom finals."

"Maybe so," Bea says. "But I've already fitted them to Ruby."

This makes Vesper fume, and I notice that for her project, Vesper has basically copied Bea's idea. She's making backpacks out of the pressed leaves, and glider covers that can withstand any sandstorm. Her items aren't exactly clothes, but still, she cuts the patterns from templates and sews them together like Bea does.

Vesper hates me more than ever. She corners me in the halls and hisses spiteful comments of all stripes. "Your skin has ugly moon craters," she'll say, or "You're shriveled like a dead lizard," which doesn't bother me. When she says, "Your brother's a real troublemaker. We'll get rid of him yet," this bothers me. I never answer her. That would egg her on.

Thorn spends all of his time out in the western quadrant, coaxing the Red from its perch, high in the tallest plant that juts above the tarp.

Sometimes it sits on his narrow shoulder and preens its leaf-like wings. I ask him all about it: "How big will it grow? Has anyone else aside from the two of us seen it? What does it eat?" But he's stopped talking again. There's compensation though, because the ever-present humming in my head fills in some of the blanks. *We're growing, we're growing, we're growing* it hums.

What's growing? I ask silently.

Babies, babies, babies, babies is the answer.

Babies, huh! Yet, I only see one Red, flopping around in the high branches, poking its beak out of the tarp, blinking its huge brown eyes at Thorn with something like admiration. How is this even possible? I'm just glad that no one else from The Greening has seen the Red. Surely they would want to steal it, claim it as their own project. I again warn Thorn to keep the Red concealed. He nods and grins, nods and grins.

~

Blane returns from sentry duty one morning, claiming that he's seen a hovercraft repeatedly cycle by. His pistol is still tucked in the hip pocket of his burnsuit, and the sight gives me a ripple of furtive desire mixed with dread. Blane and guns—a worrying mix.

"What color was the ship?" I ask him.

"Don't remember," he says as he lays the pistol down on a dining room chair, lifts off his mask and climbs out of his burn suit. His wide, rocky face gleams with sweat.

I swallow hard. My bad dreams had hovering ships, but those weren't real, they were sick, coma dreams. "Were there hairy men with beards in the ships?"

Blane sniggers. "Hairy men? You have a filthy mind, Cult Girl." I don't like that he's reverted to his early disrespectful nickname for me, and the glint in his eyes makes me furious.

"My name's Ruby," I remind him. "And I have a serious reason for asking."

"Ruby," he echoes, with bite. "What could that be?"

"Never mind." I won't tell him about my strange dreams. I'm tired of his teasing, and his insults. He had a nerve being hurt when he saw Armonk helping me walk.

Blane marches toward the kitchen. I hear him guzzling from the precious store of water, and I have a mind to scold him for drinking from the jug, to tell him to wipe off his mouth prints, but I hold back. Snapping at him is as unfair as him teasing me.

Instead, I call from the dining room, "If you see the ships again, let me know."

"You're going to help me shoot them down?"

The urge to scold is on my tongue for a second time. Something like, Is all you can think of ways to be violent? But I may need his protection again in this dangerous place. "Maybe so," I say cryptically.

He emerges with a half-grin. I've pleased him, and that's not an easy thing to do.

Later that day a bunch of us are working in the project room. Thorn is down with Nevada, who has offered to give him the rare writing lesson. Radius is on sentry duty, Bea has a bad headache and is napping, and Armonk's downstairs repairing his bow.

I'm up here with Vesper, Jan and Blane, and tension is thick. Blane, who's been poring over something on his laptop, comes over, slides Thorn's stool toward me and sits on it. My traitorous body pricks to attention. He tries to see what I'm working on, but I cover it with cloth.

"Secretive, secretive!" he says.

"Tell me what *you're* working on," I dare.

He cocks his head in a quizzical manner. "You'd be surprised. It's deep. You think you have a claim on deep, but you're not the only one."

Blane always manages to annoy me. He's right that I'd be surprised if his project is deep. He seems more brutish than brainy. Then again, there's often a crafty light in his gaze. As if he can meet me at any level. In that way, I guess he has the advantage because he knows I underestimate him.

"Blane is brilliant," says Jan.

"His father was a brain surgeon, you know," Vesper claims.

"His mother was a gene scientist," Jan adds.

I want to tell them all to shut up, quit bullshitting and stay out of our conversation. In the midst of my disdain, I feel oddly possessive of Blane, as if Vesper and Jan don't know the real Blane. This makes zero sense, as I don't either. "Okay, why'd you come over to my workspace?" I tease. "Got something to tell me?"

"Since you're so interested, I forgot to tell you before that I saw another hovercraft, a few days ago," Blane announces loudly. And then, leaning in, he whispers in my ear, "The bearded man leaned out of it and asked me about our projects."

"Is this a joke?" I ask. He makes an exaggeratedly insulted face.

"Ooh, Blane saw a hovercraft," Jan echoes.

"With a hairy man inside," Vesper cackles.

Blane's told everyone about our earlier, private conversation? I could punch him, and for announcing this to the whole room. "Okay, so if you saw another ship, what color was it?"

"Pearl blue," Blane answers. "And when I didn't answer the guy's question, the ship disappeared into thin air. I'm not kidding."

"That's absurd." I shiver hard. Pearl blue! How could Blane know the exact color of the ship from my sick, coma dreams?

His eyes gleam. He's found a cat toy and I'm the cat. "I'm giving you information like you asked me to. Want to go out to the field tomorrow and see if the bearded man comes by again? Do some target practice?"

I sigh and turn away from him. Jan's rough laughter rings out, mixed with Vesper's. Blane isn't laughing though. If only Thorn was here, he might be able to pick out the lies from the truths. I'm not so good at it anymore.

I decide to search for a pearl blue hovercraft myself. When I get downstairs I'm tempted to go outside without my suit. It's such a burden—ten tons of armor blocking out the light of day. But once I'm out there, I'm glad for it, because in the front yard next to the field of Fireseed and out further, among the dunes, the wind's whipping up funnels of sand.

Nevada said nothing about a coming sandstorm, but if the wind keeps up, sand will cover the compound, the gliders and the yard, and the tarp will get dangerously heavy.

I mount a crescent shaped dune, hoping to feel a moment of radiance between blasts of sandy wind. Waiting, I lower the clear inner visor in my mask, to shield my eyes from the sting.

Peering upward, I scan the horizon. Nothing. I turn right, toward the western part of the fence. Look above it. Not even the usual passenger ship, cobbled together from old cars and copter parts. Turning left, I see only the darkening purples of an impending storm, filtered through grainy gusts.

I'll have to come back out to search the sky after the storm. In the meantime, I hesitate here, hungry even a few minutes of solar energy. I'm not hungry for food, yet I feel weak, so needy of sun, as if my arms are branches that are withering.

Turning toward The Greening, I shiver to see Blane staring down at me from the Project Room window on third tier. He quickly turns away.

At dinner, when Radius passes the serving bowl to Bea, I watch her arrange a fat orange yam in the center of her plate and a circle of plump, yellow sea apples swimming in sugary juice around it. Looks like a pretty abstract painting, but my taste buds aren't salivating, and my belly isn't rumbling for my own portion one bit.

"Want some, Ruby?" She hands me the bowl, and I dole out a small mound. Mine doesn't look artful, and it excites me as much as a pile of sand. What's wrong with me? I have no desire to stick any of that near my mouth. It's as if I forgot how to chew and swallow. Have I lost this ability between breakfast and dinner? Is this a delayed effect of the Fireseed's toxic pollen? Has it scrambled my senses into thinking that food is non-edible putty? In all of my days matching minerals and plants and insects, and in all my days of testing the mixtures, I've never come across this symptom. It scares me.

Bea's staring at me, and nodding her head toward my sea apples in a sisterly attempt to get me to eat. "They're delicious," she reassures.

Blane's gaze lands on me, and a cloud of troubled emotion moves across his face. "Aren't you going to eat?"

"That's my business," I snap, and instantly regret it, because he looks down at his plate and his expression hardens. I don't want anyone thinking I'm a head case, and I don't want to say what I'm really thinking.

That I pray Dr. Varik comes here soon. I need to see a doctor.

A forkful of yam in her hand, Nevada looks my way. "Ruby, eat up. You need your strength to work."

She's right, and it's nice that people care. Stabbing a sea apple, I bring it to my lips. Force them open with the pressure of the pliable fruit. Push the round, warm blob back with my tongue and then down with a compression of my throat. Swallow again, because the damn thing won't move any further down.

Coughing, I excuse myself from the table and head upstairs to dislodge the apple. Eating it feels wrong.

All I want to do is to go outside and stare at the sun. Even if it burns my irises and skin, the sun would heal me. I can't say why or how, but it's an elemental urge. It's dark outside though, and the wind is still furious. When I go to the window and study the pools of sand that the storm has whipped up on the tarp, the strange humming starts. It's as if the plants under it are speaking to me, but also inside my head: *Tomorrow, tomorrow, tomorrow* they hum.

Tomorrow you will eat.

17

The next morning I feel a little better. I manage to stuff a cup of grain in and wash it down with mineral mead though I'm still not hungry. I suppose that's what the humming meant when it said that tomorrow I would eat. The Axiom Stream blast announces a clear sky:

Huzzah, Fireseeders! George Axiom here. Only days until the finalist picks! I trust that you are polishing up projects on this sunny morning. We're preparing fun swag for all our favorite finalists. Free drink coupons at Tiki Beach Lounge and entry to Simi-Surf Ride! Surf's up today, huge breakers by the piers.

Brought to you by Simi-Surf. Catch a wave without breaking your leg.

After breakfast we all go to the field and help clear off sand from the tarp by pushing at it with rakes. Then Nevada sends Armonk and me out on a convoy.

Nevada has washed her hair, which used costly stores of water, and I wonder what the special occasion is. It's flowing freely, and the wispy blond tips are freshly dipped in green dye. She's dressed in her best iguana-cell fatigues and form-fitting shirt, cinched with an emerald scarf. Her eyes are rimmed with smoky kohl and she's wearing her fringed lizard-skin boots.

"We need two dozen water pellets, the large blue size," she explains. "Also, some northern grains, and vegetables for the next two weeks. Sea beets would be nice."

Armonk says, "You have to get them from a depot with connections to Northern Dominion, above the border wall."

I panic, thinking we'll have to fly back to Depot Man who gets shipments from the north. No way would I go anywhere near that jerk again. As much as I'm longing for a junket, I'm about to tell Nevada I can't when she gives us directions.

"They sell sea beets at Skull's Wrath Depot, seventy miles due southwest," Nevada informs us. I heave a sigh of relief.

The minute I get outside and that strange thrumming starts, I want to fling off my burn helmet and lift my head high. Somehow that makes the humming sweeter, like a thousand tiny violins played by sand fairies. But Armonk would scold me so I keep it on in the glider.

His hair is in one long braid woven through with a red twine. It slaps against his sturdy back when he walks. Limps, I should say, as it's painfully clear the limp is getting worse.

Still, his mood is good. His frequent smile reveals perfect white teeth against touchable, magnificent mahogany skin. I blush inside to have these thoughts, and to be keyed up to spend time with him, as he steers the vessel out of the hanger and guides it to the runway. It reminds me of when my dad and I went on hunting junkets, of how precious our time was together.

Soaring over Skull's Wrath, we survey the desolation of craters and stark red rock formations that rise from the sand like monstrous beings. Some, like the ones Thorn and I saw on that first night, are shaped like glowing skulls. Others are cabbage-headed ogres and sunken-eyed hunchbacks. There's beauty too: dunes in gently sloping pyramid shapes, and arching crescents facing windward like a hundred rusty scabbards. After a sandstorm it always seems the world is reformed.

We fly over yurts, where nomads have stopped to rest on their way westward. Armonk explains to me that for a yurt, people dig a wide hole in the ground and then erect a tent above it using heavy solar-cell fabric. The fact that the living area is underground helps it stay cooler.

As Armonk's talking, we begin to hear a persistent thwack, thwacking from just outside the cockpit. "Is our glider making that awful noise?" I ask him.

He cranes his neck forward, and then to each side to assess the damage. "I think it's one of the propellers." He points to the yurts. "Might be interesting to talk to the nomads after we look at the glider."

Before I can tell him I'd rather not, that I can't risk any more strangers telling my old compound where I am, Armonk galumphs down, the propeller bang-banging, and lands near the circle of yurts. While we're out inspecting the bent propeller, three men step out of a tent and venture cautiously toward us. One of them is shouldering a rifle.

"They're armed," I hiss at Armonk. Not sure he's heard me. He has his quiver and bow but he's preoccupied in forcing the propeller blade back with a wrench from where it was scraping against the glider body.

The man with the gun aims it at us as he grows near. They're dressed in cloaks bound together by rags cinched like belts, and with clumsy handmade masks. They're surely poor and hungry. Oh, Save us, Fireseed! All of my earlier, paranoid fears of cannibals flood into consciousness, as I picture the two of us being roasted over a spit.

The man's eyes are bloodshot and his beard is unkempt. Is he the one I had coma nightmares about? He levels the rifle at my forehead. "Who goes there?" he calls. "What is your business?"

"We're only here a minute," I promise as I slowly raise my arms skyward. "We'll be gone as soon as we fix our ship."

"Remove your masks!" He swings the gun in a loop to indicate that Armonk should wheel around and remove his as well.

Armonk lifts his head from the repairs. He drops the wrench, raises his mask and arms. "No need for the gun," he reassures, "we're not here to harm you."

The man's grip stays firm on the rifle. "Where are you from?"

"A school in Skull's Wrath," I say, avoiding its name.

"We're headed to the depot," Armonk explains. "We're not here to cause trouble."

Finally the man lowers his gun and nods to the others to stand down. A woman emerges from the yurt. She stares out from a weatherworn, sallow face. "They're just two overgrown kids," she murmurs to her husband and then nods at us. "You two thirsty?"

"A little," Armonk admits as he wipes his brow.

Wonder of wonders, they invite us in for a sip of homemade mead.

The inside is cozy, much more so than I would've ever thought. A colorful wall hanging decorates the yurt and even a framed photo of the family—in happier days? We tell them a little about the school, and how the students go out to the depot to help with chores.

The woman's small girl leans against her side as she strokes her cheek. The girl looks puffy and red with fever. Her parents must notice me staring at her, because as soon as we're out of the girl's earshot, the father reveals their concerns.

"We've given little Moori teas," he says. "We've kept her out of the heat, she sleeps as much as she needs, yet she only gets worse. She has a strange virus. We don't know what else to do for her."

"A doctor's coming to this area soon," Armonk reveals. "I could let you know when he gets here."

"We'd like that. It's very nice of you," the man takes Armonk's hands in his and gives them an appreciative shake.

"I can bring you my healing tea," I offer. "I'm... an herbalist." He nods gratefully.

People literally scurry from the sand like spiders, because before we fly off, two more yurt dwellers approach us to describe their own medical woes. One has a recurrent bellyache from eating rancid meat. Another man has infected, oozing insect bites. I realize there must be dozens of people in need, in Skull's Wrath and beyond that only at first glance seems devoid of people.

We fly off with a repaired propeller that the yurt guy helped us bend back to its proper position. About twenty-five miles east of Skull's Wrath depot we see another large structure jutting from the sand.

"An old-fashioned house. Look!" I point down at it.

"That's a rare sight," Armonk remarks.

On closer approach, we see that the house is perched at a crazy angle, as if it's been lifted off its foundation and dropped down hard, perhaps by a wicked sandstorm. I've been made brave by the good interaction with the nomads, and I'm not quite ready to be done with discovering new things.

"Want to go down? Take a quick look at it?" I ask Armonk.

He slows the glider for a landing and we get out. "Anyone home?" he calls as we reach the open front door. Each time he gets a hollow silence in return. He ventures in first, taking care to lift his prosthetic leg high enough to overshoot the hill of sand and sharp piece of broken floor molding that's angling out of it.

I climb over next. It's spooky, but thrilling, this private space in the middle of nowhere, and I can't help wondering how many more half-buried sanctuaries there are in Skull's Wrath.

The first room was painted long ago in earthy yellow ochre. It's faded and crackled in places, lending it a pleasing softness. Two other rooms are the mottled blue of Bea's eyes. There are drawings on the walls, as if this place was a shelter for many before it got buried in sand. Nudie art—a crudely drawn woman with bulging breasts—makes me blush. As if the people taking shelter were men, missing their women. But in another room there are also children's drawings—of a boy throwing a dog a stick. There's scribbling too and words scratched out.

"Look! A calendar," I exclaim. I pull it out of the floor sand, and we peer at it together. Certain days are Xed off.

"March 2078," Armonk reads, "Three years before I was born."

"Four years for me." I read the legible notations: "Sealy's birthday, depot trader coming by." And the last, disturbing one: "I shot a thief who stole our water."

"They wrote that two days after the trader visited," Armonk notes, looking over my shoulder at it. "I wonder if the trader came back and stole their water."

"Hope not." I think of Depot Man. How he took Stiles' bribery money to talk. I imagine if he were desperate enough he would steal, even kill. How we all might if we had to.

Armonk and I dig out other things: three chairs, a small bureau, a busted stove, chipped coffee mugs and random shoes. One is a man's boot, one a child's slipper, and finally a matched pair of medium sized hiking boots. I pack them up for The Greening.

"A family must've lived here," I figure. "Wonder whether they got out alive."

"Hard to say." Armonk examines the man's shoe from various angles, as if that will provide answers.

"I hope they made it to Vegas-by-the-Sea. I like imagining that."

"Me too, I hope they're all safe and chowing down on fresh skyfarmed perch." Armonk turns the shoe face down, and pours the sand from it. He places it by the door.

We sit on the chairs, still not quite ready to leave.

"What's your project? Do you think you'll make it to the Axiom finals?" he asks.

I describe my various elixirs, including the one that healed his face. "What's yours?"

He's pensive, picking at peeling paint from the side of the chair. "I have a theory about Fireseed, something that Dr. Varik wrote to me about it."

"What?" I persist.

"How it's a fire-starter. How something makes it spontaneously combust. He said that inside the rock formation where he found it there were a whole bunch of charcoal stumps—old Fireseed plants—that would have had no reason to catch fire. He said that his father had made a reference to it being a fire-starter in his research paper. Varik never knew why."

"Wow! How will you find out why it catches fire? Did you ever see it self-combust?"

"One night when I was on sentry duty, I heard the whirring of a hovercraft, really low, as if it was right over the tarp. I hurried outside but by the time I inspected the roof area the craft was gone."

"Sounds scary, but what does that have to do with Fireseed combusting?"

"Because when I went back to that section of the field, one of the plants had burned to the roots. No one lit a match. No one else was there." The intensity of Armonk's eyes seeking out my reaction sends a shudder through me.

"You never told Nevada?"

"No. I need to do more research and experiments before the final picks. I want to discuss it with Dr. Varik." Armonk's face spreads into a crafty grin. "How badly do you want to see Vegas-by-the-Sea?"

"Very badly!" I tell him about my hope to win the prize money in order to rescue my friends and mother from the cult—that's how I think of it now. "I'll buy a shiny blue house in Vegas-by-the-Sea and move them all in. We'll get blue dishes and blue tablecloths and eat blue crabs. Ha! What would you do with the money?"

"Help my sector dig wells. Black Hills has no more drinking water, and most can't afford enough water pellets. My mom said that George Axiom used to be in the oil business before the border wars. He knows drilling. George Axiom could drill incredibly deep wells that may still actually hit water." Armonk sighs wearily. "I'd also pay for my mother to get better medical help. She has bad breathing problems, we're not even sure what it is."

"That's terrible," I say.

"I hope Dr. Varik comes soon." Armonk adjusts his leg. "So many people need him here."

I'd like to ask the doctor about the humming in my head, whether it means I'm going insane. And about the strange greenish tint on my bite wound, plus my eating problem, or should I say non-eating problem? I examine the scar. Whatever it was, it's healed normally. "I should ask him a few things myself," I say.

Armonk looks over at me. "You're getting awfully skinny. You could use a check up."

I hug myself, embarrassed. "I hoped no one would notice. I'm never hungry," I admit.

"Really? Nevada has such good food at The Greening."

"Have you spoken to Dr. Varik recently?"

"Sorry to say, I've lost touch."

My gut sinks, and then rises, with an idea. "Let's ask if anyone's heard of Dr. Varik at Skull's Wrath Depot. They'd know of any news, any new residents."

"Quick thinking, you're—"

Just then, we hear the whirring of a low-lying hovercraft, as if it's landing on the roof of this cockeyed house. In a panic, I run toward the door. As I do, I catch my pants leg on a broken doorframe, and go flying, headfirst. My forearm cuts against a sharp edge of a metal scrap, buried in the sand. I brush myself off and spit out a mouthful of grit.

Outside, whatever hovercraft was overhead has zipped away. How is that possible, when it was so incredibly loud only a few seconds ago?

As Armonk and I exchange mystified glances, Blane's words when he told me about the time he saw that pearl blue hovercraft flit through my mind: *when I didn't answer the guy's question, his ship disappeared into thin air.*

My arm is smarting. I turn it over gingerly to survey the damage, and gasp. It's not bleeding red—rather some thin, greenish liquid. My insides freeze. "Armonk, I need to find that doctor now."

He rushes over. His pale, frightened expression tells me he agrees.

18

When we reach the depot, we hurriedly shop and pay, stuffing the sea beets and other groceries in our reusable bags: a sack of grains, jug of oil, sea potatoes, a hefty bundle of northern kale, a new sponge, and of course, two-dozen Axiom Blue Water pellets.

Then we prepare to ask the proprietor our questions. She's a gargantuan woman in a thick, grey burnsuit with a tattoo of a rock formation on her left forearm. She pulls her burn mask down to get a better look at us. "Ain't seen you 'round these parts."

"No, we only moved to The Greening a couple of months ago," Armonk says.

"Ah, yes, I know Ms. Pilgrim. Now, what'd you want to ask me?"

"Have you heard word of a Dr. Varik Teitur moving down this way, or news of a clinic being built?" I ask. *"Anything?"*

I've bandaged my cut with a twist of cloth from Nevada's glove compartment, and the depot lady eyes it. "Calm yourself," she says, "no reason to get in a flurry, it'll make you sick and then you'll really need a doctor." She laughs at her own dubious joke.

"Well, have you?" Armonk asks impatiently.

The depot lady rests her trunk-like arms on the counter. "Seems to me I did hear of a clinic being built by a crew that comes here looking for work."

"Yes?" My heart pings.

"They's mighty happy to have the work. Seems that this man has some deep pockets, you get my sand drift?"

"Sure!" I laugh for good measure. "Which direction is it from here?"

"Well, now…" She eyes our clothes, as if to see how expensive they are. "Depends on if you have, uh, compensation for a poor ole gal, alone and raising five hungry sons."

Armonk and I exchange looks in an unspoken awareness that she's likely lying through her teeth—that is, the few she has left. If she owns this depot, she's pulling in all kinds of cash. But we need to play along. Armonk paws out the rest of Nevada's shopping money. We've been frugal so there's almost a third left for another shopping expedition.

When Depot Lady grins, I picture the faded echo of the younger and fairer lady she must've been, with dimples and auburn hair. Grabbing the cash, she stuffs it down the front of her burnsuit, between her ample breasts. Then, she produces a pen from her shoulder pocket and draws us a surprisingly detailed map on the flap of a produce box.

She tears it off and hands it to us. "Doctor's been around for a while now," she admits now that she's flush with our cash. "His compound's almost done. Tell the good doctor ole Marney says hello. Good luck, be well." As we depart, she points to herself and winks at us. "Marney's always ready to answer a question—for a fair price."

In studying the map we realize that Dr. Varik's place is a mere seven miles from Skull's Wrath Depot!

From the sky, we see his sprawling compound. It's comprised of three connected buildings complete with its own landing strip, on which we glide down. The entrance is paved with tastefully smoothed oblong stones, and a sturdy beige awning shades against the blistering sun.

We ring. After a moment, the door swings open. A man that I assume is Dr. Varik stares at Armonk for a few long seconds.

He glances down at Armonk's pants leg where the prosthetic leg bulges out, and up at his twine shell necklace. An expression of shocked recognition transforms his long face. "Armonk?" he asks, "from Black Hills?" In answer, Armonk rushes toward him and they embrace. Holding Armonk at arm's length, Varik takes another look. He states the obvious. "You're no little boy anymore."

Armonk laughs. "It's been ten years."

Varik is no young man either. He's not the sprightly blond that Armonk described on the way over here. His hair is streaked with brown and his shoulders sag as if they carry an invisible weight. He's wearing the curious dark clothes of the northerners—a navy blue shirt and black pants. His skin is mottled, nothing new for folks who live down here, but Varik's not. I notice round nubs that look like shaving stubble, but in places where men have no facial hair—on his forehead, his upper cheeks, even on the bridge of his nose. What is Dr. Varik shaving off?

He glances at me, with blue eyes, still crystalline and curious. "Who's the lovely lady?"

"Dr. Varik, this is Ruby. We live at The Greening, Nevada's school. Do you—?

"I know of it," he answers, abruptly interrupting Armonk, as if he doesn't want to talk about the school, or about Nevada. Why?

Dr. Varik takes a step back, and waves us on to a kitchen that stretches out from the foyer. "Let's sit." Varik nods at Armonk's leg. "How's it holding up?"

Armonk shrugs as he limps to a seat. "Not too well. I had to solder on lifts, as I grew, you know." He pulls up his pant's leg to show Varik where he lengthened the leg with welded metal scraps. "It's taken me through lots of adventures. Practicing with the bow you made me, hiking to The Greening." His hand brushes over the deepest gash—where Blane tripped him and almost broke the artificial calf in two.

"And the sensors?" Varik inquires. He reaches out and presses one of the round dials that run down the leg. As he does this, I notice more strange nubs on his forearm and hand.

"The sensors are long gone," Armonk tells him. "So the leg is much stiffer when I bend it. I was wondering if I could pay you, would you make—"

"Don't even think of it." The doctor sees me staring at his arms and tugs his sleeves down.

Armonk turns to me. "Dr. Varik was my childhood hero when he visited us, and told me that he fished in real ocean waters." He holds out the shell on his twine necklace. "That last day Varik was in Black Hills Sector he pressed this into my palm."

"Something from the ocean!" I say. "That *is* miraculous."

"You flatter me," says the doctor, and claps Armonk on the back "This guy taught me how to beetle hunt!"

"For a first timer you were pretty good at it. I wonder if you could take a look at something else." Armonk's smile turns serious as he takes my arm in his. "My friend, Ruby has a cut on her arm that looks suspicious. "

"Sure." Dr. Varik rotates my arm until the scraped part near the elbow is showing. Syrupy, green liquid is still oozing from the cut. His jaw stiffens. "Is this the first time you noticed your blood shift color?"

"My blood was always red. Then it changed a couple of weeks ago—"

"Weeks?" Armonk exclaims, "why didn't you say something earlier?"

"Continue," Varik remarks in doctorly fashion.

"Someone bit my hand a couple of weeks ago," I say.

"Bit you?" Dr. Varik frowns. "A person?"

"A man from my old compound attacked me. But that's another whole story. Anyway, the bite mark developed a green tint to it. At first I thought it was gangrene, but it healed normally, so I just forgot about it."

"Forgot about it!" Armonk exclaims.

"This cut though, it's more extreme in color. It's scary. Also…" I hesitate, but decide to come clean. "You should know, I'm not hungry—ever. Could it be related?"

Doctor Varik places my hand gently on the arm of my chair and goes to a cabinet. He returns with sterile gauze, syringes, and other medical equipment. The blood samples he takes—if you could even call it blood—look weirdly chartreuse in the vials, and I silently scold myself for waiting so long to get help. What if I've waited too long to be cured? What if I have an incurable disintegration brought on by one of my own risky experiments with an elixir?

Dr. Varik inserts the blood vials into a shiny device that spins. He also takes skin samples. Then he logs onto a handheld info pad and addresses me. "Have you spent time around Nevada's Fireseed plants?"

"We collect them, and we're making things with the leaves. For a contest."

"Ah, the Axiom Contest."

"How did you know? And how did you know about Nevada's Fireseed crop?"

"I've known Nevada for a while now."

Armonk pipes up. "She was the one who saved Dr. Varik when he crashed inside that rock formation."

If Dr. Varik is so friendly with Nevada why hasn't he visited The Greening yet, since he's obviously been here for a while, overseeing the construction of his clinic? I wonder if Nevada knows he's here?

"Let's get back to Ruby," Dr. Varik advises. "Try your best to remember, did you have any cuts when you worked with the plants?"

"Not that I know of." I think of Thorn and his amazing Red, how he made it out of stuffing his fingernails into the plants stamens and whatever other strange magic he performed. I need to keep that secret though. Otherwise Thorn's chance of winning the Axiom prize will be about as big as a grain of sand.

"Was there any other way you may have been… contaminated by the Fireseed?" This time Dr. Varik's concerned stare truly spooks me out.

"They attacked her," Armonk blurts out. "They stuffed pollen up her nose."

"Tell me about that," Dr. Varik urges, over the whine of the blood device. "Who attacked her and how much pollen are we talking about?"

"A lot," I admit. "I'd collected a whole bag. It was jerks from The Greening who had it out for me."

Clearly he's not interested in *who* did it. "Did you have symptoms afterward?"

"I was horribly sick, with fevers. I was in a coma for a week."

"For more than a week," Armonk corrects me. "We were very worried for her, that she might not wake up. Thankfully, she did."

"How did you feel when you came out of the coma?" Dr. Varik writes holding his fancy holo pen just above his info pad. Flipping off the tiny blood readers, he waits for my answer.

"This may sound odd, but, um... I felt good." I remember those early days after the coma, my incredible bursts of energy, how I practically flew through the Fireseed fields. "I felt incredibly light on my feet. I could walk super fast, but then I lost my appetite."

"Maybe she got a parasite," Armonk guesses.

"And the sun?" asks Dr. Varik, echoing my very next thought. "How did you feel about the sun—how do you feel about it now?" Scanning the holo printout from the blood reader, he grits his teeth.

"I love the sun. I crave it."

"She stood in it for hours," Armonk says. "See her scars? It burned her face something awful."

Dr. Varik tilts my chin up and examines my scars. "I have a diagnosis." He glances at Armonk and then over at me. "Ruby, would you prefer to discuss it one-on-one?"

"Will it frighten me?" My pulse speeds up. It's pounding in my neck.

"It may startle you," he admits.

"I'd like Armonk here then." Armonk shifts closer to me and takes my hand. "Ready," I say. Unbidden, the humming starts in my head. I haven't told the doctor about that part. It's embarrassing; he'll think I'm absolutely bonkers. *You're one with us, with us, with us,* it sings.

"Fireseed has very unusual properties," Dr. Varik reveals.

"Figured it might," I breathe.

"It seems that the pollen, well, has meshed with your system. I mean to say that you are part Fireseed now—part plant based."

Even before I do, Armonk lets out a gasp and presses my hand to comfort me.

I squeeze his hand back. My heart races with every emotion: shock, fear, even a strange kind of joy, and finally, finally an understanding of the ever-present humming. *The freaking plants are talking to me in my head!*

"H—how is that possible?" I slide my hand out of Armonk's and move it to my face. I suddenly have a need to feel my jaw, my cheek and the curve of my brow to make sure I'm still identifiably human.

"My father, Professor Teitur, who was a marine biologist, created Fireseed with an almost magical breeding ability," Dr. Varik explains. "He created it to withstand desert conditions—"

"To feed the climate refugees in the Hotzone," Armonk finishes. "To be a super-plant and proliferate where nothing else would grow."

"That's right." Dr. Varik nods. "And due to the nature of my interaction with the plant, I was one of the first transgenic, um, products, for lack of a better word."

I gape at him. "What do you mean?"

"I crashed inside the rock formation and staggered around, eventually finding the first Fireseed. I passed out, hugging one."

"I don't understand," I say.

"My arms had lesions on them—gaping wounds from my struggles in the desert. That's a whole other story, as you say."

"The Fireseed pollen migrated into your lesions," Armonk finishes. "It merged with you!" His dark eyes glitter with the realization that Dr. Varik is more than he ever imagined.

"In so many words, yes. Its pollen invaded the wounds. Changed me."

"But how?" I ask. "Are you healthy?" The hum in my brain has turned to uneasy static.

He snorts. Rubs his hands. "Healthy in the sense that I'm not on my deathbed," he answers grimly. "But I go through a daily regimen to stay healthy."

This is really scaring me. Maybe we shouldn't have come here. I glance down at my own arms to see if there are any lesions, or things growing out of them. Nothing now, but when?

"What kind of health regimen?" Armonk asks him for me.

Dr. Varik waves away the question. "I won't burden you all with my problems." He attempts a hopeful yet unconvincing grin. "Because Ruby's had a very different transmission than I did. You, young lady, should not worry about your health."

But he *does* have me worried, quite worried, and also for my brother, Thorn. I tell Dr. Varik about Thorn, and he makes more notations in his holo tablet. "I'll run more tests on you both," he promises. "I'll make sure I keep you two healthy."

I hold out my arms. "Will I, um develop lesions or—?"

"No, Ruby. He shakes his head slowly, too hesitantly for comfort. "It sounds as if you've gotten more of the benefits of the *blending* than I did. As I stated, there seem to be different *varieties* of this, um condition."

"What do you mean?" Armonk asks.

Dr. Varik studies me with his crystalline eyes. "You say that you run really fast?"

"Yes."

"And that you crave the sun?"

"Yes, is that bad?"

"You're getting nutrition from it—you're photosynthetic. You'll need less food. But you still need some, you're still half human, so make sure to eat at least one small meal a day."

"One small meal?" Armonk says incredulously.

I grin. No more stuffing food down three times a day. "Sounds good to me. Can I... sunbathe?"

"Yes, but not for hours." Dr. Varik smiles. "You still have partially human skin."

As he gives me a thorough checkup, Armonk sits there with a glazed, worried look. It's funny, now that I know what's going on, unlike Armonk; I'm relieved—relieved that I'm not going crazy or dying. For the moment my fear flips to giddy joy.

I'm part plant! I'm literally one with my god, Fireseed!

Ha! How the elders would envy me now.

After Dr. Varik is done consulting with me, he gives Armonk a thorough once-over and has him remove the worn, too-short leg off to take new measurements. I avert my eyes and move over to give them space. To see Armonk with one leg missing is like seeing him naked, and makes me ache. I think of all he's been through: not being able to play soccer to the best of his ability, getting twice as winded by trekking through the fields as he goes on sentry duty at night.

Dr. Varik fits Armonk for a temporary prosthetic. He promises to deliver a new one in a couple of days. As he makes final adjustments to it, the doorbell rings.

We all startle, even the doctor at this prospect of company. This place seems so private and new, as if no one yet knows about it and we're in a safe cocoon. Dr. Varik jumps up, with a guilty frown, or is that only my overactive imagination?

Before he can get to the foyer, someone enters from a side door and calls out in a cheery voice, "Varik, are you in there? I'm looking forward to this." It's a familiar wispy tone in the rangy drawl of folks from Skull's Wrath. The hair on the back of my neck stands up when it dawns on me who the voice belongs to. Armonk and I exchange uneasy glances.

"Hello," Dr. Varik calls.

Nevada bounds in, in her ornate fringe boots. Now it all makes icky sense—why she washed and colored her hair and dressed in her finery.

"Welcome, Nevada." Dr. Varik ushers her to a chair.

She stops in her tracks at the sight of Armonk and me. "Oh!" is all she says at first. Her cheeks and neck bloom into a blotchy rose as she struggles for words. "Ruby, Armonk! This is a surprise."

"What are you doing here?" Armonk blurts.

Nevada looks from Armonk to Dr. Varik and back to Armonk, clearly at a loss at how to deal with her students, catapulted into this radically different setting. "I um, well, the doctor and I ran into each other recently and we, well, wanted to visit." She giggles nervously. "It's been a very long while." As she stares at us her expression hardens. "I don't remember saying you could take hours to sightsee. You were to get groceries and come back. We only have two gliders and we need them in an emergency."

I step forward. "We needed to see a doctor, Ms. Pilgrim. I haven't been eating right, and Armonk needed help with his leg. The lady at the depot said there was a doctor nearby."

"Ah, I see." Her voice softens as she looks over at Armonk. "You could've asked me. I would've been happy to arrange for a house visit."

Armonk can't walk over to her without his prosthetic, but he calls out, "House visit? Why didn't you tell me he's been here for weeks? I *have* asked you about that!"

Now it's Dr. Varik's turn to be flabbergasted. He wheels around to Nevada, who's looking mortified. "Armonk's been asking about me? Is that true?"

Nevada casts Armonk an exasperated, desperate look. "Yes, but we've been so busy with the Axiom Contest, I didn't want them to be distracted—they wouldn't have forgiven me for it. Armonk, I know you need your leg fixed, and I know the doctor's a family friend. It's been on my mind since I ran into him last week. I was going to take you over there the minute your projects were finished."

"To heck with the projects, Nevada!" Armonk bellows. "It should've been my decision, I'm eighteen. I'm no child anymore."

"Right. I'm—" Nevada appears on the verge of tears. "I'm truly sorry. I feel terrible."

Dr. Varik goes to her and puts a protective arm over her shoulder. Have they been seeing each other for a while now? They do make a handsome couple—him with his serious eyes and noble stature, Nevada with her stylish desert clothes and pixie green hair tips. "I'm sure that Nevada wants the best for all of you," he says. "Like the students at The Greening, she fended for herself as a teen. She's trying to give you kids something she never had."

Armonk sighs. "Nevada, I appreciate you giving us the opportunity to compete for the Axiom prize. God knows, Black Hills Sector needs the cash. But—"

"Exactly," says Dr. Varik. Why is he so quick to speak for Nevada? There's something irritating about that. Perhaps I'm too touchy about her, ever since she quarantined Thorn. Perhaps we're all too touchy.

Nevada walks over to Armonk and pats his shoulder. "I'm so sorry I didn't tell you immediately. Forgive me? I'm trying to do my best. I was never a parent, I'm not good at it."

Armonk offers her a thin smile. "I suppose I never made it clear how badly I needed to see Dr. Varik. How badly my leg hurts being so uneven."

"He's not a complainer, like some of the students." I roll my eyes, remembering Vesper always comparing how much food other people get, about getting her share of Axiom tools, about how people are always short-shafting her. In contrast, it's clear how much Armonk chooses to endure in patient silence. It's impressive and it binds me to him.

Nevada brushes her long hair out of her face. "Yes, well, I'm glad you're getting a new prosthetic. Dr. Varik is very talented in that regard."

The doctor sits down by Armonk. "I'd better finish adjusting this temporary leg, so that this *young man and woman* can get back to The Greening." He winks at Armonk. "Nevada, make yourself at home in the other room, I'll be a few more minutes here."

When she's out of the room, Armonk says, "That was awkward." He pauses. "Whatever happened to Marisa Baron? The lady you were with when I first met you at my place?"

"Oh, Marisa's still working for the rights of climate refugees—to get them fair hours and housing. Admirable, really." Dr. Varik gazes off into the distance. "I suppose we grew apart. Haven't seen her for a few years now. Time passes so quickly," he adds wistfully. Then, as he looks back at us, he brightens. "I'm looking forward to finding out what your projects are."

"Will you be attending the ceremony in Vegas-by-the-Sea?" Armonk asks him.

"Afraid I have too many irons in the fire here."

We tell him about the yurt people we met and their sick daughter Moori. He promises to visit them. Then he helps Armonk secure the leg that he's created out of hardened putty. I shy away from studying the details. "You'll have to fill me in on who wins," adds the doctor.

"As a matter of fact, I'd love to talk to you about—" Armonk glances through the open door to see if Nevada's milling about within earshot.

"Talk about what?" asks the doctor.

"I'll come back to talk another time soon. Would that be okay?"

"Of course. I'll need to fit your final leg and," Dr. Varik turns to me, "Ruby, you'll need further testing and monitoring. So will your brother, Thorn. Perhaps I can come to the school."

"It'd be best to have privacy here, it's a delicate matter," I insist. "Our classmates would press us with too many questions if you visit us." God forbid every student at The Greening find out what we're up to, what we've become, we'd never hear the end of it.

"Yes, of course." Dr. Varik ushers us to the door. "I'll talk to Nevada about letting you borrow the glider, come for office visits. Surely she'll understand."

I'm not so sure at all. Armonk and I leave with only a perfunctory goodbye to Nevada. She'll have to earn back our trust.

19

Whatever Dr. Varik said to Nevada after we left did the trick. We're free to take the glider and go for checkups, and take Thorn too. I could kick myself for not insisting the doctor keep my medical condition secret from her, because she tiptoes around me and gives me long, sorrowful looks fraught with sympathy as if I have the plague.

I'm not pathetic, I'm not dying; I'm frying amazing! There's no need to look at me as if I'm going to disintegrate in the wind. I'm able to climb to the top of the Fireseed stalks in seconds, even the ones that wind way past the tarp holes. I revel in choosing a perch and basking in the sun—but not too long—just a half an hour or so, long enough to fill me with supernatural energy and speed. And all the while the plants hum at me: *Pretty Ruby, pretty plant lady.* And I hum back: *My beautiful star plants, I send you love.*

Thorn's getting lean and tan and fleet-footed. In the mornings, he hurries through his chore of sponging off the breakfast dishes and then he charges off to the fields to fertilize the Fireseed with a new compound I concocted.

After all, the plants now tell me what they need! *Minerals, minerals, minerals from shale,* they hum. I go out and pulverize those particular rocks. Well, thanks to George Axiom's decision to donate a grand rock smasher we now we have an Axiom device that does it faster and in more quantity than I ever could.

One day I'm up in the tallest Fireseed stalk when I see Jan round the perimeter of the field on his sentry duty. He's still a bitter guy, not talking much. He always wears a faint sneer, as if he forever disapproves of what you say or do, or how you look. At least he's not chasing me! Not like Blane, who I often catch staring at me with a raw, troubled look, even after my scars have made me blessedly flawed. I hardly know what to make of it.

I'm in the western quadrant by the field's edge when I raise my face to the wide gaps in the tarp and soak in solar vitamins. We've slashed them wider after realizing how much healthier the Fireseed is that way. The only problem is that now the crops are more visible from passing ships. Everything's a trade-off, it seems.

Jan is marching along the perimeter as he does his sentry rounds. He's a lean figure in a burnsuit, silver pistol holstered at his side. My eyes are lowered in lazy joy, when I hear a whirring off to my left. A glider has stopped by the field's edge and the helmeted pilot calls out to Jan. I distinctly hear someone shouting his name. Who is this guy?

I jerk upright to full alertness when I realize the vehicle's color. It's the pearl blue of the ships from my nightmares.

By the way Jan and the pilot gesture sharply with their hands it's clear that they've launched into some type of animated exchange. The man hands Jan something—a flipping of Dominion bills—and Jan points my way. My heart beats hard against my ribs as I duck behind a canopy of leaves. Where could the pilot be from and what business are they conducting? Is Jan giving away contest secrets? Can't say why but that's the first thing that crosses my mind. Or, god forbid, it could be one of Stiles' men.

Thorn, Thorn, Thorn, hum the plants. *Thorn, Thorn!*

Reds. Reds, Reds, comes the refrain, and repeats, *Reds, Reds, Reds!*

Squinting at Jan and the pilot, something else catches my eye: a red blur of motion rising from the back of the field— frantic, flapping, driving forward like an arrow from its quiver. The Reds! Not just the one that Thorn's been caring for but an entire V formation as big as a tent top, making its way toward Jan and the pilot at warp speed.

They race through the air and determinedly down. Jan's arms shoot up to cover his face and he emits a high-pitched scream that has me gasping with shock.

How did the creatures replicate so fast? Why didn't Thorn tell me he was growing a veritable Red horde, and why did he let them out? Jan can't know about the Reds! But now he's seen them. Does Thorn know about this attack? Does he have any control over them? Are the Reds turning violent? Bloodthirsty?

"Off! Get off!" Jan screeches as they form-fit their wings to his body. It's quite spectacular, really, a breathing exo-skin made up of dozens of Reds glommed onto his writhing torso. But it won't be beautiful for long because Jan is trying to wriggle his arms out from under them in order to fire his gun.

Meanwhile the strange ship rolls upward like a monstrous pearl and disappears behind a hazy vapor cloud. Jan curses as yet another formation of Reds dive-bombs him. He's managed to grab his pistol from the holster and he's aiming up at them. No! I can't let him shoot! Where's Thorn?

Scrambling down the Fireseed stalk, my panicked limbs become clumsy. My heart fairly chokes me as I race toward Jan. There's a deafening shot, then another. A plaintive squealing turns me inside out. Crashing through the dense field, I finally see it. A limp Red is dangling from Jan's hand, it's snout or whatever it is exactly, is agape in a display of tiny teeth.

Jan stumbles forward, the fluttering, squealing mass of Red wings still clamped onto his skin. I can't quite see what they're doing with their snouts. Are they biting at his burnsuit? If Jan doesn't kill them, Nevada will surely put them to sleep with an injection when she finds out they attacked one of the students. That can't happen! The Reds are Thorn's—his project that we pray will win us enough money to save our family and friends back home and get them to safety.

"Jan, put your gun away!" I yell. Too late, I hear another sickening pop. "Stop your shooting! The creatures are friendly," I insist, though I know nothing of the sort.

This time, he hears me. He wheels around with the Reds still stuck to him like so many Vampire bats.

My mind calls out to them: *Off! Off! Off!* And then, in a desperate appeal to Thorn to come fast from wherever he is: *Thorn! Fast. Fast!*

Off! Off. Off! Comes the refrain, not from me, but from my brother. Though I don't know how I know, until I see him, tears streaking down his face as he pulls one of the carcasses from Jan's fist and cradles it in his arms.

Jan wastes no time in yanking the Red out of Thorn's arms and stuffing it in his latchbag. In the flash of movement, there are no drips of blood, only a drool of green on Jan's burn glove. "Whatever the hell that thing is, it scratched clear through my suit sleeves," he growls. "I'm taking it to Nevada for identification."

Thorn turns bright crimson. He kicks Jan in the thigh, again and again. Thorn's small but these days he's a powerhouse. I can tell by the way Jan flinches he's doing a bit of damage. I'm caught between blurting out the truth: that the Reds belong to Thorn, that they're his creation, and between silence and simply trying my best to get the limp corpses away from Jan. That's what Thorn seems to want.

En masse the Reds alight from Jan's suit, and make the strangest, mournful *yeep* sounds as they flutter off into the forest. The Fireseed is humming its own tumultuous refrain. I sense the Reds perched in the shadows, waiting for another command from Thorn to attack.

With one hand, Jan bats Thorn off. With his other hand, he tosses the second Red body in his latchbag. Again, Thorn charges forward and lands more kicks. Jan groans but isn't deterred. He grasps Thorn by his slender shoulders and pitches him down. Thorn's head clunks against the woody trunk of a Fireseed stalk.

"Stop that!" I yell. "You'll give my brother a concussion." I begin to pummel Jan with my balled fists.

"Crazy woman!" He catches my fists and holds me there.

I shake him off and step away. He's too strong for me, plus my eyes have caught sight of his pistol, undoubtedly loaded and ready to kill again. Another tactic will have to do. "Give us back those animals, they're—" is all I dare say.

Because Thorn, having scrambled up and brushed off, is frantically shaking his head at me. Beet-faced with silent rage, he's begging for me to shut up.

"What? You think these are your pets?" Jan yells. "No way I'm giving them to you. They may have infected me, they need to be tested."

Thorn inches up, ready to land another kick. Brave, hotheaded soul.

Jan slides his gun from his holster and slowly levels it at Thorn. "Don't you try anything more," he warns low in his throat. "So help me, I'll shoot you down."

This overgrown bully better put his goddamn gun away. In my head, the plants scream, *Go, go, go!* I lift my head to the internal racket and breathe in... the smell of fire. What next? A thin, smoky coil is wafting up through the leaves from just beyond. Is the field on fire? Taking Thorn's hand, we run back to The Greening.

~

About ten minutes later, Jan reports that the blaze is out, though a sweetish smoke lingers, scratching the inside of my nostrils. Everyone crowds around the patio table, gaping at the two Red carcasses. They're a sight up close. So eerie with their human eyes staring at nothing, their mortal wounds running with the same greenish liquid that swims in my veins, and their delicate leafy wings and stamen-like tufts, now partially flattened with gore.

Thorn is screaming and screaming inside. I hear it even though his lips are pressed together in a thin line. Clasping him tightly to my side, I'm hoping that the pressure will provide him enough comfort to impel him to stop. The Fireseed is still wailing too, as plaintive as if it's bleeding out. These two Reds are its half-breed infants. My eyes fill with tears. If Jan could hear them, would he feel something, anything?

"I've never seen the likes of them," Nevada remarks. "I've seen the lizard species Ruby calls Spatters and the beetles she calls Antlered Purples, but these?" She shrugs in bafflement. "You're our resident naturalist, Ruby. Any idea what we've got here?"

Thorn pokes my side with his thumb. But what makes me even surer to stay quiet is the humming. *Not now, not now, not now* it insists. Who knows whether it's coming from Thorn or the Fireseed or from my very own instincts? "No, Nevada," I mutter. I hate lying. It gives me a nasty cramp in my gut. "I could run some tests if you let me—"

"No way!" Jan exclaims loudly. "Ruby and her brother wanted to steal those things from me. They want them as some freak trophy. I don't trust her. No way," he repeats.

"You're making up stories," I scold.

Blane leans over the carcasses. With a stick, he carefully stretches out one pair of leafy wings. Its wingspan is the length of one of my arms. "You could ask George Axiom to take one in for analysis."

"Yes," Nevada breathes, still staring. "That's what I'll do."

"Doctor Varik might know," Armonk says. "I could take them over to him."

Nevada shoots Armonk a prickly look. "I doubt he's been down here long enough to know the wildlife." Is she that possessive of Dr. Varik's time? Doesn't want his expert help?

"He's been here long enough, he's a quick study," Armonk answers.

"What do you know, Peg-Leg?" Jan growls.

"Yeah, you're no expert," Vesper gripes.

Bea sighs. "Would everyone just shut up?"

Only Radius is silent, holding close to Bea's side.

Vesper sniggers. "They sure are ugly fuckers."

"Well, I think they're cool," Blane counters.

We're all one happy, cooperative group at The Greening.

"Hey, Jan, let's see your bite marks," Vesper says. He raises his sleeve enough to show her a run of scratches.

"They're not bites and nothing's really swollen," I note. Otherwise I'd have to consider letting Jan use one of my salves, but no need.

"Jan, what happened out in the field?" Nevada asks. "What was all of that smoke?"

He coughs and spits. "Two Fireseed stalks burned to the roots. Then the fire fizzled out."

"Was someone sneaking smokes out there?" Nevada regards us, one by one. "You all know that's strictly forbidden."

"No evidence of any smokers, pyros or matches," Jan insists. He glowers at me. "No nothing, except this crazy thing and her brother out there kicking and screaming for me to give them the critters." He nods to the Reds.

"Why would we want those creepy things?" I lie. If Thorn wants his creations back, we'd best act completely disinterested.

"You change your tune and lie through your teeth," Jan spits.

"Enough!" warns Nevada. "That's quite enough from all of you." She covers up the Reds with a remnant of tarp. By now, there's a pool of slowly congealing green liquid under them. "No one goes near these, got it?"

"Got it," everyone echoes.

"They're staying out here," she instructs. "Until I decide what I'm doing with them I don't want that glop messing up our floors and rugs. Now get inside, make dinner and work on your projects. George Axiom's coming to pick the finalists in two days."

In two days! With all of the uproar, I almost forgot.

For a flighty, airy type, Nevada sometimes rises to the occasion and cracks the whip. This is one of those times.

"Immolation," Armonk whispers as he and I set the table.

"What?" I whisper back.

"My theory about the plants. My contest project."

"Ah, that they set themselves on fire? How will you prove it?" I whisper.

"Trying to figure that out."

"Well, hurry! I want us both to make the cut for finalists."

"Me too," he says with a grin. I wonder if Armonk likes me as more than a friend. He never touches me in that oily way that Stiles did. Never strokes me with his eyes like Blane sometimes, when the heat of his body seeks me out and his eyes try to read me. Do I like Armonk in that way? It's not easy to trust any guy after Stiles. I hardly trust my own feelings. Armonk is handsome and kind. Yet mostly we're like left and right arms—friends who match up. Blane? Blane is fire, turbulence and hurt emotions. The playful tease. Blane is the one who frowns down at me from the window as I bask in the sun.

At dinner, there's more banter about the contest. I'm hoping that the excitement of it all makes people forget about the Reds slowly decaying on the garden table outside. I need to figure out a way to help Thorn recover them, even if it's only to lay the bodies to rest under a sand dune because they're his contest entries. It wouldn't do to have George Axiom claim them.

"There will only be four finalists from The Greening," Blane reminds us. "And one will be me." He stretches, revealing a taut set of abs. I can't lie; the sight makes me swallow hard.

Bea frowns at him. "What makes you so sure you'll make the cut?"

"Just a hunch." He grins and sneaks me a look. He's always sneaking a look and asking me questions with his mystery gaze. I don't know what his questions are so there's no way I could even attempt to answer them.

Since my talk with Dr. Varik, I've calmed down enough about my condition to at least eat one small meal, usually at dinner. In the morning, everyone's too busy to notice I'm not eating, but at dinner, it's harder since we all sit together. I choke down sea potatoes and work to move them past my throat.

Only Blane seems to notice these days. His eyes narrow and his face mists over in worry, but he says nothing. After dinner, people rush up to the workspace, eager for one of the last chances they'll have to work on their projects before Axiom comes with his judges' panel. Nevada goes up too, for last minute mentoring.

Lingering on second tier with Thorn, I kneel down to be eye level with him. "I've got a way to make it seem like someone else took the Reds," I murmur in his ear. "You want that?"

He nods, following me with his eyes.

"Do you want to bury them? I'll leave them at the roots of our lookout tree."

He nods again. This time there's a grateful grin on his face.

"It'll take some doing," I whisper. "Have to find a lizard to work my magic." I squeeze his hand. "Go up and distract them, okay?"

He starts right upstairs, his little boy hand inching up the banister. On my way out the garden door I hear a racket from third tier.

"What are you doing, Thorn? You spilled that oil all over my boots!" Ooh, he's in for it. That was Nevada yelling, and she's wearing her best fringe boots.

Anything for the proper burial of a Red.

20

Those dead bird things are gone!" Bea clomps into the kitchen still wearing her burn suit and mask. It's the morning after I've done my deed, just after breakfast and Bea was sent out there to check on the Reds. We scramble into our suits and clamber outside. The patio table is empty except for a smeared green blob and a trail of tiny footprints in greenish gunk that lead from where the Reds were, out to the field.

"Lizard prints," Bea declares. "Lizards must've hauled them off."

"Weird," Blane mumbles. "Those red things were three times the size of any lizard."

"What kind of lizard would want to eat rotting meat?" Radius screws up his face in repulsion. "Those red things were already kind of stinking."

Nevada wears a skeptical frown. "Ruby, do lizards eat meat? Dead meat at that?"

"Dragon Lizards don't," I report earnestly, "but I'm not familiar yet with the feeding habits of the Spatters." It's not a lie, not really, even though judging by their tiny teeth and the lack of meat around here, I highly doubt that's their daily fare. Not even carnivores eat rotted meat except for vultures. And they don't live down here.

Thorn's eyes dart over to me. There's hilarity in them. If we lock eyes for any longer I'll burst out laughing. Yes, my mind says to his, I found a lizard last night and dunked his feet in the creatures' green runoff. And yes, I lay that perfectly devious trail.

"Ruby and her brother set this up," Jan grumbles.

"Now how would we do that?" I ask with feigned innocence and syrup. "We were upstairs on third tier all evening, working hard on our projects."

"True," Bea defends me. "Ruby was trying on my outfits for last minute fittings."

"It reeks," Vesper glowers at me. "We all know drug addicts are crappy liars."

"Enough!" Nevada snaps. "Who said Ruby was an addict?" Vesper and Jan snort. As sharp as Nevada has become, there are things that she'll never find out. Besides, after a few more white-knuckle evenings pacing and talking with Bea about my old nightmares of the elders at midnight, and sweating out the last perilous particles of Oblivion, I finally kicked it. I felt triumphant, buoyant, newly determined to do something good in this world.

Bea told me during one of those long nights, about Vesper's past, how both of her parents got hooked on black market pills from up north, how they let their kids run amok like famished beasts while they used up their hardscrabble money on pills. And then, how her parents wasted away to hollow, lifeless stalks. No wonder Vesper hates druggies. Now that I know, I don't take it personally. I almost feel sorry for her.

"Well, I hope that stupid lizard chokes on those rotten carcasses," says Jan.

"Jan, I said enough," Nevada snaps. "You're on dish duty today." With that pronouncement, Nevada has regained my approval.

~

I run distraction while Thorn slips away and does what he needs to with the Reds. Besides, Jan is busy sponging off the dishes and he's a lot slower at it than Thorn. By the time Blane heads out for sentry duty, Thorn is back inside. We have lessons later, and then one last chunk of time to polish our presentations for George Axiom who will arrive tomorrow in his glitzy caravan of white gliders with his judges.

I'm itching for the sun. My energy is flagging and food; even sea apples in sweet berry jam don't make up for it any longer. I sneak outside to the dunes beyond the yard. They are spectacular sand crescents that slope outward toward the pink horizon. Removing my mask, I raise my head and open my arms.

Energetic pulses of light sink in as healing lotion, liquid vitamins. My arms spread wider, like vines unfolding. My lungs drink in the luscious warmth.

The humming starts, like tiny violins with choruses of sand angels. *Beauty, beauty, beauty. Drink, drink, drink.*

The lizards and beetles chirp. And, in harmony, Thorn's band of Reds thrum at the edges of the field where they perch in the plush leaves. *Beauty, beauty, thanks for burying our own.*

Abruptly my back overheats with the awareness of curious eyes on it. Footsteps startle me—booted, sturdy and resolute. The soft slap, slapping of boots rousing up sand.

"What's happening to you, Ruby?" asks a familiar husky voice. "Why are you always standing out here without your mask?" Blane steps in front of me. His hazel eyes, flecked with gold and brown, sear my skin. He picks up my mask. "You already got burned once."

"I didn't know you cared," I tease. "Do you?"

He shrugs. I know Blane can't answer those kinds of questions. Instead of answering, he places the mask on my head. His fingers, fastening the straps at the back of my head shoot fire through me. His body, so close makes my chest swell with confusion and desire. Why am I so sensitive to his presence?

I press him. "Why do you always stare at me from the window? Why do you ask me questions with your eyes and not your mouth? What do you want with me, huh?"

He stands his ground, his boots planted apart. His silent confidence angers me.

"I asked you what you wanted. Do you want to kiss me? Huh?" I ask with more fury than I intended.

He lowers his head and kicks at the sand. "Why are you such a tease? You're either too remote or flirting in an angry way. What happened to you at that place, Ruby? What did they do to you?"

"What did they do to me? Hah! What *didn't* they do to me?" I barrel on, looking over Blane's shoulder at one of the dunes. "That man you saw claimed me when I was five. He beat me." I hold up my bad hand. "He cut off three of my fingers. He would've assaulted me if I hadn't run!" I pause to catch my breath. My knees are ready to cave. As at peace as I was before, the memory of what I went through renders me a furious, quaking catastrophe in seconds. "And you have the nerve to ask me why I'm such a mean tease?" That hurts. Armonk has said as much, about me being seductive. But why should I tell Blane that he's the second guy to tell me this? "I have a question for you," I fire back. "Why are you such a brute?"

He flinches. Hurt dims the light in his eyes. Is that what we are to each other? Punching bags? No, I won't play that game. There's good in Blane. He dragged Thorn and me in to safety when we passed out in the sun. He saved me from Stiles that night. He defended me against Jan. Blane might be a brute but brute force is sometimes what's required. And I sense that there are more layers below.

"I had to get strong to survive," he whispers, so low that I need to move closer to hear him. "I couldn't protect my brother, Percy. I couldn't protect my family. I vowed to always be stronger after that."

"You got too strong, too mean," I tell him.

"You too, Ruby."

"I don't try to be a tease. I learned it to survive. How do I unlearn it?"

"I don't know. Be more aware of when you do it?" He sighs. "I don't mean to be a brute either. I hate that you see me that way."

"You helped me get rid of Stiles," I admit. "And I never really told you what that meant to me."

"No, you went off with Armonk."

"You didn't give me a chance because you stormed off so fast," I tell him.

"Do you like that guy with the arrows?" This would be funny if it were someone else unable to say Armonk's name. With Blane it makes me sad because he knows I like the both of them.

I raise my head to Blane's solid neck, to the honey-brown stubble on his chin and up to his eyes—locking gaze-to-gaze, fire-to-fire. "I do like Armonk, as a *friend.*" Why am I admitting all of this? Why?

I feel Blane's heart beating out of his suit. Or is it my heart that's beating out of my chest? He steps closer. His warm sea apple breath drifts onto my cheeks. I breathe him in. This is dangerous madness. He reaches for me, hungrily, desperately. Our masks bump awkwardly against each other as we kiss. The taste of his tongue is as delicious as the sun pouring down. Wrapping my arms around his head, I run my fingers through his soft, cropped hair. Oh. My. God, what is happening to me?

"Ruby," he moans. "Ruby."

In a panic, I pull away and run. As I look toward The Greening I see Vesper, staring out the window at me. What have Blane and I done? Armonk will know, everyone will know and I'm not ready for that.

Not at all.

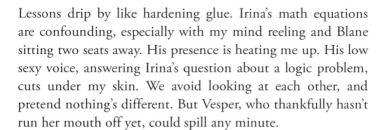

Lessons drip by like hardening glue. Irina's math equations are confounding, especially with my mind reeling and Blane sitting two seats away. His presence is heating me up. His low sexy voice, answering Irina's question about a logic problem, cuts under my skin. We avoid looking at each other, and pretend nothing's different. But Vesper, who thankfully hasn't run her mouth off yet, could spill any minute.

After math, Nevada takes over and gives us a history lesson. We learn more about the earthquakes that rattled through the land before the border wars. We learn about the museums that got sacked and the skyscrapers that fell. We also learn about how farmers down here are farming underground. How crops are beginning to thrive. How devastated enclaves are growing into brave little towns. How the air is slowly, slowly improving with more density of oxygen per cubic feet. But what's mostly on my mind is that if Blane and I win spots as finalists, I'll be riding in a hovercraft next to him.

I look over at Armonk and he grins at me. He's so handsome with his black hair spilling over his shoulders and his white teeth gleaming. Why can't I fall for this nice guy who takes adventure rides and talks with me in our cockeyed desert hideaway? Armonk doesn't scare me. He doesn't make me ache or fill me with longing.

I turn away from Armonk and Blane and toward Bea. We draw cartoons of Nevada—as a tall, warty desert lizard in fringed boots and as a fairy with green wings and green-tipped braids. Bea giggles behind her hand. She's so much fun. Why can't I be content just with my friends like I used to be with Petal and Freeblossom? When Blane brushes up against me on the way out of class and my heart sparks again, I know it can't ever again be that simple.

21

The Stream blast wakes me even before Bea does.

Huzzah! Huzzah, Fireseeders! Today's the day for the finalist picks. Put on your game face and display your best projects for Axiom Coastal. Ready? Set, Go!

Brought to you by Solar Flares, where the fireworks aren't just for holidays.

Where are my good shoes? Where's my lip-gloss?" Bea wails. "Oh, frying hell, one of the Fireseed dresses creased overnight." Clad only in her bra and lizard print boy panties Bea dashes over. "Ruby! Get up. George Axiom and crew will be here any minute." I watch her as she heads toward her rolling garment rack of project clothes and irons the dress in question for the third time.

Scrambling out of bed, I check the elixirs on my desk. They're in pretty labeled bottles I scavenged from that strange cockeyed house Armonk and I found. We went back and dug up three antique glass bottles, and an old-fashioned toaster too. We even found Thorn a pair of sneakers.

Two of my ointments I've tested well. A Spatter Lizard waits in my latchbag for the demonstration of the newest ointment. I hope it survives. I only tested this formula once.

Whirring outside announces the caravan of gleaming gliders. I dash to the window and stare out as they make a smooth set of landings on the front yard landing strip. There are three ships. Five judges, including George Axiom, in Axiom's favored beach whites, step out and head to the school. They seem to gravitate to the lone woman in the crowd. She's taller than most of the men and she carries herself regally. Unlike the men, she's like a lovely painting in my favorite color, blue—a flowing blue dress with blue pearl buttons. Her dark hair is swept up off her neck, and she has on blood red lipstick. Intimidating, really. I wonder what job she has in her everyday life.

I know what Bea, Vesper and Armonk's projects are, but I've no idea of what Radius, Jan or Blane have in store. I worry about Thorn's. How will he lure the Reds inside The Greening, and once there, prove that he has any control over them? Will he make them do a trick? And most importantly, how will he prove they're his special Fireseed offspring? I asked him over and over if he needed help and he shook his head defiantly every time. This is an intriguing new side to

Thorn. My little brother's growing up and it makes perfect sense that he wants to be proven competent after years of being mocked as slow.

But how will he, if he won't talk? I fret enough for the lot of us.

Racing downstairs, I run into Vesper and we almost collide on the stairs. "From liar to slut," she leers. Vesper never showed any sign of liking Blane, so what's she complaining about?

It's hard to imagine all of the horrors she experienced as a child, but she's so bitter she's hard to take. I can't lie though. Vesper looks sharp as always, in a skin-tight solar-cell jumpsuit and thigh-high desert boots. She's bound her tresses with a twisted lock of her own hair, and sandstone earrings dangle from her ears. It's a toss-up as to whether Vesper has the better earring collection or Nevada has the superior boot collection.

"Come in, everyone, enjoy some breakfast!" Nevada has set up a deluxe smorgasbord in the parlor, where Axiom and his people are already milling about, sipping special coffee that Nevada splurged on from the north, checking their holo tablets and munching on oats with candied sea apples.

Way too hyper to eat, I huddle near Bea, who flits around, arranging her fashion line on the rack. Thorn trots in with Radius who reports that he helped Thorn get cleaned up in a nice jacket and pants. I thank Radius, who's already flirting with Bea. The two give each other hugs and pecks on the cheek for good luck. "You make a cute couple," I tell Bea, when Radius is distracted.

"What about you and Blane?" She winks.

I flinch. "Who told you that?"

"Word travels fast when Vesper's involved."

"Ack, does Armonk know?" I whisper.

"If he doesn't, he will soon."

My belly clenches as I glance over at Armonk. Just another thing to deal with after we find out which classmates made the finalist cut.

Blane arrives last with his holo tablet in hand and a brooding expression. He's freshly shaven and I can't help resting my gaze on his brown sugar freckles and soft upper lip that looks delicious enough to nibble on.

Heading to the food table, he lights up when he sees the steaming coffee. After he pours himself a cup, he seems unsure of where to sit, but he gravitates to a chair near me. I smile awkwardly at him. This seems to shift his mood and he ends up beaming at George.

Armonk comes in last, a sheaf of notes and sketches tucked under his arm and his braid strung through with narrow stone carvings. The carvings a handsome coal black, and I figure he chipped them out of Black Hills Sector rock. He and Radius have become friendly, so Armonk joins Radius and Thorn on the sofa near Bea. Armonk puts a benevolent arm around my brother. It makes me feel good that Thorn has found at least partial acceptance here at The Greening after being such a pariah back home. I don't have to worry about him as constantly. My eyes move to Jan, by the window staring at Armonk and Thorn with narrowed eyes. Well, I do have to worry some. We're not one happy family. Not even close.

But things are shifting in interesting ways.

George Axiom rises to the podium, as I remember him doing on that first big day. He's wearing his trademark pastel suit with shell buttons and his platinum hair in a pouf. With the air of a proud father on his sons' and daughters' graduation day he begins.

"Today, dear Fireseeders, is the day we judge the first round. Four lucky finalists will be chosen from each school, and only four, so present well." An enthusiastic, yet nervous murmur rises from the students and teachers. Nevada is sitting with Irina and another of our tutors, a wiry, over-tanned lady who sometimes teaches us poetry.

"One by one," George continues, "when we call your name, you'll proceed into Nevada Pilgrim's study and present your project. Pretend you are onstage, and project your voice." He demonstrates by fairly shouting his next line: "If you mumble, you'll lose points!" Bea and I mock-frown at each other.

"Before we get started, I have a quick question. Have you enjoyed the Stream Blasts?" This question is met with a roar of approval.

Can't say that I'm roaring with everyone. I've never gotten used to the sudden, startling noise in my head, or the ads, which make me long for things I can't afford or have no access to. I feel more akin to the Fireseed hum that I hear when I go outside. It talks to me softly and directly with far more lyrical messages.

"That's the spirit!" George pumps his fist in the air and the guys follow suit from wherever they're sitting. "Huzzah! Huzzah! Huzzah! Pretty soon you lucky finalists will dine in Vegas-by-the-Sea's famous Crab House Delights, and take a whirl in the Axiom Skye Ride over the beautiful Pacific." A cheer goes up.

That's what I want. Blue waters. Shutting my eyes, I breathe in and ask Fireseed to please deliver it. After all, Fireseed is part of me now.

"First up, Vesper Engel," George calls. A visibly less confident Vesper saunters to the front of the room and into Nevada's parlor. George and his panel of judges follow her. Nevada goes in last, closing the door behind her. In the parlor, talking lulls to a murmur, as we all try our best to eavesdrop.

Either the golden door is too thick or they're talking too softly. Blane and I exchange hesitant glances. He's shy in a way that he never was before we kissed. I have to say, I am too. I want to talk to him, but I fear we'll revert to our mean teasing. So, perhaps it's safer to stay quiet around each other for now.

When Vesper emerges from Nevada's office with a sour pout, I avoid her. Clearly, it didn't go so well, and the last thing I want is for her to use me as a scapegoat. She still hasn't run her mouth, at least in public, about seeing Blane and me together and I'd like to leave it that way.

They call Jan in next, who also comes out prune faced. I suspect, from how short a time he's been in the office that he's never come up with a project at all. Radius goes in next. He stays in there longer than Jan and comes out busily packing up his gear.

Axiom calls Blane. My heart pounds the whole time he's in with the panel. I'm silently rooting for us to make the finalist cut. A big part of me wants that private Skye Ride with him. He comes out swaggering, holo tablet in the crook of his arm. He reminds me of the early Blane—overconfident and wearing it with relish. Seeing that, my heart pounds even harder. I worry that he's ruined his chances, acting like that. No matter what his project, judges see through a braggart, don't they? I worry that he's brawn and little brains after all, and I'm ashamed to still feel that judgmental. If I only knew what his project was.

Next, it's Bea's turn. I'm one of her models, so I get to come with! Nevada, anticipating Bea's fashion show, has set up a folding screen where I quickly wriggle into Bea's outfits. I'm so skinny that it's easy to slide them on and off.

The woman judge can't hide her enthusiasm, but even the men nod their heads admiringly at Bea's clever garments. She's tricked them out with sun hoods, utility pockets and secret places for spare burn masks and food packs. I steal peeks at the panel, making their marks on their holo pads.

As I do my best strut down an imaginary catwalk, Bea narrates with a dramatic flinging of her hands. "Now we have my reversible sun cape. As we know, Fireseed can withstand punishing desert sandstorms and 180-degree heat. So this cape made from large, breathable top leaves is the ideal outfit for a rough overland trip or a scalding trek to the depot in summer. You never know when a sandstorm might blow up and…" Bea pauses while I lower the blue-tinted sun visor that's tucked under the hood top. We grin at each other and enjoy the surprised intakes of breath from the panel. "You're always ready with the extra slide-down visor."

George Axiom, leaning forward with his mouth open, seems riveted. After all, he's a clotheshorse *and* a businessman. Money signs practically gleam in his eyes. When the panel forgets to be neutral and starts to clap I'm sure Bea's clinched a spot. As we walk out, we give each other a congratulatory hug.

In the parlor, we receive hateful glares from Vesper and Jan. Obviously the enthusiastic clapping has filtered through the door.

Armonk is up next, and his presentation involves the judges trooping through the parlor and out to the Fireseed field. Fingers crossed for him. I can only suppose that he's trying to invoke a Fireseed plant to immolate, as he calls it. How does one make a plant burn itself? The last time Armonk spoke about it, he wasn't sure.

When he returns, he walks stiffly with a set jaw. I get an uneasy feeling about it especially when Thorn bounds over to him and he doesn't say much. I want to ask Armonk, but it feels like bad form while we're still all waiting for word. I don't have much time for speculation because I'm called in next. Bea wishes me good luck and Armonk gives me a thumbs-up. Blane offers me a sympathetic grin, which helps steady my quaking knees.

I march in, arrange my wares on a table that Nevada's set up in front of the panel and launch into my speech. Sometimes I can get nervous, but not when I get a chance to delve into my passion—the making of my salves. "Since I was four I've been making potions and salves. You could say I'm a modern herbalist. I used to make them from crushed rocks, Dragon Lizard venom and Fireagar." I pause to smile broadly and gauge the impact of my words. So far so good, the judges are listening intently. "Since Nevada's taken me in, I've noticed new life springing up in the desert, such as this Spatters Lizard." I reach in my latchbag and place the clear box containing the lizard on the table. It peers out at the panel. "Also these new beetle species I dubbed Antlered Purples for their antler-like protrusions." I place that box next to the Spatter's.

The chilly female judge, whose name I've learned is Stazzi, wags her arm for my attention. "Excuse me, but how is this connected to new applications for Fireseed?" Another judge nods in impatient agreement.

"I'm getting to that," I say cheerily. "Fireseed, as we know, is an incredible plant in so many ways. We know it's super fertile, and survives without water in high heat. But I found a new talent: for its use as a medicine." The panelists, now anticipating I'll put two and two together, relax back in their seats, readying their holo pads for notations.

"Elixir #1 is a combination of Spatter Venom and pulverized Fireseed." I raise my left arm, which I held under a candle flame last night until I was practically screaming. The judges gasp at the sight. "As you see, my left arm is badly burned. It's runny and blistering."

I take a flattened spoon, dip it into the mixture, and then spread it over the burn. When it touches my skin it stings and tickles all at once. "See how fast it works?" Holding my arm out for everyone to see, the elixir hisses and bubbles and within a matter of seconds my skin is pink and tight with no burn just the way it worked with Armonk's injury. Everyone starts to ask me for the recipe at once. I hint that I will reveal all if picked as a finalist.

For the next demonstration, I'll be winging it. "Elixir # 2, a mix of pulverized Fireseed and beetle antler powder can be used as a powerful sedative. Who knew that Fireseed also had this property in its leaves!" I announce as I open the vial, and lift the Spatter Lizard from its box. Gripping the flattened spoon in my two-fingered hand, I dredge up a hunk of the buttery mixture and spread it across the Spatter's arching back. Its madly cycling legs slow dramatically and its snout freezes into a gaping grin. "Now I can safely place him on the table. Elixir #2 renders the patient temporarily motionless, which is handy in a variety of situations."

"Such as?" Axiom twiddles his holo pen.

"I know a co-worker I'd use that on," sniggers a judge.

I stifle a laugh. "Well, it could be quite useful during medical procedures, or situations where you need to subdue a person, or—"

"Will the lizard snap out of it?" George Axiom frowns at its motionless body.

Good question. I hope I didn't kill it. This mixture's so new I didn't have quite enough time to work out the proper dosage. "I, um…" Just then, the lizard slowly raises its head and rotates its beady eyes. By the time I catch it and hold it aloft, it's again madly cycling its legs.

With relieved satisfaction, I see that the panelists are all taking notes. I'd so love to win this competition, and a fledgling dream is forming in me to replace my old Stiles nightmares. My new dream is for a man to love me not for what I look like, but for what I *do* in the world.

Could that be Blane? Way too early to tell, but the excitement over my successful demonstration has my legs wobbling and my heart bouncy with glee.

"Thank you, Ruby." George gestures toward the door. "Please pack up and wait outside for the judge's decision."

That's it? No hint of their early response? I could've shown the third elixir, a drug similar to Oblivion, but my druggie days are behind me, and I'd hate to encourage anyone else to use.

Marching out, I close the door behind me, pricking up my ears as I go. Alas, the judges have reverted back to savvy silence.

No time to catch my breath before they call my brother. "Thorn, um, Fireseed, your turn to present," calls the female judge. Once again, my nerves jump all over the place.

Thorn looks at me with a mischievous gleam as he skips toward the parlor. I see now: his shirt is bulging in a place where he has no fat. In fact, the bulge is shifting as he walks.

Oh, how I wish I were a spider on the wall in there.

Bea elbows me. "What's Thorn up to, Ruby?" I dare not say, so I simply play dumb.

Next Armonk pulls up a chair. "How're you holding up?"

It's hard to concentrate while I'm watching the shadows move behind the office door, but I'm glad that Armonk wants to talk. Does that mean he hasn't heard about Blane and me? Or that it doesn't bother him? "My presentation went well, except they got impatient with my rambling explanations. You?"

He sighs. "I couldn't get the darn Fireseed to burn, and I know it does, I've seen it happen. No way they'll pick me. So much for seeing the great Vegas-by-the-Sea."

"You might have misjudged…"

Armonk starts to fiddle with his long braid. I jiggle my foot. Blane is sitting on my other side, picking at the armrest, but I don't have the wherewithal to worry about what he thinks of me spending time with Armonk when I'm also worried about Thorn. Besides, it's not as if Blane has claimed me.

Just then, we hear screeches—of delight or fear? Nevada's office door flies open to more screeching as a Red soars out and careens toward the ceiling to perch on a light fixture. The Red flaps its leafy wings and peers down at us as it squeaks like a rusty hinge.

Stazzi rushes out, craning her neck to get a good look at the Red. The other judges clamber out and stare too.

"Watch out!" I cry as the Red lifts its plumed tail and lays a pink turd that plops down on Jan's shirt. Cursing, Jan bats the turd off, smearing it on the floor. The Red, frightened, lifts off of that light fixture and flaps around until it finds a higher perch, on a ceiling rafter.

The string of judges look absurd in their fancy outfits, as they leap upwards in clumsy attempts to grab it.

"My. Red!" Thorn warbles.

We all gape at him. "He spoke!" Bea exclaims, "he—"

"That thing crapped on me," Jan yells. "It's going to meet a bad ending."

"Enough, Jan," Nevada warns. She reaches up slowly for the Red with a long-handled scoop she uses for cleaning sand from the tarp.

From above, the Red cocks his head at the scooper, and then down at Thorn. It blinks its brown eyes and flutters down to sit on Thorn's shoulder.

"My word!" exclaims George Axiom. "My word!" he repeats dumbly. He sticks his finger out for the Red to sniff… or bite or whatever a Red might do.

The Red must not like what it smells. It squeezes its eyes shut and tucks its head into Thorn's messy hair. Stazzi, the female judge guffaws at the sight. Does she know that George Axiom has cheap taste in cologne or what?

"Thorn, can you show us where this creature lives?" Axiom suggests. As the students and even the teachers try to follow them out to the Fireseed field, Axiom holds up his hand. "Judges only, please." We sigh loudly and trudge back to our chairs.

On their way to the burnsuit porch I hear Axiom asking Thorn how he created the Reds. Thorn doesn't answer. Has he stopped talking?

Now I'm not only wiggling my foot, I'm rocking like a lunatic. The suspense is way too much. After ten minutes of this, I busy myself with cleaning up the pink turd.

"So, are there more of those things out there?" Blane asks me.

"I guess so," I say.

"I'm going to slaughter every last one of them," Jan threatens.

"The hell you will," says Armonk. "Whatever they are, they're miraculous. I mean, this desert's been barren for so many years."

"Miraculous as a pink turd," Jan sniggers.

"Oh, will you all shut up?" Bea presses her temples with her palms. "You're giving me a frying headache."

"One big happy family," I say.

To which the other guys laugh.

~

Thorn comes back beaming and runs into my arms. I slide over and share the chair with him. He's gotten bigger in the last month, still there's room enough for both of us.

I whisper into his tousled hair. "Did you show them the new buds and tell them how you made the Reds?"

He cups his hand around my ear and whispers back. "No. Keep. Secret."

"It'll give them something to look forward to then. You'll still be in the finals for sure!"

He nods, confident. I'm amazed at how much the Red's eyes resemble Thorn's. It's incredible, these tiny half-human beings.

And me, half human as well. How many varieties of half-human are possible? Am I the same person I was a year ago? How could I be?

22

A xiom and the judges return from the Fireseed field engaged in a heated discussion. They file back into Nevada's office. As they deliberate behind closed doors, she brings them cold mead on a tray. Gazing at the Axiom poster, I imagine Thorn, Blane, Armonk, Bea and Radius out at the Vegas festivities, even Vesper and Jan. All of us swimming at the beach.

Except it can't be all of us. There aren't that many spots.

Nevada's doors open and the judges emerge. They form a semicircle around the podium. I grip the sides of the chair as George Axiom begins. "The first student finalist from the Greening is Bea Wynter, with her stupendous Fireseed fashions. They are fun and also functional, and will help many, many people combat the heat." Bea yelps joyously. Radius and I get up to hug her. Nevada too.

"The second finalist is Radius Quist." Bea runs over and gives him a bear hug and we all cheer for him. I'm thrilled that Bea will get to party in Vegas-by-the-Sea with her boyfriend. Fingers crossed I'll be as lucky.

"The third finalist is Blane Tralfant." Strange, I never knew Blane's last name. It's an elegant, mysterious name, and he's wearing a mysterious grin. What on earth did he do to win that spot? "Blane's advanced genetic work on Fireseed will help sort out this complex and changing plant, and we look forward to more of his work."

Advanced genetics? Holy Fire! Clearly, I underestimated him.

Nevada heads over to shake Blane's hand, and I do too. The touch of his hand in mine sends heat all through me. I think he feels it too because neither of us wants to let go. I break away just as Axiom announces the last finalist.

"Miss Ruby, um, Ruby… Fireseed wins the forth spot." Laughter erupts from all corners of the room.

"That's right," I explain. "Where I came from, we all shared that last name." It was a hallmark of our society. My neck burns with anger. And excitement!

"Well, Miss um, Fireseed," Axiom stumbles, "we appreciate your medicinal elixirs."

"You mean, her *drugs?*" Vesper mutters from the facing couch. Sore loser.

Thorn squeezes my arm. Armonk, Bea and Nevada congratulate me. Then Blane comes over and surprises me with a hug. He feels good. I can't lie. I inhale his scent of sweat and musk as his strong arms fold me in. From the corner of my vision, I see Vesper studying us but I can't put my finger on her expression other than it's coldly blank.

When Blane heads over to talk to Radius, Thorn jiggles my arm. I'm so excited that it doesn't dawn on me right away. They haven't called my brother's name. "I was sure you'd be picked," I tell him, "It makes no sense." His creation is the very pinnacle of what we've done here. It's so obviously a winner.

Big tears start to roll down his cheeks as I clutch him to me. "I'll talk to them, okay? I'll ask them what happened." He nods, swiping a hand across his nose.

I dash after the judges, packing up their holo pads and latchbags in their fancy gliders. "Is there some mistake?" I ask Axiom.

"Meaning?" He whirls around looking taller and more wizardlike up close with his pouf of hair and disc-shaped eyes.

"My brother, Thorn made those Red creatures. Shouldn't he have won a spot? Aren't they the most incredible things you've ever, ever seen?"

"They're quite impressive." Axiom looks down at his hands.

"So, why didn't he earn a spot? I mean, how could—"

"The judging process is not up to me alone. It, um, has many factors," he says, still examining his cuticles. "I'm not at liberty to reveal the processes."

"But…" Doesn't he run this whole thing?

"George?" Stazzi peers out of the glider and glowers at me.

"I must go." He offers me a harried handshake before stepping into his glider. As if he feels guilty for brushing me off, he calls out at me through the window. "I look forward to seeing you and the other Greening finalists out in Vegas-by-the-Sea." He gives his driver a hand signal to take off, and the caravan makes a steady ascension into the sky.

It feels as if the wind's been slapped out of me. What can I tell my brother? I haven't the heart to go back inside. Turns out I don't have to. Thorn bursts from the front entrance, followed closely by Jan, who's dressed in a burnsuit. Jan is cursing at Thorn.

"I'll smear those bird poops in your hair! Get back here, you little creep!"

Thorn is very fast on his feet these days, but Jan has long legs, and could've been a professional runner, if there were any down here.

I start to chase after them when an incredible thing happens: there's a frantic rustle in the Fireseed field. A band of at least forty Reds alight from its canopy. Their madly fluttering wings are framed against the bright coral sky as they charge toward Thorn and Jan. But instead of the Reds attacking Jan as before, they link their wingtips to form a fluid, rolling rectangle. Soaring closer and closer to Thorn, they swoop him up on their airborne carpet, just as Jan has caught up and reaches out to grab Thorn.

The Fireseed hums its approval *Safe, safe, safe, safe! Fly, fly, fly.*

I cheer from the dunes below. "Go, Reds!"

A distinctly more human cheer erupts from behind me. Spinning around, I see Blane, Armonk, Radius and Bea pumping their fists by the entrance to The Greening.

Today Thorn spoke for the very first time in front of his classmates and now this flying red escape hatch. It's unfathomable that Thorn didn't get picked, and I sense the real reason could be disturbing. What other bizarre wonders and terrors await us I can hardly imagine.

23

Armonk, Thorn and I take one more trip to Dr. Varik before I pack for Vegas-by-the-Sea. This is Thorn's first trip here and he's excited to meet the well-regarded doctor. He skips along the tasteful stone path and raps on the door.

Dr. Varik is delighted to meet Thorn as well, and they seem to hit it off—this all with few words, though Thorn is talking more. The doctor examines Thorn, peering into his ears and down his throat. "Have you been eating much?"

Thorn holds up one finger. "Bowl. Fireagar."

"One bowl a day?" Thorn nods. "You have questions for me?" Dr. Varik asks as he sneaks in a quick blood sample and genetic swab from Thorn's tongue. I see the blood sample is as greenish as mine.

Thorn's liquid eyes shimmer. "Reds. I made them. Part plant. Part human. Like me?" Impressive that my brother can stay silent for so long and then easily find the words he needs. From his shirt he produces a Red and holds it out. We all do a double take. The critter was so quiet on the way over—not one peep—that I had no idea he was swaddling it. It's true; the Reds are incredibly calm around Thorn. This one flaps its wings once and then, with a twiddling of its stamen-like tufts, it settles into itself.

Dr. Varik reaches out a gloved hand, palm up. "May I?"

Thorn moves his hand toward Dr. Varik's. The Red flicks its head at Thorn. It seems to be asking Thorn if this man is safe. Having transferred an unseen, unheard okay from Thorn to the Red, the Red hops onto Dr. Varik's hand, and then on his crossed knee. It nibbles the doctor's pant's leg. Deciding it not very tasty, it closes its snout and blinks up at Dr. Varik.

Just above the rim of Dr. Varik's gloves, I see more blunted nubs on his wrist. The sight makes me wince. His movements seem slow and stiff, as if he's aged in the span of a couple of weeks. I don't know what to make of it, and a cold, hard shiver runs down my spine. I again glance furtively at my own arms. No nubs. I heave a sigh.

"The Red sure has a giant personality," Armonk notes.

Dr. Varik makes a few funny faces at it to see if it'll react. The Red just blinks back at him. "Uncanny blend of Thorn and the Fireseed," he decides.

"Yup, it has the same serious, yet cute expression as Thorn," I say.

"The eyes are a lot alike," Dr. Varik agrees. "Irrefutable evidence of the Fireseed's capacity for transgenic breeding."

He takes a tiny genetic sample and then observes it as it hops back onto Thorn. "Makes me nostalgic for my dolphin, Juko. I had to leave him up north."

"Can. I. See. Juko?" Thorn pronounces each word as if it's in its own sentence.

Before we know it, Dr. Varik has guided Thorn and the Red to a couch in front of a holo screen. Thorn yelps with delight as the doctor plays a video of the dolphin tapping a ball with its prosthetic flippers.

While Thorn watches the film over, Dr. Varik does final fittings to Armonk's leg. He also advises me on what I'll need to stay healthy when I travel. "Go outdoors daily. Drink in solar vitamins. You'll need this extra supplement." He hands me a liquid vial. "Steer clear of cake and fancy contest foods that could make you sick." He pauses. "Anything you want to ask me?"

"Yes. It's um, hard to talk about. It sounds nuts."

"Try me," he says. By the way Armonk starts stops fiddling with his already adjusted leg it's clear he's curious.

"Okay, I *hear* things," I check the doctor's reaction. He's still waiting patiently. "I hear the Fireseed talking. That sounds really odd. But I do. My brother does too, I'm sure of it. I hear Thorn's thoughts in my head and even the Reds. As if we're all connected."

Thorn glances over at us, and nods before he goes back to watching Juko breech the waves. Armonk, on the other hand, looks quite worried for me.

Dr. Varik's grin is wise. "I've studied this phenomenon because I've witnessed it too."

"You have?"

"Occasionally I'll hear silent words when I'm in the lab, surrounded by my plants. Especially when they've been disturbed."

"Disturbed?"

"Emotionally affected."

"But plants can't feel!" At my statement, Thorn busts out laughing. He's looking at me, not at the dolphin. "What's so funny?"

"Plants. Feel," Thorn announces.

"I'll second that," Dr. Varik agrees. "Plants have something called stroma. A ventilation system; pores or ports or a network; however you choose to describe them. My theory is that in addition to the stroma providing ventilation, the plants' electrical impulses travel through the stroma, and that is fueled by their reactions to their environment. A primitive nervous system."

"Wow!" So cool that the Fireseed have a million tiny pores that feel things, think things.

"You could call it a stromanet," Armonk says.

Dr. Varik nods. "Correct. Good name for it. So, Ruby and Thorn, you're actually communicating with the plants, gaining sensitivity toward them."

"Could the... the stromanet warn someone of danger?" I ask.

"I imagine it could."

"And you said that plants communicate their stress, right?" Armonk asks. "Can Fireseed set themselves on fire when they're upset?"

"Yes," Dr. Varik answers. "The ones my father planted in the desert many years ago burned themselves up when he left. I think they felt abandoned."

"I knew it! The judges didn't believe me," Armonk complains. "I didn't make their finalist cut. I won't get to see Vegas-by-the-Sea."

"That's too bad. I suppose the concept was simply beyond their scope. Perhaps another time." Dr. Varik says.

"You still have a valuable role," I remind Armonk. "You'll be at The Greening to keep Thorn safe from Jan and Vesper. To protect the whole school!" I know it's not enough of a consolation, but Armonk's such a sport that he simply nods and shrugs.

Then he throws an arm around Thorn. "Stick with me, bud." This prompts the Red to a flurry of enthusiastic sounding squeaks.

As we leave, I hug Dr. Varik and he wishes us well. I notice his gait is stiff and slow, which again makes me sad for him. He's not that old. I wish I knew what was wrong with him.

But there are other pressing worries. Heading back to school, I'm already fretting about leaving Armonk and my brother when I go to Vegas-by-the-Sea. If there is a stromanet, I worry that I won't hear it signal danger from so very far away.

24

Axiom's gliders arrive to ferry us to the coast. We load the cargo hold with Bea's fashion line, the angled sections of Radius' flyer, a case of my lizards and salves, Blane's holo tablet and a holy mess of brimming suitcases. The last time I traveled I had only my latchbag.

This time I feel like one of the fairy queens that Bea draws. I've packed a filmy red cocktail dress that she designed for me, a pair of fancy heels Nevada lent me, and flirty decorations for my flyaway hair; and I'm only going away for a weekend.

I'm teary at the sight of Thorn and Armonk waiting by the landing strip to see me off. "Take care of Thorn, will you?" I plead with Armonk for the tenth time. We hug and he gives me his word. His presence feels like a rock—strong, unshakable and reassuringly familiar.

I lean over Thorn, and mash my head in his sweaty mop of hair. These days he smells less of boy and more of sweetish Fireseed musk. "Don't get in trouble, okay? Don't wander off, stay close to Armonk. Do everything he tells you to do." Thorn looks down at the ground and nods. He's still uncomfortable with gazing in someone's eyes. Probably always will be.

Blane comes out dressed in snug white pants and a plaid shirt that shows off his powerful shoulders. He's packed his burnsuit, only wearing the mask part. My heart thuds at the sight of him. He cleans up well. When Armonk steps aside to let him by, there's an obvious flicker of pain in his eyes. Does he know that Blane and I have kissed? I should've told him, but there was never a kind way to broach the subject. I push down a huge wave of guilt. Who knows if Blane and I will end up a good fit? All I know is that I'm itching to find out.

Blane and I sit facing forward, Bea and Radius facing us. As the gliders take off, my heart does too. I'm filled with a lightness and joy I haven't felt since I was little.

"We're double dating!" Bea gushes.

"Huh?"

"Silly Ruby, you've never heard that phrase? It'll be so fun to hang out, the four of us."

I glance over at Blane. He's blushing down to the scalp underneath his cropped hair.

Radius and Bea are already making themselves comfortable in each other's arms. Bea's blond hair is spilling all over Radius' shoulder as she nestles in. He places soft kisses on her forehead. Blane and I smile awkwardly. We rushed into each other's arms way too fast, and now we need to get to know each other better.

"So tell me what your project is," I jab him playfully.

He smiles at me, and then down at my dress as if he's still a bit shy for longer eye contact. It's so unlike Blane it cracks me up. "My lips are sealed," he claims. "You'll have to wait until the contest presentation."

"It has to be good to win a spot," Radius says. "Give us one hint."

"Like father like son," Blane says mysteriously.

I nudge him again. "What's that mean?"

"Remember what Vesper and Jan told you about my parents in the project room?"

"That your father was a brain surgeon and your mother was some kind of scientist?"

"You got it."

"No way! Vesper was joking around."

"Was she?" Blane arches his brows. For a moment, the big, hulking man next to me is elevated to a higher level. He's just teasing, though, the thing he accuses me of doing.

"Your old man was no brain surgeon," Radius scoffs.

"Was so, and my mother was a geneticist."

"Hot damn!" Bea remarks.

Worlds turn, and spin away. The desert below is aglow with unearthly light as we speed westward, over yurt communities and dead cities, pockets of cave gardens surrounded by more yurts. Radius discovers an embedded drinks bar in the side panel of the glider. Clinking our unbelievably tasty iced lemon sodas, we make a toast. "Here's hoping one of us wins the Axiom Contest. Hear, hear!"

"Huzzah, Fireseeders!" I exclaim, in an echo of Axiom's trademark cheer.

Nearing Vegas-by-the-Sea, we see a large, close grouping of cone-shaped towers and whirligig warehouses, spinning like carnival rides. We see neighborhoods of solid blue agar buildings and in the city center, rising sandstone statues of what must be famous people—a long-legged lady lifting her face to the sun, a man with a wide brimmed hat, and a clown with puffy cartoon lips.

Swooping lower, the gliders whoosh into an underground landing pad. It turns out to be the basement of a hotel. We are whisked into its glitzy lobby with fake palm trees, grand pastel-colored sofas and well-dressed clientele lounging on those sofas and settees. I've never seen such women with chunky jewels and spiky heels. Doormen wearing Axiom pastel jackets with shell buttons cart our cumbersome baggage.

Bea and I share a room, and across the hall are Blane and Radius. "I wonder how closely we'll be chaperoned?" Bea says with a smirk.

"Hopefully not so much," I answer, with my own smirk. "At least Nevada's not here, breathing down our necks."

We buzz around, marveling at the marble bathroom, the floor-to-ceiling picture windows and the plush quilts with wave patterns on the wide beds.

We're told to get dressed and meet the group in the lobby. I put on the fancy dress and some red lipstick. Bea helps me adjust my special hair decorations.

She leans over my shoulder. "You look incredible. Blane's in for a surprise." Normally I prefer looking plain, but tonight, I'm glad I'm sparkling.

～

George Axiom wasn't exaggerating when he bragged about the ornate feast. Crab House Delights is a candlelit cavern whose central attraction is a broad table brimming with culinary delights: steamy rolls, crunchy crab cakes, rice mixed with peas and faux-shrimp, sea apples dripping in honey, sautéed Fireagar, vats of icy mead and teas, and desserts sprinkled with chocolate and berries, the likes of which I've never seen.

The place is packed with kids, all dressed in their finery. Bea and I link arms and stroll in, followed by Blane and Radius, who are already chattering about the food. Bea's adorable in a hand latticed yellow dress that shows off her curves. Her purse is strewn with handcrafted textile flowers. We snake around to find a free table, no easy task, as others are searching for a spot too.

"You can tell who's from Baronland South," Radius snipes. "They're wearing northern pants and suits." Indeed, a group of kids already eating at a large, round table are wearing the ponderous navy blues and grays that look so alien down here in the desert.

"Their clothes look expensive," Bea says. "Wish I had access to that kind of fabric."

"Let's steer clear of them," Blane decides. "Hey, over here." He spots an open table and throws his jacket over a chair to save it. We follow suit and then head over to the food.

I haven't had enough time to soak in my solar vitamins so I figure I'd better try to eat a decent meal. I choose some sea apples, one of the crab cakes and a mug of icy mead. Blane shovels on a portion of just about everything.

By the time we return to the table, three kids are sitting at the chairs we didn't reserve. The girl has stringy red hair, one of her guy friends has glasses, and the other boy has shoulder length brown hair and a tan jacket with coral buttons. They eye us warily.

I grant them a smile, no need to start out with a feud. "Where are you all from?" I ask the one girl.

"Vegas Central High. You?"

"From The Greening."

Her eyes widen. "Whoa, I've heard it's really desolate out in Skull's Wrath."

"More space to invent big contest pieces," Blane retorts.

"I guess so." She returns to the rice dish she calls seafood paella.

"Just look at those rich kids from Baronland South," scoffs her friend in glasses. They stare at the table of rowdy kids that we were just talking about.

"As if they need the prize!" the longhaired guy huffs.

Radius snickers. "Our feelings exactly."

"But you guys have it good here in Vegas," Bea notes.

"We don't get feasts like this every day." The spectacled guy wolfs down his fish.

"Who's paying?" Blane asks. "Does Axiom cover this?"

The longhaired guy shrugs. "I think it's a consortium, underwriters or whatever."

"Like who?" I ask.

"Rich business tycoons," replies the red haired girl between mouthfuls of cake.

"Are there a lot of rich business folk in Vegas-by-the-Sea?" asks Blane.

The longhaired guy nods. "More and more. It's becoming a boomtown."

"Do they have a say in the voting?" I ask him.

"Probably." The longhaired guy raises his mug. "Hey, may the best person win."

"I second that," Blane exclaims.

We end up clinking glasses, all toasting each other. The red-haired girl is Haddy, the longhaired boy is Tib and his friend wearing glasses is Van. People in Vegas-by-the-Sea might be almost as well off as the ones from Baronland South but they're super-friendly, and it makes me want to move here even more.

~

Bea, Radius, Blane and I waddle out of Crab House Delights like stuffed lobsters punch drunk on mead. Axiom's white limo glider ferries us to the Skye Ride at the wharf. Stepping onto the seaside dock, I'm aware that I'm stepping into my longtime dream: to finally see the sea dazzle with its infinite blues. Breathing in its marine scent, I picture starfish, octopi and waving clusters of anemones below—a paradise of creatures that I've only read about in old books.

The sun is setting. Gold and pink crescents of sky reflect blithely on the ever-moving waves. The shimmering curves make their way out to the horizon until they disappear beyond it.

"Ocean!" I call out, lifting my arms in joy.

"It's beautiful!" Bea calls out behind us.

"So are you," I hear Radius tell her.

Blane steps up to me. "It's so vast." A troubled expression casts a shadow over his face.

"What?"

"Nothing, it's just…"

"Thinking of your family?"

He gazes over at me, pain evident in his hazel eyes. "Reminds me of how the waves took them. The tsunami. Oh, god, Ruby."

"It's over, it's safe now." I slide my arm around his waist. I don't need to wait for him to take the lead. He needs someone to care about him, and I do.

Our Skye Ride whooshes down for us. It's a white hovercraft with a cab just big enough for two and a rounded, high-arching top. This cab is attached to a great looped track in the sky, as the other cabs are. The ride master opens the door and, with another swipe of his arm, invites us in. "Belt up," he advises.

Blane helps me in and I arrange my red dress under me and cinch the seatbelt. Suddenly, I'm tingling with anticipation and fear, and my heart is rapping hard against my ribs.

We're borne up, soundlessly and more grandly than in any mere glider. We soar so high that the wharf and the people walking on it look like tiny beetles. Turning around, I see Radius and Bea snuggling in the hovercraft behind us. We wave.

Higher and higher. Delicious songs play inside my head, like the thrumming of the Fireseed. Only it's the humming of my own heart, filled with joy and lightness. Or is it? I hear it again, exactly like the Fireseed: *pretty one, pretty one, pretty one.*

Ocean, ocean, ocean!

How is that even possible, all the way out here on the coast? We're hundreds of miles from Skull's Wrath. Can the Fireseed sense me here, flying above the sea? How could the message be as strong as it would be if we were back at school? There are no sure answers.

Blane presses me to his side, and I feel his heart throbbing against my arm. Relaxing into his shoulder, I nestle there. What would he think if he knew what I was now? I'm afraid to tell him, but do I really need to?

He nuzzles my forehead, planting soft kisses on it, and moving his lips down to kiss the tip of my nose, and then each wind-burned cheek, and finally grazing his lips softly over mine, like a velvety leaf. With his tongue, he playfully guides my mouth open. We kiss until flames lick at my entire body.

We're flying in the heavens now, the city so many radiant specks below, the ocean a filmy, celestial blanket.

But the humming gets louder and more insistent. Abruptly its cry turns pleading. *Help me, help me, help me!* In my mind's eye, I see a tiny Red, fluttering, trying in vain to stay aloft in the powerful bluster, but falling, falling, falling. Falling away.

Looking down, I search for a real set of red wings. I swear I see them, spiraling lower, and my breath catches in a frightened gasp. When I jerk my head upward, and look over at Blane to see if he's seen the Red too, the corner of my vision catches on something else outside the other window. It's enormous and curved, pearly and anonymous, and I lean toward it. A monstrous orb is floating right next to us, the size of an entire small planet. It's way, way too close, as if we're about to crash.

"Blane!" I scream.

He whirls around to see where I'm looking, and squints out the window. "What, Ruby?"

"It was there. Now it's gone, behind the mist. I don't know… I swear that I saw something."

"What, Ruby? Describe it to me." Now Blane is fully upright, his eyes wild, scanning the darkening sky in all directions.

"It, it's gone." How could a huge glowing orb just disappear? Or how could I have seen an actual Red, all the way up here, out on the coast, struggling against these violent air currents? How could any of this be happening? "I'm going crazy."

"Ruby, talk to me." Blane grasps me by the shoulders.

"I'm scared," is all I can utter.

"Scared of what?"

"Scared something terrible is happening." The humming is back, inside my head. Not humming exactly, more a shrieking. It eats at my heart.

"What?" He's holding his own terror in, but he shudders under his glaze of control.

I shake my head, as much to get the bad omen out as to shake sense in. "I don't know, Blane, I don't know. Just hold me. Please."

What is this strange screaming static? Is it some kind of radio interference from that orb I just saw? Or is Thorn in some kind of trouble back at home? Is it the stromanet sending a message? No, the noise is nonsensical now. There's no language attached to it like there was with the Reds, with the Fireseed. Could it just be my amplified fear at being a mile above the ocean?

Blane wraps me in his arms and lets me sink into him. "It's okay now," he whispers. "We're okay." I breathe his scent of spice and sweat and a fledgling kindness—clean and flowing in, stronger and stronger. The static in my head lessens and I see no more glimpses of that ghastly orb—as if was a stark, frozen nightmare that evaporated in our warmth. I want to forget it, let go of my past troubles. We stay entwined for the rest of the ride. From abject terror to a sense we are solid; I've never felt so loved or safe.

Back at the hotel, Radius slips into my room to be with Bea, and I slip into the guys' room to be with Blane. In the wide bed with silky sheets there are more sweet, passionate kisses, and tender hugs, but we'll heat up the bed another night. Tonight, Blane knows what I really need is to be held and protected, and I know what he really needs is to feel love, respect and that he has an unshakable ally.

25

B lane Tralfant, representing The Greening," calls the announcer.

Stepping onto the stage, Blane sets up his holo demonstration in front of Axiom's large white demo screen. The bars and graphs of Blane's design shimmer in three-dimensional complexity. He's wearing his best suit, a beige solar cell one with a melon color shirt, which sets off his freckles in the most charming way. I'm nervous for him as I glance around at the excited crowd of kids, judges and city officials in this luxe auditorium that overlooks the ocean.

Blane clears his throat. "I've been researching the genetic formation and structure of Fireseed," he starts. "You see, my mother was a geneticist, and after my family perished in the great East Coast Sector flood, well, I…" He glances over at me, and I nod to egg him on. "I feel the desire to carry on my mother's work." So he was telling the truth about her! It wasn't just his mad boast. I lean forward, eager to catch every word.

"You see, Professor Teitur, the marine biologist who created Fireseed, used very special ingredients in his hybrid. We all know he needed a plant that withstood extreme heat and harsh conditions. But it might surprise you that he also wanted to create a *smart* plant. And one that had strong *emotions*." The audience has an immediate and loud response to this news.

So that's why the Fireseed bent down and stroked my back that first night at The Greening. That's why it hums when it's happy and screams when it's scared. And why the Fireseed might destroy itself if it gets upset enough.

When we settle down, Blane continues. "To that effect, Professor Teitur blended his own human DNA with plant RNA." More shocked gasps. I look around. People are exchanging heated remarks with their seatmates. "This human-plant hybrid mutated into a new species entirely. One that feels emotions, thinks, even talks in its own way." More loud exclamations from the audience. "And because Teitur created Fireseed to have amazing powers of reproduction, it now produces transgenic chimera. What does this mean exactly?" Blane pauses for maximum effect. "It means that Fireseed can breed with humans to create varieties of human-plant beings. My holo software not only maps the gene sequences but through its unique algorithm it predicts at least twenty more varieties of chimera." With this, Blane taps a glowing button and twenty kinky images fill the screen, from the kind of hybrid I am, with greenish blood, to a variety where the being's skin is actually vibrant green, with leafed out hair.

The audience bursts into spirited chaos. Dr. Varik told us that we'd mutated, but no one knew that his father had already created a mutated being on *purpose* so many years ago!

I'm proud of Blane. With this, he's a sure winner. I'd like that prize money, but wow, he deserves it too.

Utilizing his floating graphs, Blane describes the genetic codes, which I can't begin to comprehend. I'm no geneticist, but I *do* know that Thorn, Dr. Varik and I are all living proof of Blane's theory. The Reds too. How did Blane determine all of this just from the Fireseed leaves? Clearly he compiled major data from Teitur's experiments as well.

I underestimated Blane, that's for sure. He's not the person I thought he was; he's a lot smarter, a lot more soulful. Maybe now I can tell him the truth about who I am, *what* I am. Will he be fascinated or repelled?

I'm so deep in thought that I hardly hear the audience clap and the next student come up to talk about his project. In fact, a string of students from Spokane Way and Vegas Central come up, present, and sit back down, and it barely registers. Until a guy in a stiff navy suit from Baronland South steps up to the podium. They call him Alex Dean. He has a high forehead and a humorless, waxy expression.

"The Fireseed is a perfect military tool," he starts. "It's strong, easily reproducible, of amazing genetic material, as we've heard Mr. Tralfant of The Greening explain."

"Let me demonstrate." From a large cargo bag Alex Dean extracts what looks like a thick white target. He sets that up on the back wall. Then he takes out a hollowed Fireseed stalk, injects something in one end and aims it at the target. A shuddering blast startles the audience, and the target starts to break down like hardened sugar in water. Gradually, the target dissolves into thin air. The audience bursts out in reaction.

"Forget about drones that damage huge swaths," he says, "just pick your target and dissolve *only* that target. This can be done from a long way away, as the Fireseed-based material has intelligent tracking ability. Imagine what power you'd have against an enemy. *Your* enemy." With this, Alex Dean stares out into the crowd, a dare etched in his blocky chin and steely eyes.

I break out in cold gooseflesh. This guy scares me. What enemy do we have, and do we really want to vaporize anyone who gets in our way?

The audience erupts into a furious discussion. Bea leans over to me. "Since when were we supposed to design military weaponry?"

"I know. Disturbing." I think of my own salve that can incapacitate someone. But that's not for war, that's for medicinal purposes, or calming a rowdy criminal... and it's temporary.

I look over at the judges, half expecting them to disqualify this guy. They're deep in whispered discussion. But they only thank him and call me up next!

My knees knocking, I present my elixirs. The stage is so vast that even my most dramatic demonstration— temporarily freezing the Spatter Lizard in one position—can hardly be seen at such a distance. I wish I'd set up an oversized demo like Blane. Even the burn on my arm—the second red, puffy burn that hurt like anything this morning as I prepared—seems so insignificant compared to what he revealed. Nonetheless, people are leaning forward, squinting their eyes to get a good look at the burn as it transforms into pink, fresh skin.

There's a respectable smattering of applause. Still, I leave the stage deeply disappointed. No way will I be able to afford my fantasy blue house in Vegas-by-the-Sea, not even a tiny studio apartment. I'll never get the money to help my family and friends back home escape. When I sit back down, Bea pats me on the back and tells me what a great job I did. She's a good friend, but her glued on smile can't fool me.

Bea's up next, so there's no time to mope. I'm glad for that. The time whizzes by as I hurry into one outfit only to shrug out of it into another, and burst out again on the red carpet catwalk that Bea's set up onstage. There is thundering applause for Bea, and the female students are clapping especially hard. I bet they would all love to dress in her fashions. This bodes well for her chances to win. No doubt, sales of Bea's clothes would be brisk and bring in boatloads of cash to this city, and for Axiom, even after he doles out the prize money. Nevada would win the bonus to fix up The Greening as well.

We sit through about four more presentations, including Radius' small hovercraft. He has a hard time with one of the wings, which keeps sagging to one side. Still, he earns an enthusiastic response when he gets it to rise unsteadily above the stage.

Afterwards, we're steered into a ballroom, filled with steamy teas, coffees, crumpets and cookies while we await the judges' determinations.

A crowd of mostly guys huddles around Alex Dean. Bea and I eavesdrop. He says that he hails from a long line of military brats.

"Brats?" I scrunch my face at Bea. "I wouldn't brag about being from a family of brats."

She breaks out in delighted laughter. "You learned nothing in that cult. A military brat is someone who grew up with a soldier mom or dad."

"Oh. I've never thought about military stuff. Nevada told us there were border wars with the north. But that's over. Who's our enemy now?"

Bea shrugs. I guess she doesn't know everything either.

Radius is also a popular guy, with kids asking him questions, and some curious grownups too. A flock of pretty girls start to surround Bea, asking her where they can get their hands on her fashion line, and if it's in Vegas stores yet. They also compliment me on my modeling.

As for my presentation, I have a generous handful of admirers, including a turbaned healer named Caprice from Vegas-by-the-Sea. She adores my salves and insists that her clients would pay good money for them. Nice! Perhaps I can eventually raise enough money to move without winning an actual prize. I forgot to bring my holo tablet, so Caprice jots her address down for me on a slip of paper.

Blane comes over and wraps an arm around me. "How are you holding up?"

"I'm good, and you were great! I had no idea how smart you are."

He laughs. "You thought I was dumb?"

"No, but you were so incredibly secretive about your project. Smart is sexy, you!" I stand on my tiptoes to kiss him. He kisses me back and my senses are fully attuned to the sensual movement of his powerful arms enfolding me, the currents of his fierce, independent mind.

We decide to head over to the dessert table where he loads his plate with cake and pastry. With all of the mandatory activities I still haven't been able to sift in enough solar vitamins, so I compensate by eating a sliver of chocolate cake. As miniscule as my appetite is these days, the chocolate still melts on my tongue.

Blane and I watch the judges emerge from a blue door at the end of the room and gather behind a long table there. The crowd begins to gravitate toward the table when it becomes clear the judges are preparing to announce a winner.

The three students from Vegas Central High that we sat with that first night at dinner drift toward us.

"Fancy meeting you here," quips Van, pushing his glasses up the bridge of his nose.

"Your presentation was great," Haddy tells me. "I so need that miracle skin salve."

"Sure, I can spare a little."

"Really?"

Blane pops in the last bite of chocolate cake and brushes his mouth with his sleeve. "Here we go! The judges are ready to make an announcement."

The judges have chosen their seats. Their heads turn to George Axiom as he steps out from the blue door. While he confers with them in a hushed voice the crowd settles down as everyone waits for the verdict. I realize, momentarily, that whatever type of discussion they're having is fast turning into a nasty argument. Stazzi, the lone female judge has gotten up and she's having at it as she wags a painted fingernail at him.

"Ooh, I wouldn't want to be Axiom right now," I say.

"What are they going on about?" Tib asks.

Haddy shakes her head. "Whatever it is, it's bad."

Abruptly, the panel of judges rise and file back behind the blue door. In response, the whole room sighs with impatience.

Tib turns to Blane. "I'd bet a load of cash that you win."

"It's pretty incredible, all the genetic decoding you did," Van admits.

"Our resident bodyguard brain," boasts Radius, clapping Blane on the back.

"Wait! Here they come again," Bea exclaims. It's true; the judges are marching back in, ominous determination on their faces. George Axiom yanks down his suit jacket as he scowls at Stazzi. What's going on?

Stazzi, not George gets up and proceeds to the center podium. Her long skirt rolls in waves behind her. "This was a very hard decision," she starts, a theatrical smile spreading across her face. "We were not unanimous. But we did reach a clear decision."

Is it my imagination that George Axiom has just rolled his eyes at Stazzi? I scan the room. No one else seems to have caught it. But I did, I'm certain.

Stazzi continues. "The grand winner, from Baronland South, is… Mr. Alex Dean!"

The audience erupts in loud objections. Seems like everyone is arguing now.

"What the heck!" yells Tib, "a rich kid from Baronland South? What a sick joke."

"Doesn't seem right that someone should win for a military weapon," I say.

Blane, who's been holding it together, bursts out, red-faced, "This contest was rigged. Everyone knows that my project was better than that military brat's."

"Much better," Haddy agrees.

"By far," I chime in.

Van growls, "Those Baronland South snobs shouldn't even be in the competition. They don't need the frying money."

Apparently lots of kids feel this way, because heated variations on this theme explode all around us. Amidst the clamor Alex Dean marches up to the podium in his official looking navy suit and collects his prize money, in a bulging white envelope Stazzi hands him.

I'm starting to feel sick, and dizzy. Is it the cake I ate? Dr. Varik warned me not to eat sweet desserts. I should've stuck to the liquid vitamins he gave me. Was it that chocolate cake, or is it from the sudden, distressed humming in my head?

Danger, danger, danger! It hisses. *He's lost, he's lost. Lost!*

The humming turns to abrasive static and I lose my footing. Trip into darkness.

"Wake up, Ruby!" Cold, wet sprinkles hit my face. "Ruby, it's me, Blane. You okay?"

I shake my head and raise my lids, gaze into Blane's anxious face. He's got my head cradled on his lap. One of his hands is stroking my hair, and the other is holding a cup. When he sees me looking up at him he puts down the cup and bends over, kisses me on the forehead. "You scared me, Ruby. What happened?"

In silent answer, the noise in my head swells once again. It relays no clear message the way it normally does, more like a dozen messages colliding in discordant and tangled tumbleweeds. "My head's hurting," is all I can say to describe it. "We need to get home. Something's wrong. Maybe it's Thorn. I just don't know."

"Can you stand?"

"I'll try." Blane helps me to my feet. Other people are gaping at me. I remember we're in the grand ballroom at the Axiom contest celebration. How embarrassing to have fallen in the middle of the activity. I brush off my crumpled dress. Haddy and Bea wear pale faces as they help Blane guide me to the exit.

"We need to find the chaperone and get out of here." Bea scans the clusters of people. I see the Vegas High teachers, and the Spokane group in their woodsy-inspired twine gear. The Baronland South contingent in their navy and grays are speaking to Stazzi over by the long table.

Finally, Bea locates our guide. We gather our gear and he delivers us to the lot outside. George's minions load us into a white glider and give the driver instructions to ferry us back to

The Greening. The Axiom folks seem eager to be rid of us now that we've not been declared the winners. Fine by me. I need to get back, make sure all is okay with Thorn and Armonk. A bitter taste lingers, and it's not from that chocolate cake.

~

Armonk's text pings on Blane's holo tablet when we're about an hour from The Greening. This is a highly unusual event, as they're not exactly friends and he's never sent Blane a text before. I reason that it's because I forgot my holo pad.

Reds going crazy. Thorn unwell. Won't talk. He wants Ruby. Return soon? Armonk

There's no more making out in the back of the glider. No more fun word games or flirting, no more gossip about the spoiled, entitled kids from Baronland South or theories why they'd grant Alex Dean the prize. I just want to get home, and fast.

"Oh, why did I go off and leave Thorn?" I wail. "What if Stiles came for him?"

Bea shakes her head. "Armonk mentioned nothing about Stiles. Calm down, Ruby, you need to keep your wits about you."

"How can I keep my wits about me when my head is splitting from the worst headache ever?" I press my palms into my temples and groan. If this is what the stromanet sounds like I don't want any part of it! Has it mixed signals with some other entity?

"Describe the headache," Blane says.

"Like thunder is blasting off inside my skull."

"Ever experienced that before?" Radius asks me, breaking his silence.

"Not exactly…" I've heard humming, not this, but the pain is too awful to speak.

"Lie on my lap." Blane eases me down so that my legs are drawn up on the seat.

"That helps," I moan.

"Good, shhh," Blane soothes, "get some rest."

26

I wake to the sound of high-pitched *yeeps* and the sight of literally hundreds of Reds careening every which way around our glider. We're in the middle of a red-winged tornado, hovering above The Greening landing strip.

"Watch out!" we yell to the pilot. "Don't hit them."

Without answering, he slows the vehicle and inches it to a shaky landing.

My headache still rages. Blane and Bea help me out while Radius and the pilot fetch our baggage. The pilot flies off before he even makes sure I'm okay. Which I'm not!

But it's the Reds that truly have me alarmed. Besides the ones flashing by our faces, many more are skimming over the

Fireseed field, whirling around and around, a militia of mythical, mad bees whose queen has abandoned the hive.

"It's like they're directionless," Bea notes.

I cup my hand over my brow as I stare up at them. "Yeah, they normally flock to Thorn as their... well, their king. Wonder why they're not seeking him out?" Is their connection broken somehow? If so, why?

"Their king?" Radius laughs. "That's a stretch." He has no idea, but now is no time for explanations. I need to see Thorn.

Overhead, two Reds collide in an explosion of wings and tufts. In a volley of high-pitched yeeps, they repeatedly dive-bomb and bite each other.

"Stop it!" I yell, as if I have any say over them. Now it's not only two of them biting and snarling, it's become an escalating skyborne brawl.

"They're going insane like they're ready to attack us." Radius shouts over his mask. A distinct possibility if this keeps up.

Halfway down the path toward the school, Armonk runs toward us. He's raised his bow to his shoulder as if he's prepared to use it—to kill a Red? When he sees us he lowers it, but keeps on racing forward.

"What the hell's going on?" Blane asks him. "Where's Nevada?"

"The Reds have become mutinous," he answers. "They won't listen to Thorn. They won't listen to anyone." Armonk looks up at them with a frown. "It's as if they're rebelling. And Nevada? She's been away for a few days. I thought she was with you."

It's unlike Nevada to check out. Something's really off. "Are Vesper and Jan around?" Blane asks. "Have they been on good behavior?"

Armonk sighs. "As good as they ever are. They took off in one of the gliders." At this, Blane shakes his head in disgust.

"Where's Thorn?" I ask, racing closer.

"Sick in bed," Armonk answers. "Can't get a word out of him, he's stopped talking."

"Did you take him to Dr. Varik?" As I open the front door the Reds continue to swoop and dive, nipping at each other and at us. I bat one away that's winging inches from my face.

"Not yet, he only came down with an intense headache this morning. No fever."

"Headache—odd coincidence—that's what I have." It's some relief to hear that Thorn hasn't been in pain long.

I speed upstairs with Armonk, followed by Blane and Bea. Radius stays on first tier to sort out the luggage and cook up a meal.

Thorn rolls over to face us as we hurry in. His covers are rumpled. His face twists into a pained grimace as I sit by him on the bed.

"Thorn, what's wrong?"

He doesn't answer in words, only in movements. He shifts his head into my lap and folds up, arm-to-arm, limb-to-limb, like a Red fetus.

I jiggle his arm. "Talk to me, please. I can't help if you won't tell me how you feel."

"I'll give you guys space," Bea whispers. "He might talk if it's just you." I nod, which prompts Blane and Armonk to pad out too, though I sense them hovering in the hall.

"What's going on?" I comb Thorn's tangled hair with my fingers and rub his back. "I'm so sorry I left without you. Did Armonk take good care of you?" I hear a pointed rustle in the hallway. Clearly Armonk doesn't appreciate the question.

Thorn shifts his body so he's gazing up at me. He unsquints his eyes as if it hurts to do so. "Armonk. Took good care."

"Then wh—?"

"Sucking at my brain."

"Sucking your brain! What's sucking at your brain?" My pulse pounds in my neck.

"Sucked out," he breathes. "Dreams eat my thoughts."

Icy shudders wrack me. What in holy hell? Has my brother finally gone raving nuts? If so, I'm not sure that me always watching him like a mama hawk would have made any difference. Tears threaten to slip over my lids and down my cheeks but I force them back. If my brother is broken, I can't fall apart too. One of us has to stay strong; we're the hinge between the Fireseed and the Reds. We need to honor whatever we've become. Did Jan have anything to do with how my brother feels? "Where's Jan? And Vesper? Have they bothered you?"

Thorn blinks up at me. "Jan friendly."

"Oh, really?" This makes me immediately suspicious. "*How* was he friendly?"

"Candy."

"Candy, eh?" Dr. Varik's cautions about me eating cake and pastries in my condition as part plant roll through my mind. Plants don't tolerate sweets well. Could Jan have poisoned Thorn, even unintentionally? "We need to get you to Dr. Varik's right away."

"No!"

"Why not, Thorn? You like Dr. Varik, remember?"

"No Dr. Varik." His eyes grow so wide I see the whites around his irises.

It almost seems as if someone's brainwashed Thorn, but how's that possible? We don't have a hypnotist at the school. That idea would make me laugh if I weren't so worried. Maybe Thorn's decided that he doesn't relish checkups any more than most kids. Still, it's out of character since last time

Thorn was fawning over Dr. Varik. "Why are you scared of going to see the doctor?" I ask him gently.

He covers his face with his hands and rocks, a sure sign of his terror.

I get up and stare out the window, watch the Reds rampage in the violet-streaked sky. "Why are your Reds flying all over the place? They normally stay in the Fireseed field, in their perches."

Thorn slowly rises to a sitting position and props himself up with his hands. "Reds. No more listen to me."

"Why not?"

He shakes his head, clearly as baffled as me.

"What should we do then?"

"Clean my head, Rube."

I frown at him. "What on earth do you mean by that? Wash your face?" He only repeats the request. We need a trip to Dr. Varik's whether or not Thorn approves. "I'm going to let you sleep while I think about what to do."

"Stay near," he murmurs, his eyes still wide. "Dream of blue ships. Take me away."

My heart stops with a thud. "Blue ships?" Holy effing fire! Like the ones in my own sickbed dreams? I scramble out of the room, and crash straight into Armonk. "Did someone come here and mess with my brother when we were in Vegas? Someone in a pearl blue ship?"

"No," says Armonk, "I've kept my eye on him the whole t—"

"But you may want to see what Jan has in his desk drawer," Blane cuts in as he marches up behind Armonk.

We step over the mess on Jan's floor: socks stiff with dried sweat, Nevada's pistol manual, spent bullets and two crusty sea apples in a bowl. Inside Jan's pants drawer is a wad of cash, as thick as a Fireseed stalk. Blane counts it out, while Armonk stands lookout in the hall.

"Frying hell! This is close to 2,000 Dominions," Blane exclaims. He has a hard time gripping the cash in one hand there's so much of it.

I don't bother to ask what Blane was doing snooping around in his bureau drawer. In fact, I start to unearth pants, shirts, Jan's lone jacket stinking of gun metal, and old papers, crumpled and refolded to shreds. Nothing notable, though, until my eyes fix on a familiar image in his sock drawer: a card with the pearly globe logo. "Hold on, I know that."

"What, Ruby?" Blane leans over me, scanning the card.

I shout, "This logo was on the Stream implants that George put in us. But there's no address on this card, no nothing."

Armonk peers out of the window. "Ask the culprit, Jan's coming in now." Reaching for his bow, Armonk slips behind a dresser. He nods to Blane, who stuffs the bills in his pants pocket and ducks behind Jan's door. Are they really going to make *me* deal with him?

The clatter of Jan's boots and the sight of his acerbic face glowering at me as he stomps in make my insides curdle. "What are you doing in my room?" he accuses. Glancing around, he notices that his things are strewn even farther afield than he tossed them, because he says, "What'd you do with my stuff? I asked you a question, Cult Girl."

"What did you do to my brother?" I growl, and hold up the business card. "And where did you get this?"

Without answering, he stalks toward his drawer and yanks it open, rifles through the pants. "You stole my cash!" He grabs me with his sinewy arms, and squeezes hard as he shakes me. "Where's my frying money, witch?"

Armonk slinks up behind him and puts an arrow to his

neck. "Let her go," he warns. "Or I'll put this point through the back of your throat."

"Oh, you think?" Jan sneers, not moving. "What if I don't feel like it?" His hand inches steadily to his hip. Jan ducks as the arrow flies into the air and thwacks into the wall. Whirling around, Jan lifts the gun he just grabbed to Armonk's face.

"No!" I crouch and then dive into the hall, as Blane leaps from behind the door and tackles Jan. They plunge down together as a gunshot explodes, piercing my eardrums. Impossibly loud, its bullet blasts a ragged hole in the floor near the window. The pistol slides toward me and I seize it, stuffing it inside my sock. I don't want to use it, ever. Just need to keep it from Jan.

Blane and Jan continue to wrestle. Blane is burly, but Jan is wiry and fast, with legs that wind around Blane in and chop him with karate jabs. They're both grunting and cursing. Meanwhile, Armonk has gotten back to his feet. He lets loose an arrow, which sinks into Jan's arm. Jan yelps, his other arm yanking the arrow out and clutching at the wound.

Blane gains the upper hand at last. "Ruby, get me something to tie him with!"

Running into my room, I hide the gun under my mattress and Bea and I return with two dress belts. Blane winds one securely around Jan's wrists and I bind the other around his ankles for good measure. We drag him to a chair by his bed and prop him there. Bea uses another piece of fabric as a tourniquet for his bleeding wound.

With Armonk's arrow leveled steadily at Jan's forehead, we finally get him talking. "They came one day and asked me for Thorn. I said hell no. I asked why they wanted him."

"Who? Why?" I press.

"They said for some test, that's all. I said I couldn't just fork the kid over, that Armonk was playing chaperone with him." Jan snickers as he eyes Armonk. Then he glares at the floor.

Blane prods him hard in the ribs. "Go on."

"They told me they had money. Money talks." Jan's snort turns into a long, acidic laugh.

How dare he! I slap him in the face. "So if money talks, what does it say? Get on with it."

He purses his lips as if he's poised to spit in my face, but since Armonk's arrow is still poking into his forehead and Blane is still hovering over him, Jan goes on, begrudgingly. "I told them they'd have to come here at night. They said to leave the bedroom window open." He stops. "Don't know what they did with the kid. They said they'd keep him sleeping. That they only needed to take a blood sample or some crap."

I get up in Jan's face, so close I smell his vinegary breath. "Who are they, and where do they live?"

He averts his face, as if he can't stand my breath either, or my presence so close, pressuring him. It feels dangerously good to have the upper hand with this bully, and I can see how someone could easily get carried away with that feeling. I quash my urge to give him another hard slap just because I can. "Who's *they* and where do they live?" I ask again.

"I don't frying know, doesn't it say on the card?"

"No."

"Nevada knows. She was talking to that lady, Stazzi."

"Stazzi? The Axiom judge?"

"That's who gave me the card, Cult Girl."

My stomach drops as I remember Jan talking to that pilot one day, to the transfer of what I thought was money. I'd assumed the pilot was a guy but he, or she, was wearing a helmet. So, that was Stazzi under the helmet? Did she come back again? I guess so! I gape at Bea, who's cowering in the door, then at Blane, who's staring back at me. Finally, I look over at Armonk.

"What does Nevada have to do with it?" Armonk asks Jan.

"She took half the money, fool."

"I don't believe you." Armonk prods the arrow into Jan so sharply it puckers his skin.

"I know you hate to think of your favorite teacher that way," Jan chides. "But the woman's out for the money. She's broke, greedy and weak." Jan plays a confidence game, but sweat is trickling down either side of his neck.

My mind fixes on Nevada's strange behavior at Dr. Varik's and how she never told Armonk the doctor had come to Skull's Wrath. I remember how she wasn't so welcoming at first, and how she only had a feeble hold over Blane and Jan. She was awfully excited when Axiom was describing the prize money too. Nothing in those memories provides a shred of comfort.

"Let's go talk to her then," Armonk says quietly, fiercely.

"Talk to who?" Vesper appears in the doorway like some forgotten apparition. "What the hell, Jan?" Quicker than a flash sandstorm, Blane and Armonk bind her hands as well.

"Who the hell do you think you are, Peg Leg?" she hisses at Armonk.

"Where's Nevada?" he asks, ignoring the slight.

"Out spending money no doubt." Vesper sniggers. "She got a killing from giving those people in the pearly blue ship access to your freaky brother. Hell, she got so much she probably blew this dump and moved up north to Land Dominion. I mean, who'd stay down here if they had the scratch, right Jan?" Vesper and Jan launch into a laughing fit and it's all I can do to keep my clenched fists by my side.

We dash down to Nevada's study, her private sanctum, which we now have ample reason to breach. This breaking in is all so new, and forbidden. I remember how Nevada gently washed my back after Stiles attacked me. I remember her coaxing me to eat.

God only knows who the villains and heroes are anymore.

All I know is that I need my brother to get well and I need answers. In her desk we find Stazzi's address on the letterhead of a note. It's a company called NanoPearl, and it's listed as Pacific Ocean 3, in Vegas-by-the-Sea. Pacific Ocean? How is that possible? Is it underwater? Stazzi's scribbled a note for Nevada on it: *Come see me and we'll talk business.*

Business, huh.

Nevada's desk looks rifled through—uprooted papers, and files in a mess. I do see a wad of cash stuck inside the frame of a holo calendar. I count it out—a mere 200 Dominions—not an impressive cache if it's payoff money.

Thorn has padded down. He's mumbling, clutching his head. "Clean me out. Please, Rube." My own head erupts with harsh, nonsensical sound when he comes close. This doesn't seem like the stromanet or the Fireseed, whose voices are always so clear, so harmonious. What then?

A handful of the Reds have managed to get into the compound and they're flying wildly, bouncing off the rafters, yeeping and careening near us. Unlike all of the other times I've seen Thorn with them, they pay no attention to him whatsoever. This fills me with a nameless dread.

"Let's take Thorn to Dr. Varik's now," I whisper to Armonk.

"I may be able to help," Blane says. "My father was a doctor."

"Sure he was." Armonk scoffs.

I'm tired of the tension between them, and it makes me feel guilty as if I encouraged it somehow. "I believe Blane," I say quietly. "Besides, we need all hands on board."

Armonk nods, his lips fixed in a grim line. He may not trust Blane, but he trusts me.

Radius enters the office with Bea, and we quickly fill them in on our plans.

"Can you hang tight and keep watch over Jan and Vesper?" Blane levels his gaze on Radius, no doubt to detect any wavering of his friend's loyalty.

Radius puts an arm around Bea. "Sure, just keep us posted."

"Hope you feel better fast, little man," Bea says to Thorn.

I jog up to third tier to fill my latchbag with elixirs and tools we may need on the road. On my way down Vesper yells from Jan's room, where she's bound to a wall pipe, "That doctor of yours sold out too, you know." Nevada has him twisted around her fingers." Vesper cackles. "You're all so damn clueless. Whenever you were away, Nevada had the doctor over for soirees." She laughs hard and Jan joins in.

I want to tell her that I'm shocked she even knows the word soiree but it's so not worth it.

27

Even before we land, Thorn is crying—silent tears streaming down his face. He's my weathervane so I know that something's horribly wrong. I feel it too, in the pit of my stomach, in the discordant howls in my head, that I know Thorn also hears.

We scramble out of the glider and hurry under the awning toward the house. The front door is cocked open.

"Dr. Varik never leaves the door this way," Armonk says, "even when he's in the yard, loading the glider for a house call."

"Or when he's picking his medicinal crops," I add. As generous a doctor as he is, he's also guarded about thieves.

We stand motionless. None of us have the nerve to go in. It's like the night I escaped. Once I walked toward that pyre with Stiles and later that night to The Greening I sensed that I could never return to innocence. But we're bound by the need to help Thorn, and by allegiance to this doctor who took the time to explain what we've become.

Stepping over the threshold, I gasp. We're faced with chaos. Thorn lets out a rare cry. Dr. Varik's furniture's been upended in some sort of raid, or fight. His prized antique medical books have been tossed carelessly on the floor with covers splayed. Blane sets the chairs upright, I dust off books and return them to the shelves.

Armonk calls out, "Dr. Varik? Are you here? What's going on?"

Thorn ventures into the doctor's adjoining office. He returns, tugging at my arm, new tears blotting his eyes. In there, someone has thrown Dr. Varik's holo files across the table, their diamond and octagonal jewel shapes spilled for the poaching. Whoever was here didn't want these files, though who knows how many others are missing. His monitor's still on, and when Armonk presses return, it blinks alive, onto a medical report.

I read it out loud. "Subjects display chimeric aspects upon testing. The variety of symptoms and transgenic response is stunning. Subjects have less need for food and more for photosynthesis. Each displays weight loss and heightened energy, with the blood thinning and mixing with sap. Unlike my side effect of the plants throwing off new roots, subjects Ruby and Thorn are each self-contained in one plant chimera, having no root system."

"Chimera," Blane says as he clenches and unclenches his jaw. "A genetic splicing of two very different beings." His brows shoot up as he turns toward me. "That's you!" he exclaims. "Why didn't you ever tell me?"

"I... I guess I was scared to."

A glint of satisfaction plays on Armonk's face, no doubt because unlike Blane, I trusted Armonk with my secret the whole time.

Armonk continues reading where I left off. "Each form of mutation or contamination, if you will, foments a different variety of chimera. This is an improvement on my transgenesis, as in my case, the need to cut off constant new growths has been a source of pain and embarrassment, and has rendered my skin a woody texture that must be treated with special—"

"So the doctor's part Fireseed too?" Blane murmurs. "This just gets more bizarre."

"I knew it," I blurt. "I saw those nubs."

"We need to find him," Armonk interrupts. "We'll talk about the details later."

"You're right." I scan the room for a clue to the doctor's whereabouts.

Thorn has run off again. We find him pounding on the door to the operating suite.

Armonk puts his ear to the door and wriggles the latch. "The doctor never locks the inside doors. Dr. Varik," he calls, then louder, "Dr. Varik, if you're in there open up!"

I hear a faint groan, but wonder if it's an echo off of the slick office walls. "Did you hear someone?" Blane and Armonk shake their heads so I keep searching.

Thorn tries the doorknob again. "Smell," he exclaims.

Putting my nose to the crack under the door, I breathe in. "Ack! Stinks of stale potatoes but much more raunchy." After another inhale my stomach quivers with a profound nausea.

Blane searches for a tool to pry open the lock. He finds one of Dr. Varik's surgical tools—a curved metal blade with a narrow hooked tip, which does the trick—that, and a determined kick. On the operating suite table, our worst fears are realized.

A horrible yet strangely exotic sight lies before us. Someone has secured Dr. Varik to the surgical table with his own belts, and springing from his grey, decaying flesh are tall sprays of gorgeous red star-shaped flowers. They bloom from his chest, his forehead and his stomach. Smaller, curlicue fronds unfurl from his upturned arms. One single stalk with a crimson flower head rises from his mouth in a lyrical, triumphant arc.

Armonk approaches the doctor and checks for a pulse. "He's gone." With that, tears begin to slide down his cheekbones.

"The flower roots must've invaded his organs," Blane says.

I gag and swallow. That reality is overwhelming. Those few times that I studied the doctor's exposed skin and noticed stubs now flood back to me in lurid detail. He was shaving these blooms off. He's hidden this horror from us, and now whoever secured him here and robbed him of his dignity and life, has released Varik's secret to the world.

Varik truly was Fireseed One—the first transgenic variety of the species.

Tears spill from my eyes and onto Thorn's head as we hug each other. Terror seizes me too. I know that the doctor said my transmutation was different than his but… I glance down at my arms. What if he was wrong? I hear Armonk, now crying in gasps, and Blane is frozen in place, still staring at the sight.

When I finally creep over toward the body, I'm afraid to touch it. I'm one and the same, though I'm supposedly a different breed.

"Is it catching, Ruby?" Blane whispers as he inches closer.

"No." I will myself to believe this. The doctor has to be right. "If it was that easy to get, all of the kids at The Greening would have come down with it."

"How did you catch it then?" Blane asks with a frown, as if it's a plague.

I tell him what happened after Jan and Vesper stuffed pollen down our noses. Armonk chimes in and describes Dr. Varik's pollination through his lesions. All the while, Thorn is rocking and holding his head.

"We need to help Thorn." I rush to my brother's side. "Dr. Varik would have wanted us to. We need to figure out what's wrong with him."

"I could examine him," Blane offers.

Armonk peers at Blane with suspicion, and I shake my head at Armonk. "With the doctor gone, Blane is our only chance at figuring this out," I insist, as much to myself as to Armonk. Again, Armonk nods with a dour determination.

Armonk holds out his arms to Thorn. "Come here, little man. Sit in my lap." Thorn sinks down and wraps his arms around Armonk's solid arms.

Blane collects an array of the doctor's surgical tools and arranges them on a clean towel. Sitting next to Armonk and Thorn, he examines Thorn's head, carefully thumbing through every inch of scalp, behind each ear and around the circumference of his downy neck. Blane's hand stops at the nape of Thorn's neck and he presses in. "Does that hurt?"

Thorn lets out a yelp and tries to push Blane's hand away.

"No, don't touch." Blane looks over at me, where I'm kneeling. "Ruby, do you have your numbing elixir?"

I reach for the vial in my latchbag and unscrew the top. Blane shows me the red spot on Thorn's neck and I spread my salve around the area.

"Hold him firmly," Blane advises Armonk, and he complies, gripping Thorn's shoulders and head so he can't suddenly flinch.

What a relief that Blane and Armonk have finally gotten

to a place where they can work together without sniping—even if it took the doctor's death to get them there.

After a minute to let the salve do its magic, Blane takes a miniscule scissors and a tweeze style tool and gets to work.

I'm squeamish, and on top of the foul odor wafting from the doctor's corpse, I have to steel myself not to spew. Veering away, I screw my eyes shut. My head screams with noise! It feels as if my head will detonate. Thorn must be feeling it too. Forget the nostalgic thrumming of the Reds and the Fireseed back at The Greening, what I wouldn't gave for an annoying vanilla Stream Blast right now. Anything but this searing static. Clamping my head between my palms, I count down the seconds.

"Holy fire!" Blane exclaims.

"Mother of god!" Armonk cries.

Only then do I dare turn my head and stare at the object clamped in Blane's surgical tool.

"It's a totally different implant than Axiom stapled in us before the contest," I say.

"That's for sure," Blane swivels the device in his clamps.

"Looks like a spiky space creature," says Armonk.

"Or a collection device," Blane says. "Whoever put this in Thorn wanted to get information from him. Maybe because he won't talk, they tried something else to steal his thoughts from him."

"Sucking on my brain," Thorn murmurs.

I shudder. "It's stamped with that NanoPearl logo. Who are those people?" As I say this, I realize that the dial on that horrible internal static has suddenly been turned down—no, it's off!

Thorn says exactly what I'm feeling. "Better. No noise."

We all stare at the implant, dripping with Thorn's greenish gore. "Frying hellfire," Blane mutters under his breath. "I'm sure this thing was collecting some kind of data from his brain."

"And at the same time confusing it with noise." I add. "Which I heard too because Thorn and I are connected through the stroma."

"The stroma?" Blane frowns.

I explain to Blane how the stroma works, how all of the plants and even the Reds are connected to Thorn and me. How we read each other's thoughts, how we feel each other's pain.

Blane stares at me long and hard. I wonder what he's thinking: probably that it's one thing to have a formal knowledge of advanced genetics but another thing entirely to connect that with real people with beating hearts. "You say you turned into a chimera from inhaling Fireseed pollen?" he asks. When I nod he continues with an unexpected enthusiasm. "First we need to get the other chips out of our heads, and then we have to get back to The Greening. You have more pollen there?"

"I can gather more, why?"

"If we work collectively through the stroma, maybe we'll figure out why they want Thorn's thoughts so badly, what they intend to use them for."

"You mean transform ourselves?" Armonk asks Blane.

"Exactly."

"What a smart idea." Armonk grins at Blane for the first time ever.

Thorn nods. "Stroma powers us."

I'm proud of Blane. One by one, I smear numbing elixir on the napes of our necks and Blane surgically removes our implants. This time, I'm calm enough to watch him remove Armonk's, and even his own, with me holding a mirror aimed at his neck so he can clearly see the entry site. It's surprising how precise Blane can be with his bearlike hands and thickset fingers that always seemed best suited for sports and pummeling his enemies.

Armonk is amazing too, patient and gentle with Thorn. I imagine what a great father and husband he'll make someday, to another woman—maybe even my friend Petal or Freeblossom. Thinking these happier thoughts I smile.

In the meantime, Blane lines up the implants on the towel like tiny monsters from a horror show. The new one from Thorn has a dozen spiky nodules like a lethal insect, but even the early ones that George stapled in us look alien in their smooth anonymity. How could I have been so eager to have that in my head, telling me what to think about, what to long for? I'll never again have to be startled by those awful Stream blasts, never hear any more wheedling ads hawking the latest restaurant or cleaning powder.

Instead, we'll be connected to the stromanet.

We bandage each other's wounds. The harmonious thrumming from my being to Thorn's, from Thorn's to his Reds, from the Reds to the Fireseed has already begun as we wrap the good doctor in a length of clean surgical sheet. First we pluck off the majestic blossoms and place them in a vase with a dampened sponge to save for his memorial. How bizarre that he grew flowers from his own body for his memorial, I think as I wrap the last part of the sheet under the doctor's cold arms.

Goodbye wise one, wise one, wise one, goes the humming.

The memorial will have to wait. We need to deal with NanoPearl first.

As we pack up our supplies, I hear a tortured groan. This time it's not my imagination. We stop what we're doing to listen. Another. Someone is suffering, badly.

"Is it coming from the living room?" Blane asks.

"No, the kitchen, behind the pantry door." Armonk is

already there. As he swings it open, we're shocked to see it's someone we know quite well.

"Nevada! Oh, my god!" I cry and dash forward, fling my arms around her. She's slumped, head on chest, and weaving in and out of consciousness. "How long have you been in here?"

She shakes her head in slow motion.

Thorn hides way back in the shadows of the room.

Armonk uses his pocketknife to slit her binding because someone tied her arms behind her back. She comes alive enough to bring them forward and paw at her bloody wrists. She has one black, puffy eye and her expression is glazed with hunger and sadness.

"Who did this to you, Nevada?" Armonk crouches next to her and feeds her sips of water that I've rushed to get.

She clears her throat, attempts to talk but it comes out as a grunt. Trying again, she puts a few words together. "Jan attacked me, at the school. Took me here and…" Tears wet her sunken cheeks. "Forced me to look at Varik's body. All tied down, with vines coming out of—" She breaks out in sobs. "Jan killed him. Varik… I loved him so."

My heart bleeds for her. I feel guilty for being so suspicious of her motives with the doctor. Armonk and I exchange glances. I see he feels the same way. But how were we to know?

Blane has collected a small bowl of sea applesauce from the doctor's kitchen and he hands it to Armonk, who spoons some in. After a minute or so, Nevada raises her head and drinks more water.

There's no way around asking her hard questions. "Did you know that NanoPearl was after my brother? Did they make any deals with you?" I study her; use my intuition to discern a lie or a truth.

"Nano Pearl, what's that?"

Is she kidding? "You had a note from them in your desk. That female judge, who works for NanoPearl wrote it. She asked you to come talk business."

"Oh, that pushy woman," she mutters, "I wanted nothing to do with her."

Blane kneels down, crowds Nevada's space. "Jan says you took a bribe from her." I know how intimidating Blane can be. She might just crumble if he presses her. "We found money in your desk."

She narrows her eyes at Blane. "Who told you to snoop in my office?" I understand she's our teacher but if she's truly innocent this response won't help her. "I only had a couple hundred in there, for emergencies." That's true, that's exactly what we found.

"Nevada," Armonk says in a gentle, patient voice, the one that warmed me to him from the very first days at The Greening. "This is a very serious issue. If you made any underhanded deal you need to come clean now."

"What deal are you talking about?" she shrieks. In her tone, I hear she knows nothing.

"Jan said you took a bribe from NanoPearl, and got paid plenty to let them experiment on Thorn," Blane explains.

"What?" This shriek is shriller. "I'd never let anyone touch Thorn."

"We understand that The Greening's on the verge of bankruptcy," Armonk adds wearily. "We understand how incredibly tempting it would be to collect a payoff."

"I did no such thing," Nevada spits. "Yes, that woman wanted to talk to me about some sneaky deal, but as desperate as I've ever been..." she snorts under her breath. "And I've been plenty desperate wandering alone in the desert, living on shale and spiders; I would never use my students as pawns. Never!"

"Okay, okay." Armonk sighs. "Then explain how Jan got a huge stack of cash."

Nevada's eyes grow round and feral. "You see what he did to me!" She holds up her blood-streaked arms. "You see what he did to the doctor?" With this more tears fall. "Jan's capable of anything, that murderous bastard. Truth be told, I was always petrified of him, him and that delinquent, Vesper. I tried to give everyone the fair shake I never had as a teen. But…" Releasing a bitter moan, she sags down again. "What happened to Thorn?" she whispers after a moment. "He's not hurt, is he?"

Thorn steps forward from the shadows and plops down by Nevada, takes her injured hand in his little one. "Here," he says simply, and gives her a hug. Oh, my, god. My brother is an angel here on earth. In a way he really is the second coming of Fireseed after all. As more tears fall, she mumbles about how relieved she is that he's okay.

Armonk hauls Nevada to her feet, guiding her around the long way so she doesn't have to traipse through Dr. Varik's surgical suite and see the sheet over his body. As he helps Nevada into a glider, Armonk addresses us. "Listen, Ruby, Blane, I'm taking Nevada to Marney's Depot. Marney can watch over her until we straighten things out. Nevada has no business going to the school right now as long as Jan and Vesper are there. Her condition's way too shaky."

"Meet us at The Greening?" I ask.

"Yes."

"We'll take the doctor's glider," says Blane.

With that, Blane, Thorn and I pile in and fly over the dunes to Skull's Wrath. The skeletal rock faces glower in the purple slants of sunset. Pitting myself to face Vesper, Jan and the rampaging Reds, The Greening and its environs feel more like a battlefield than home.

28

From the sky, it's evident that the Fireseed has burned whole swaths of its own kind since we left. This must be the third time they've set themselves on fire. Our intense turmoil out on the coast must've upset them. Narrow coils of smoke still drift up from the field, though it looks as if the blaze is out. It's a wonder how the plants can burn and then manage to tamp out before setting fire to the school. The human or plant in them?

Bea races down the path to the glider and folds me into a hug. Radius follows.

"Am I ever glad you guys are back," she groans. "This place is falling apart." Her face is set in a grimace of worry. I've only seen her this upset on the day I woke from my fever coma.

I hate that I can't dispel her worries, especially after we tell her what Jan did to Dr. Varik and to Nevada.

She clamps a hand over her mouth. "My god! That's so heartless."

"I'm glad you took Nevada somewhere safe," Radius says as we start to walk to the school. He snorts. "Jan and Vesper don't relish following orders. They tried to convince me I was a fool to believe they did anything wrong, a fool to be loyal to you. When that didn't work, they tried to bribe me with money." He laughs. "But that didn't work because we're holding their money now." Blane chuckles along with Radius. We need a little gallows humor now and then.

I glance over at the Fireseed field. "No Reds. Wonder what made them calm down?"

Bea stares up at the sky. "Wow, I've been so traumatized I haven't noticed, but yeah."

Thorn tugs on my arm. "They hear me."

"They hear you?"

He nods, and on cue, dozens of Reds alight from the field and fly in that amazing V formation toward Thorn, their child king. It's clear now that Blane was right: without the spiky NanoPearl bug in his head, Thorn can talk to the Reds and they, him. No more static interference, no more stealing his thoughts.

They settle on his arms, on the crown of his head, and a relieved thrumming commences.

At the compound, Radius cooks us a meal of sautéed Fireagar and sea potatoes. I'm not so hungry but I know the work I'm about to do will require massive reserves. I even remember to take a dose of Dr. Varik's liquid vitamins with my meal. While we eat, Radius ferries food up to our captives. Bea has a helpful, reliable boyfriend and I tell her that.

We discuss the decision to transform in order to work collectively. Armonk is all for it. I hug him to show how grateful I am for his help, and how important he is to me, even though I'm bound to someone else. The fierce look of loyalty and love in his eyes tells me he gets it.

Bea and Radius not so much. "Why don't Bea and I stay here and keep holding down the fort?" Radius suggests. His face stiffens into a frown that reveals his horror at snuffling up large quantities of Fireseed pollen.

Bea nods. "I'd much rather draw hybrid creatures than become one."

"Plus someone needs to keep the prisoners in grub, and I'm the only one who really likes to cook," Radius reasons.

"You're off the hook," I tell them. "Babysitting Vesper and Jan is plenty hard."

After the early dinner, while Armonk gathers supplies, Blane and I head to the field to collect pollen.

I test him. "You sure you want to do this? There won't be a way back once—"

"I'm sure, Ruby." His soulful gaze reassures me.

In the privacy of the red jungle, we take a moment before the hike to dive into each other's arms. Clasping each other tightly, we kiss. When his lips graze mine, the stubble of his days not shaving feels intimate and rough. Our passion withheld while in Vegas-by-the-Sea we give each other freely now. Our lingering kisses reveal our unfolding love and how fully committed we are to seeing this through.

He whispers, "You're amazing, Ruby. I want to feel your thoughts and all of your emotions."

I run my finger down the slope of his nose, his spray of

freckles. "I'm intense, Blane, are you sure you can handle feeling what I feel?"

"Bring it on, Ruby, all of it." His mouth on mine is hungry, pressing, taking all of me in. For all of those famished looks Blane gave me before I knew him, I feed him now with my attention, my tenderness, and the beat of my rapid-fire heart. His hard against my soft fits—we fit well together.

It's hard to break away, but we can't afford to wait until dark. We brush off and start hiking. I show him how to shake out the Fireseed stamen without damaging it, and collect its ruddy particles in the vials. Even with patches of the field destroyed and still smoking, we fill our jars to brimming.

A couple of the Reds swirl down and land on my shoulder, peck at my latchbag, and rummage their beaklike noses through my hair.

You're here, you're here, you're here they thrum.

And the Fireseed plants add their harmony. *Protect us, protect us, beauty.*

I used to hate it when people called me beautiful. But the plants aren't looking at my striking face, my long platinum hair or ample curves. They're referring to the beauty inside of me. And I feel it too, unfurling, blossoming.

"What?" Blane asks me when he sees my smile.

"The plants are talking to me," I breathe.

"Will they talk to me, when I change?"

"They will."

We hike back to the school, and proceed to the project room with Armonk. I dose Blane and Armonk with just the right amount to make the transformation into hybridism, without them sinking into the fevered, nauseous coma that I experienced. It's a fine line, and when they are done, with their nostrils stinging, ribs aching and limbs shuddering from the hard work of fusion, I have to admit I'm relieved.

Their transmutation will solidify in the hum of the sun. We file downstairs, adding Thorn to our little procession.

At the sound of our footsteps, Jan calls out, still tied to a wall post in his room, "Freaks! I knew you were a bunch of freaks from the second I saw you. I should have thrown you all out then."

Freaks, you could call us that. In a good way, I think as my inward smile spreads.

Silently we traipse outside without our burnsuits and make a beeline for the dunes. The sun's still up, though no longer at its zenith. No matter, we group together and open our arms and bodies to its vibrational food.

Eat, new ones sing the Fireseed, and the Reds join the refrain: *Eat, eat, eat, and take your fill, take your fill.*

We huddle toward each other—like a family of nested lizards, or nested humans, or nested chimera, whatever we are at this moment. The sun blends us, one into the other, and we engorge in our power and strength.

Blane's eyes turn from hazel to vivid green as his thoughts pour into me. *Tide, tidal pool. Tide, tide, tidal pool.*

Tidal pool? I ask, *tidal pool?*

Turbulence, he answers in my head, *turbulent waters, troubled sky.*

Ocean Armonk thinks, *ocean, ocean.*

I picture the ocean, its calm blue, and the infinite sky above it. Then I picture it troubled, with roiling waves, and whirling, angry clouds. *Rough troubled waters, and rough troubled skies. What trouble?* I ask without words.

Trouble Thorn answers, *over the big ocean.*

It is there the Reds call, *it is there where they stole us, stole us, stole us!*

My mind moves to *the pearl, the ominous troubled pearl in the rough-hewn sky.*

From the sharp, unexpected flash in Blane's eyes to the way Armonk flinches, to Thorn's growl of pain, it comes to us all at once, and so clearly.

I lower my arms, break away and yell, "The orb I saw over the Pacific Ocean! That's where we need to go."

"That's Pacific Ocean 3!" Blane shakes out his legs.

"The NanoPearl headquarters, where they make those bugs," Armonk adds.

I say, "When Blane and I got near it during the hovercraft ride I felt its incredible evil."

"Evil." Thorn nods.

A flock of Reds sail to us, *eeping,* fluttering, crowding in, but not too close, not nipping.

Thorn lets them land all over him. "They want to go with us."

"Let's do it," says Blane.

"I'll pack us some food and gear," I say.

"Bring your elixirs," Armonk suggests.

"Right. I'll bring the healing and also the paralyzing one. And you, bring your bow," I tell him. I glance over at Blane. "Please, no guns."

He sears me with his hot, glittering eyes. "No guns. We have other ways now."

Other ways, echo the Reds.

In the field, the Fireseed sways and whooshes in audible agreement.

29

Over the Pacific the wind screams sideways, and our glider catches on its violent current. It spins us around, and in the roll, we're thrown further and further from the gigantic orb. Helplessly, we stare out as its pearl-blue presence slides behind monstrous, humid clouds.

Armonk navigates the glider back to the cloud cluster, only to have the wind shriek sideways again and toss us mercilessly. How frustrating! We're as far from it as we were in that first airborne rollover. Howling, the bluster vibrates the glider as if it's a breakable toy. I'm starting to get airsick and again the orb is nowhere. I recall the way Blane described the pearly ship as disappearing in plain sight and this brings me to an unsettling, new thought.

"Could this wind be manufactured?" I ask as Armonk tries unsuccessfully to steer the glider back to an upright position for the third time. "Do you think the NanoPearl techs know so much bioscience that they create these unnatural winds and clouds to hide their headquarters?"

Blane, next to Armonk in the front, grips the hand rests during another abrupt upside-down spin. "That would be a disaster. What if they can even make their place invisible?"

Armonk groans. "That would mean if they don't want to be found we won't find them, and also, if we get trapped inside, *we'll* never be found."

"Guys, calm down, we can't afford to concentrate on all the negatives," I plead, feeling no surer of things than they are. The terror leapfrogs to all of us—the downside of the automatic stroma flow.

In the backseat, Thorn presses his hand in mine. *Ask the Reds.*

How? I think.

We see the invisible they answer. The Reds *eep* frantically in the cargo hold below, their snouts tap on the floor below our feet. *Out! Out!*

Kneeling down, Thorn starts to fiddle with the cargo latch as the Reds go wild underneath it. I help him lift the cargo door, and the Reds burst out, falling over each other in their haste to do the mission. Thorn picks four of them, placing them one by one on the lip of the glider window, now closed. It's no easy task to nudge the rest of the Reds back down in the hold. They make sharp *eeps* of protest. But we manage.

At least for the time being the wind's died down, so Armonk steers the hovercraft as close to the dense cloud formation as he can to make up for the distance lost to drift.

I help Thorn open the back window and the four Reds leap out in a wild flutter of wings. They burrow through the thick haze and disappear.

Armonk frowns as he stares at the clouds. "Where did they go?"

"Steer!" Blane orders. "Go in the direction they flew in."

When Armonk guides the ship into the gauzy core, we lose all sight of sky and ground as if we're stuck in the mother of all sandstorms. No visibility whatsoever.

Then comes the thrumming, very faint at first, then louder, in our heads.

Windows, windows, windows.

"Windows, eh?" With narrowed eyes and white knuckles, Armonk blindly presses forward. "There! I see the orb," he exclaims as it slides out of the cloud cover.

"I see one of its windows," I yell and point to it.

"Careful, Armonk, we're almost touching the frying thing," Blane hisses.

It's true. Armonk's guided the ship within inches of the orb's vast curved shell. The windows, if you could call them that, are long, narrow and few. In fact, I count only two on this side. Set in the huge round globe they look like sideways alien eyes. The Reds have already zeroed in on one, and are flitting madly around it.

Armonk levels the ship to that window and cranes his neck to study it. "It's sealed."

"Looks as if the Reds have found a slit underneath the window though." Blane opens his window for a better view.

"Some kind of extra ventilation system," Armonk guesses.

"It's very slim. An inch tall and about six inches wide," I gauge.

The Reds peck and fret over the slit. Clearly, they know what they're there to do. I glance at Thorn, biting his nails, and in front at Blane, jiggling his big, booted foot.

Silently I command the Reds. *Squeeze, squeeze, squeeze your way in.*

Everyone starts concentrating on my silent chant. In response, the Reds peck harder.

Thorn lets out a whoop of victory when the first Red finally squirms his head in, and wriggles in sideways, wing-by-wing. We cheer as the other three follow suit.

"No doubt there are armed guards in there," Armonk says.

"The Reds will need to disarm them somehow," Blane decides.

Feel the Reds. Direct them, Thorn thinks.

Turning to each other across the seat backs, we bow our heads and spread our arms across each other's shoulders. Our silent humming picks up velocity. Its energy directs us to a mutual point of thought, of feeling, of language. *Disarm, disarm, disarm, confuse, confuse* we chant inwardly.

In my mind's eye, I see the Reds swarm the guard closest to the window. In my chest, I feel the force of them charging him, over and over, nipping at his head, his hands. "The guard's panicking," I whisper.

"I feel that too," Blane says.

"One Red is jabbing its wings in the guard's eyes. Another one is pecking at his cheeks," mumbles Armonk.

We hear the guard in our brains: *What do you want, you crazy birds? How did you get in here?* We feel him stagger to the window and release the automatic lock in frantic hope that the critters will opt out.

The orb window gapes open.

Now, we decide. I reach down and lift the cargo door. Dozens of Reds swarm up, jabbing at the window.

Release us, release us! they demand.

Cover the security cameras, we tell them.

But first, help me get in, I instruct.

The second I open the window, the Reds zoom out. Half of them fly inside and the rest, hovering, wait for me.

"I'll go in and dose the guards," I say.

"Good luck," Armonk says.

Blane squeezes my hand. "We'll be right behind you."

I climb onto the undulating carpet of Reds they've formed like a magical woven basket to hold me aloft. They deliver me gracefully to the orb's window. I sense that the Reds who have already flown in are covering the security cameras with their pliable bodies.

My vials at the ready, I leap off and through the orb window. The burly guard, dressed in jackboots and a NanoPearl logoed jumpsuit, wheels around with a scowl and a cry of shock. He raises his weapon, an odd looking blaster with tiny blinking lights. With everything I've got, I attack him before he can fire by leaping on him and smearing elixir over his face and hands. The salve's effect is instantaneous. He groans as phlegm drips from his mouth. Drooping inch by inch to the floor, he sticks one sluggish arm out to brace his fall and then crumples like a doll that's lost its stuffing.

I yank up his shirt, and spread salve, on his stomach and back—anywhere there's exposed skin. The more I smear on, the longer he'll stay zonked. And I want him zonked a whole lot longer than my demo lizard at the Axiom contest. Then I stuff his blaster in the waistband of my suit.

Dashing back to the window, I signal for the others to enter. Armonk secures the glider to the frame, and a contingent of Reds zooms out to ferry the guys in. Once in, Armonk adjusts his bow and helps Thorn slide inside. With all of his muscle mass, Blane has the hardest time squeezing in. The Reds soar around us, forming a crimson tide.

We blink at the flickering light in the hall. Its tremulous

strobe reminds me of the carnival funhouse the elders made for us children in one of their rare playful moods.

Once my eyes adjust it's clear that the hallway itself is dark, but a series of animated holograms, at intervals, spark the darkness to light. They're almost as high as the ceiling. Some holos are spinning, while others jag maniacally up and down. As long as they don't come near me I'm okay.

"Which way should we go?" I glance over at Thorn, our truest weathervane.

His eyes run down the length of hallway, as if he's scanning what exists behind the surface. Then he wheels around and studies the hall from the other direction. Along this section, I see a few side doors. "How about those office doors—"

"No office." Thorn stops and closes his eyes. "Warehouse."

"Which way?" I whisper. He shrugs. The Reds seem momentarily confused too. They perch on the rafters, nervously chattering.

"Let's huddle," Armonk suggests. When we take each other's hands and stand in a closed circle the air around us seems to talk.

Don't damage us. We're part of you. Don't damage us.
Get us out of here, free us, get us out of here!

It's confusing because even though the message is contradictory my inner core tells me it's coming from the same source. During our huddle, the Reds careen overhead, from one end of the hall to the other as they *eep* loudly. I worry that their nervous chatter will give us away.

Don't damage us, a stranger's voice pleads.
Destroy them, destroy them runs a contradictory line.

Again, I have the same strong feeling these lines are coming from the same source. Can't say why; it makes no sense. I look around our circle and whisper, "Who wants to destroy us?"

Judging by everyone's mystified expressions no one has an answer. Yet, while we're still in the huddle, our feet begin to carry us along the first hallway.

As we proceed, the holographic ghoul closest to us skitters over. Its light is blinding at close range, but when I blink to adjust, I see it's a spinning, larger-than-life replica of the same tiny tech device that was implanted in Thorn's brain. But this one has eerie, gleaming knobs where eyes would be. Its animated prongs look truly real and terrifying, as if with a thrust, one could pierce my heart.

"Shoo!" I manage.

In response it hovers so close that its light brushes my skin, its prongs assault my torso with sharp tentacles of light. It's not that it hurts, but it's frightening in its unpredictability.

"Get away!" Armonk bats his hand at it. The holo doesn't seem to like this. It jumps forward and literally invades Armonk, its massive light making Armonk glow as if he's polluted with radiation.

"We said lay off, bud," Blane snarls. He pushes us forward, swerving around the holo. We pick up speed, moving away from it.

But it catches up. In jerky movements it launches its transparent body at Blane, and it starts to babble in a gravelly voice. "Data collection tools are a must in this dangerous era. You need us."

The Reds try to peck at it, but their snouts dive right through it. The holo goes on. "As Adam, I'm everyman, helping you discover the devious secrets of others. Collection tools are a must in this era of pre-war."

"Pre-war?" Blane scoffs, "Who the hell are you really, *Adam*?"

As if the holo *is* a man, it starts explaining the dangers of pre-war without actually explaining what pre-war is. "You'll be in danger of losing your money, your house, even your mind. You'll need every nanotool for the ramp up. NanoPearl and I, Adam, have partnered for the future."

"You're a freaking ad, aren't you?" Blane jeers. "You stupid tool! You're worse than those stupid Stream ads."

"Tool," parrots Adam. "Tool. I'm the best pre-war tool ever." Finally, with one glazed stare back at us, Adam bumps down the hall from the direction "he" came.

Blane wipes sweat from his brow. "Holy Fire, that thing was obnoxious." Clearly, the transparent stalker has unnerved him. Blane is used to knocking down enemies with two solid legs and a fleshy torso that he can neatly tackle and pin to the floor.

"If this is who we're fighting, get ready for a different kind of fight," Armonk warns. "An arrow or elixir won't work on a stalking hologram."

The next holo, a black, oblong device with two red nubs for eyes, also babbles about the ramp-up. But it signals a worse problem. Right behind it, a real flesh and blood guard is marching our way, doing his rounds. He's got a massive neck and shoulders, and he's holding some type of futuristic looking weapon.

"Crap!" Blane whispers. "Why'd I let you talk me out of my gun?"

"Halt," orders the guard when he sees us. He raises his weapon.

The Reds rocket into action, swarming the guy. He stumbles as he fends them off.

Blane dives, tackling him at the ankles and they crash down together. As the man's weapon bounces away, I see Armonk reach for it and stuff it in his side pocket. I join the melee, desperately smearing elixir wherever I can, across the guard's wide face, his callused hands and, yanking up his uniform pants, over his legs. He slumps down like a sloppy drunk. Blane clambers up and asks Armonk for the guy's weapon. I guess Blane gets a gun after all, if he can figure out how to use it.

We only have a moment before the third holo whirs our way. This one is shimmery yellow, with wormy fronds spiraling out of where its head and torso would be if it were a man. "Nod here. I'll be your seventh sense during pre-war. I have teamed up with NanoPearl in this dangerous ramp-up time." Its "eyes" rudely ogle us up and down.

The Reds charge it, but their leafy wings sail right through its ghostly core.

"Nod, here, Nod, here," it repeats. Somehow the Reds have flummoxed its promo rap. "When you need to ferret out the enemy, use Nod here, Nod here."

Thorn barrels right through this holo, and runs to the end of the hall. With that, the holo spins away and dissolves.

Warehouse door thinks Thorn, and his thought shudders through us all. *In there, in there, in there.*

An infuriated chorus from behind it strikes back at us. *Destroy them, destroy them!*

There's no one standing between that last door and us. We can power into that warehouse now, finally see what the stroma wants from us. Except that a forbidding wash of danger crashes toward us, warding us away. It's so strong that it nearly knocks me to my knees.

I brace myself with Blane's hand, and he, in turn takes Thorn's. Thorn reaches for Armonk's. We all sense it, a fearful machine.

Fearful machine whirs the stroma. *Fearful machine, fearful machine.*

Fear not, I'm part of you. Fear not comes the retort from inside the warehouse, trying to convince us.

Destroy them, destroy them, destroy them another invisible wave rolls through the door, sending us all into baffled confusion.

Two parts of the one breathes Thorn, deep in his stroma trance. *Two parts divided.*

So that's why I sensed it came from the same entity! Thorn's ability amazes me.

Blane breaks the human link to march over and jiggle the door handle. It's not budging.

I point to an outline of a hand embedded on the wall. "ID pad, upper left."

Blane curses under his breath as he scrambles back to the guard, still passed out down the hall. He drags him toward the door by his limp arms. Armonk helps haul him by grabbing the guy's jackboots. Blane pauses before pressing the guard's hand on the ID scanner. He gives us each a pointed look. "Once I do this, we'll need to be ready for anything. Got it?"

We nod. As he matches the guard's hand to the flat screen print, the door clicks open to a scene more frightening than my worst Stile's nightmare.

30

We look down from a platform to a vast stretch of factory, larger than anything conceivable are rows upon rows upon rows of monstrous Reds, each in its own pod, custom-molded to its massive wingspan, its hawkish head and leathery torso. The way they're hooked up to sensors and what look like feeding tubes reminds me of carnivorous dinosaurs, half-grown, yet still nested. These beings are clearly derivative of our Reds, but they're not cute and leafy. They are geometrically jagged like the rocks of Skull's Wrath. Their blood red wings have scaly, angular planes as if they're designed to fly as swiftly as the rockets the world knew before the Border Wars, the rockets Nevada drew diagrams of in her history lessons. Rockets of fire that were meant to populate other planets. These beasts bask in the glow from the skylight above.

No, these aren't the Reds we know and love. Not at all. These beings are as big as giant gliders. They raise their necks, narrow their beady eyes at us and gnash their sharpened pickaxe teeth.

Jaws gaping, they snarl at us. The clamor eats at my brain: *Enemy dares come here, enemy dares come here, enemy dares come here!*

And their own baffling counter refrain: *I am you, I am you, I am you.*

Why is their message so ambiguous? Are their ranks divided? Blane and I exchange troubled looks, and then we glance over at Armonk and Thorn to see if they understand. We all have the same desperate impulse: *go into the huddle.* But there's no time.

Because live human watchmen are rising from a handful of the pods.

Armonk flies into action, raising his bow and aiming, firing, aiming. A few of the watchmen go down, but others are stalking toward us.

Blane fumbles at the lights and levers of the pilfered weapon to figure out how it works. Our own Reds, in the meantime, glom onto the watchmen who are reaching for their same narrow-barreled guns.

One guard flips open his holophone to call for backup. "Main office? Reporting a—" he starts until our Reds dive-bomb his face.

I creep up from the back, reach around and slather elixir in his eyes. Nasty move, but we need this to work instantly.

"Frying hell!" the guard scrabbles at his eyes, trying to wipe them clean. As he does this, Armonk lands an arrow in his back. The guard grunts, falls and his holophone clunks to the floor in a stark splotch of his blood. That'll keep him down. I race on to my next mark.

Blane has figured out how to shoot the weapon. It's a taser with all of the bells and whistles, including a high-pitched digital shriek as the thing hits its mark. The next two guards seize up in spasms, while I swoop in to paralyze.

We must be venomous and swift, and we are, because there are five more men coming at us. Thorn guides the Reds to create interference, Blane tackles, Armonk shoots his arrows, and the moment I see a watchman down I smear my elixir in his eyeballs, his mouth, on his exposed neck.

The last guard manages to trip me. I hit my chin hard on the textured floor. He whirls around and zaps me as I try to deal with the throbbing pain in my jaw. As I convulse from his taser, I see Blane, firing at the man's torso.

Blane hauls me to my feet as this last watchman goes down in fits, clutching at his chest. Turns out I've only been hit on my shoulder. It burns like crazy but I can function.

All during this time, the monstrous Reds continue to struggle against their thick restraints. As they writhe, they release terrifying, ear-shattering roars.

You! You! You will pay for this invasion.

Who knows how much more time we have before they explode out of their binding. If they do, we'll be crushed.

We did not come here for murderous, bloody slaughter I think.

Thorn looks my way. *We need to use our real power. Remember what we are.*

What we're capable of Armonk joins in without speaking.

Raising my arms and face to the skylight, I soak in the sun and gather my strength, my shared power to transmit silent messages. *Let's ask the monsters questions* I suggest to my friends. *Trump them at their games.*

Armonk, Blane and Thorn receive my message, I know this by the way they pause, head my way, and raise their own faces to the skylight—for energy, for direction.

The monsters can hear us, Thorn says silently. *So, talk to them.*

Who are you? I try to ask them. *Who are you and why did they create you?*

For war, for war, for war they shoot back.

We are you, we are you, we are you they also insist.

But who do you think we are? Armonk asks them. *We were not created for war. You're different.*

The monsters snap their backs up and down. *How dare you, how dare you!*

No different, no different, no different than you comes the retort from their very own faction.

You are killing machines, killing machines and that's all! Blane scolds. His silent proclamation blazes through the warehouse, inspiring a fiercer rally amongst the monsters.

We are you, we are you, the power, the power, the power of Reds, of the Fireseed, the Fireseed they insist as they writhe and thump their massive wings against their pods.

You are only part from us, part from us say our friendly Reds.

If you're us, then you cannot be war machines I say without words.

They're us and they're not us our own Reds explain as they soar overhead. *Us and not us.*

If you're made for war Thorn tells the monsters *you must destroy yourselves.*

Destroy yourselves. Destroy yourselves to save the stroma from contamination! we chant fervently in our heads now that we've begun to figure things out. The part that *is* us, NanoPearl stole from Thorn's mind and from the Reds they captured. The parts that aren't, well, those are gruesome adaptations designed to wage war, for mass slaughter. God only knows what lethal weaponry they contain. I never want to find out.

We are more than copies, more than copies the Red beasts insist. There's a deafening pop and we see that one of them has broken his neck binding. He swings his massive head toward us and roars. We stumble back, shaken. Our Reds are shaken too. They lunge at the great beast's eyes to taunt him.

Time is running out I try to convey privately but the beasts hear me too.

Running out! Running out, the emboldened one roars. *Your time is running out!* He struggles mightily against his remaining leg binds. Raising his snout, he snatches one, then two more of our Reds and clamps his powerful jaw closed, gobbling them whole.

The rest of our Reds shriek but keep their distance.

How dare you! I scold silently.

The Reds are ours to eat the monsters insist.

We are not yours our Reds *eep* back as they careen around the monsters.

These mutants are, in truth split, tortured souls. They must know, in their core, just as the Fireseed does, as Armonk always insisted, that if there is enough emotional turmoil and contamination in their ranks that their sacred duty is to immolate and self destroy.

You must immolate. Self destroy we chant to them inwardly.

We raise our rallying cry until every part of us vibrates as one. One hive, one solar battery, one mind of the great Fireseed.

Our Reds swarm overhead, squawking in a manner I've never heard before now. They're reprimanding their monstrous counterparts. *You cannibals, cannibals, cannibals!* The warlike Reds still trapped in their binds, snap back, their teeth gleaming.

Immolate, immolate, immolate our little Reds screech while they race in faster and faster circles, as if they're stirring a boiling pot brimming with healing elixir, designed to fix something irretrievably broken. *Immolate!*

Blane steps out of our circle and raises his gun to the monster that has just broken free of its leg bindings. "You'll pay for killing our Reds," he growls.

"No, Blane!" I shout. "Come back."

"This thing will kill us all if I don't do it first," he insists.

But he won't kill the beast with a taser; he'll only aggravate it. A wave of sheer terror crashes through me when Blane steps closer and fires. The monster unleashes a torrent of infuriated howls as its claws reach out like curled sabers.

And then, its jaw gaping, one of its sharp teeth ejects at Blane. *Made for war* it growls. Its tooth rockets through the air, plunging deep into Blane's thigh. Blane moans and drops, blood spurting onto the floor.

I want to shoot at the thing so badly. It's hurt Blane, and killed our Reds. The second taser is tucked in my sock. I could reach down and grab it. But it won't kill it; only rouse it to further rage. We need to keep working together to raise the energy of the stroma. It's the only way. My heart batters hard against my ribs.

Armonk, Thorn and I increase the decibel of our silent chant: *Immolate, immolate!* My head pounds as sap and blood press against my ears. My legs shudder under me and threaten to buckle.

From the corner of my vision, I see a flame ignite from one of the monster's mechanical nostrils. Then a dozen beasts are beating at creeping flames! They wail, plaintively, pathetically *we are you, we are you, do not destroy us.*

I sense Armonk's momentary hesitation. *Don't listen* I command my friends.

We renew our chant. An entire row of monstrous wings light up like dry kindling, and then another three rows.

Armonk and I dash over to Blane and help him stagger back to our circle. We agree not to remove the projectile in his thigh until we're safely in the glider, if we make it back. The danger of him bleeding out is too acute.

The warehouse rings out with monstrous *eeps* and snarls, the great thrashing of wings and teeth. With this, it's all we can do to keep our concentration on the message at hand: *The stroma is divided, contaminated by warmongers. Immolate!*

We hold to our circle, vibrating, sweating and coughing from the smoke until the whole army of vicious Reds detonates into flames. Our lungs scald with smoldering chemical particles as we struggle back through the hall, plunging right through the holos who still stalk us as they bark out their warlike wares. Our own Reds blanket us, providing a protective layer as we go.

Making our way out of the window, wounded but triumphant, we ride on our own devoted Reds to our glider before the warehouse can explode.

In the vehicle, it takes all three of us to yank the monstrous tooth from Blane's leg. He moans in pain as I slather on my healing elixir, bind the raw flesh with my jacket and dose him with numbing salve so he'll sleep through the worst of it.

The Reds are sad, telling us silently that they hated to kill spawn sprung in part from their own genes, no matter how horrifying the beings were.

But we know that we did the right thing, because a harmonious, relieved thrumming stirs in our hearts.

Thank you, beauties, thank you sing the Fireseed from a thousand miles away.

You're welcome, we sing back.

31

George Axiom's secretary serves us iced sea-grape mead in goblets, and it flows down our parched throats faster than she can sneak in her next furtive peek at us. We look a fright, with our clothes torn and bloodied and purple bruises galore. Not to mention the four Reds clucking and eeping on Thorn's shoulders. Thorn insisted on taking these with him if he had to leave most of them in the cargo hold. I don't argue with my brother. Surely he's got a good reason for it.

The secretary, in a breezy shell-buttoned dress, looks up from her holo tablet and says, "He'll see you now."

As she escorts us to his penthouse office I think about our earlier escape from NanoPearl. We slithered out of the narrow window just as the first guard shook himself from his stupor, and from a mile away we could see the flames engulf the orb, like some mad planet in its death throes. We raced down in the glider to the hovercraft piers and stretched out, exhausted, on a sliver of beach behind the Skye Ride lounge.

We soaked in as much solar food as we dared before it fried our skin. Then we bathed in the brackish surf and combed our hands through our tangled hair until we looked half presentable. I let Blane sleep until the elixir started to heal his flesh. Truth be told, I could've slept on that beach too, for hours. But we're here to take care of unfinished business.

As we enter George's suite, he rises to greet us, shaking all of our hands and even stretching out a friendly finger to one of the Reds blinking at him in midair with curious eyes. "What brings you Greening students back to our city?" George asks, as he looks us up and down. I sense him almost remark that we're looking fine but then deciding that between my horribly swollen chin and Blane's ripped burnsuit and homemade leg bandage we aren't looking anything of the sort.

We hesitate in front of his plush sofas until he gestures for us to grab a seat. Armonk starts. "We need to report a crime, well actually a slew of criminal activity." Armonk levels his famously dark, intense look at George.

"A crime at The Greening?" George clears his throat. "That's not quite my jurisdiction."

"Then who's in charge over there?" Blane sends George an equally stony stare to rival Armonk's.

"I suppose we could stretch to include Skull's Wrath, since there's not much of a government over there aside from Marney at the Depot," George answers with an arch of his brows. So Marney's larger-than-life persona has filtered all the way to Vegas-by-the-Sea. "Tell me what the problem is."

I say, "It seems that Stazzi, your judge from the Axiom Contest has not only stolen a student contest creation, but has illegally implanted a phishing device in this student's head to suck out that concept." Blane wraps an arm around Thorn, who nods at George.

George's face contorts into a disturbed grimace, but he says nothing.

Thorn says slowly, "It was me, my project. These Reds," he murmurs, gesturing to the Reds, now nuzzling his hair.

"Your project? With those... those birds?" Is George's memory that bad? I distinctly recall talking to him at The Greening before he flew off and confronting him about Thorn not winning. Or is he willing himself to forget?

"They're not birds," I remind him. "They're half Fireseed and half human, as I told you before you left The Greening on finalist pick day. And I said that they deserved to win your contest, hands down." I pause for this to sink in. "Clearly NanoPearl wanted that concept without paying for it."

The spark of recognition in George's eye suggests that maybe he doesn't think too highly of NanoPearl either; that he may have had his own run-ins with them. Though he snaps, "You're making some major accusations here. What gives you the right?"

Blane reaches in his latchbag and presents the device he surgically removed from Thorn's neck. "Ever seen this type of Nanotech?"

George rotates it gingerly between thumb and index finger. Taking a napkin from his desk he places the implant on it as if he's afraid it may contaminate him. "Can't say I have. This does have the NanoPearl logo on it but anyone could have implanted this. What exact proof is there that Stazzi from NanoPearl stole your, uh, concept?"

Blane holds up a wing section from the monstrous NanoPearl Red he managed to break off at the warehouse. "As you may recall, I'm an expert at decoding genomes, and this sample from NanoPearl will prove, when decoded, that their formula for this hybrid chimera is a blatant and direct thievery of this young man's invention."

George rubs his forehead as if this news has just given him a horrendous, throbbing headache, which I'm sure it has, metaphorically if not physically. "M-my word!" he stammers.

"In addition to the illegal actions of NanoPearl and Stazzi," Blane says, "A Greening student named Jan should also be arrested for accepting a payoff from Stazzi to put young Thorn in harm's way."

"Yeah, and a student named Vesper, for being an accomplice," I add.

With this, George begins jotting down info on his holo tablet. "I'll look into these matters."

"Right away, please," says Armonk. "These students are tied up and under watch at our school, but we'll need immediate help removing them before they cause further harm. They are quite dangerous."

I stare at George. "By the way how did you decide on which judges to use? Did they give you perks or what? Because we all remember the little, um, last minute disagreement with Stazzi over the Axiom prize. I mean, you're a *governor* of the sector, and as such, you're not supposed to favor one corporation over another, right?" My brother is furiously shaking his head at me.

"I don't know what you're insinuating," George retorts. He scowls at me and then at Blane. "May I ask, how you happened to get a piece of the NanoPearl hybrid?"

It's my turn to flush from nerves. My brother isn't just shaking his head at me; he's pinching me. I went too far by suggesting that George let Stazzi and NanoPearl buy him off. The chain could totally crack if we unspool all of it now. I suppose everyone has his or her price. It's a matter of degree.

We need to catch the most poisonous lizard first. I smile. "Let's just say that we had unexpected and unprecedented access."

"We have our ways," says Blane, pointedly flexing his muscles. "There are many underhanded things happening at that, um, NanoPearl warehouse," Blane shakes his head, "that the head of a big sector like yours would not want to be associated with in any way."

"Well, no, I have a good name," he mumbles. "My family's been here for generations."

Armonk nods at George. "And I'm sure you'd like to keep it that way. A scandal would do you no good. Ruin your chances of reelection."

With this, another spark of understanding gleams in George's eyes. He snorts. "Stazzi *can* be a bit overbearing." So, it wasn't my imagination that he was rolling his eyes at Stazzi during that ballroom dispute. By the sound of his snort, he'd love nothing more than to slap a pair of handcuffs on her if he has ample reason. "I'll get on these claims immediately." He pauses to really look at each of us, one by one, as if he's seeing us for the very first time. "I'm so sorry you experienced these difficulties. Is there anything else?"

Oh, yes, there's more, a lot more. I explain that Jan attacked our teacher, Nevada, and that he murdered Dr. Varik. I tell him we're going to set up a memorial for the good doctor and that George and his people are invited. Then I ask him about the nature of Alex Dean's prize. "The fact that it's military," I say, "is disturbing, given that Axiom was a *student* contest."

"Yes." George sighs deeply as he tugs on one of his shell buttons. "I regret making that, um, decision." In his weighted pause, it's obvious that he was bought off, not only by NanoPearl but also by the well-heeled faculty at Baronland South. I feel sorry for him. He desperately needs a stronger rudder. He's so much weaker than I ever suspected Nevada of being. In contrast, Nevada is a mighty goddess who could hold up The Greening in her own bare hands. "Under the circumstances I'd like to suggest that you rethink the contest prize."

Armonk, Blane and Thorn gasp collectively at my pluck. I'm shocked at it myself.

I've inspired a flow though, because Armonk says, "What's all this war talk anyway? What is pre-war exactly, and the *ramp-up*?"

A look of astonished mortification comes over George as he jiggles his holo pen. "We've had skirmishes," he confides. "In the northwest sectors with Land Dominion. Some in our sector feel that we need to arm ourselves. Get ready for the moment our bounty's bigger than that in the north, because heaven knows, we were very unprepared before the Border Wars, unprepared for the wall they built, barring us from northern dominions." George looks weary, even his suit looks droopy and sad. I'll be an adult in a year, but I feel sorry for some of them, the ones who aren't totally grownup after all, yet playing dangerous war games.

Armonk pipes up. "I like your ideas better."

"Which ones?" George puts down his holo pen and leans forward.

"When you were so excited about all of the good things you were going to build in your city, all of the ways you would improve life down here." Armonk stops. "If the contest funds were reallocated, some of them could be distributed to

Nevada to fix up The Greening, and some sent to my home sector, Black Hills. There's no water there. People are suffering. You said your family drilled for wells. You'd be such a hero to so many."

"Young man, you make good sense," George scribbles down more notes on his holo pad.

"Oh, one last thing," I tell him. "I'd love to send word to my family back at the... the Fireseed compound in Chihuahua, that I'm okay. Will you please have a letter carried there for my mother?"

"The Fireseed compound, eh?" His disc-like eyes widen. I guess everyone knows about that cult. "Of course, glad to do it." George says, and squeezes my hands. He seems relieved that this last request is simple, and doable.

By the time we leave his office, we're bubbling with new ideas and hope. And George seems almost excited to have an expanded philanthropic role. He even assigns a trio of his armed guards to accompany us back.

We take one more hour at the Vegas beach to bask in the sun as the guards pace back and forth on the sand. Thorn splashes in the surf, Armonk does yoga and Blane's eyes shimmer ever more emerald as I apply one more dose of healing gel to his injured thigh. After our ordeal we deserve a few extra moments to soak in solar minerals. I grin as I imagine the looks on Vesper and Jan's faces when we return with an armed escort. But my glee fades to sadness when we discuss plans for Dr. Varik's memorial.

32

We hold Dr. Varik's memorial at our school, in the
fields that we deck out in strands of Fireseed
blossoms. The most spectacular ones, plucked
from his body, we display in a vase by his casket. He'll be
cremated and join the soil to fertilize it. The field could use
some help, as great swaths self-destructed during our turmoil
out at NanoPearl.

Moori's yurt family attends, as do many other dune
dwellers that Dr. Varik attended to. Moori is healthy and
pink-cheeked now, and her villagers are no longer suffering
from uncured insect bites. The people spring to the memorial

like lizards from their cave gardens. I'm amazed that Doctor Varik touched the lives of so many.

Earlier that morning, we took turns consoling Nevada, who was completely heartbroken by the doctor's death. We cooked her a breakfast in bed and Bea and I helped braid her hair.

"What would I do without you kids?" she'd asked as she gazed at the bunch of us circling her bed.

"We're not exactly kids," Armonk reminded her.

"Young men and women." She squeezed his hand.

"I think we've earned a few days off from lessons," I said.

"We all have." Nevada sighed and took a bite of yam loaf with sea-grape jam. "Delicious bread! The chef?"

Radius beamed. "That would be me."

After the memorial George Axiom helps perk up Nevada by donating a generous sum to The Greening for renovation and state of the art student labs. Nevada is deeply grateful.

Jan, Stazzi and Vesper are in holding cells in Vegas-by-the-Sea awaiting the trials of the century. When they first saw Axiom's guards marching with us the day we returned they were dumbfounded—at a loss for words. That is until they realized the guards were coming to escort them off to jail. Then, all manner of filthy curses broke loose from Vesper's mouth. Jan added in a few choice ones too.

"Lousy druggie," Vesper screeched at me, "I should have finished you off with the rest of your poison powder."

"You're the one who belongs in jail," Jan snarled at me as the guards cuffed him. "You and your brother invaded our school and ruined everything. Criminals!"

No one bothered with an answer. Not even the guards who dragged them off. How do you reason with four scoops of crazy? All I know is that we breathed a major sigh of relief when that Axiom glider took off for points west.

The guards told us that the prison overlooks the great blue Pacific. Picture the view! Funny, I imagine that Vesper and Jan's jails are cushy. Everything's glitzy in Vegas-by-the-Sea, so why not the jails? I bet they get tasty fried fish dinners and fancy jail outfits with shell buttons. Perhaps Jan will have some kind of great human turnaround, but I won't hold my breath.

I've gotten in touch with Caprice, the turbaned healer lady out there. Caprice wants to buy cartons of my elixirs for her clients. She wants to brainstorm with me to develop more outrageous cures and potions. Elixirs that make your wrinkles, depressions and love troubles disappear forever, and salves that enhance hearing and sight. Potions that could even make you fly. Sky's the limit, and that suits me fine.

I'm going to save every tarnished coin and crinkled Dominion bill, until I collect enough to set up my wave blue house with sky blue curtains on the coast. It'll be a sanctuary for friends and family, who I'm going to rescue from the cult, the second I figure out a foolproof plan.

First, I have to graduate. One more year—education before enterprise.

~

Today we're reseeding the decimated field. We have brimming satchels of seeds that George helped buy. We reluctantly donned our burnsuits and masks because it's a long, laborious job. We should really head out to different quadrants; it'd be so much faster that way. But we want to be together, after so much. Plus Armonk's heading to Black Hills tomorrow. George will fly him there and help drill his people their wells. That part is exciting. If I dwell on Armonk leaving, though I'll start bawling. We'll never return to the cockeyed house for talks, never again cook together as we share our innermost secrets.

But I have Blane—man of fire and soul. It makes sense, after all, that I ended up with the one who was a brute, yet blossomed into a sensitive, smart man. After all, I started as a drug-addled tease, whose method of connection was manipulation and seduction. You start with the tools you have at hand, but you don't have to end up using those same tools. We both transformed, not only our personalities, but through and through, as hybrids.

It's funny, the world and what you can become in it if you try.

As if Blane can hear my thoughts—of course he can—he leans over and plants a soft kiss on my forehead. I stand on tiptoes and kiss his too.

We work in a line, reaching in the bags and tossing out the pretty red seeds like confetti.

"Don't make yourself too scarce," I tell Armonk. "You'll have to visit me in Vegas-by-the-Sea next year. I want to introduce you to my best friends, Petal and Blossom." He's dark and tanned, but his blush peeks through.

"Your best friends?" Bea teases as she tosses a handful. "What about me?"

"Well, you're already spoken for, *best* friend."

"True," she says, and with this, Radius raises her mask and gives her a kiss.

Thorn tugs on Armonk's hand. He takes his dinosaur toy from his latchbag and hands it to Armonk.

"Really? You sure you want to give me this?" Thorn nods. Above his mask, Armonk ruffles Thorn's hair. "Okay, fair is fair. Got something for you too, little man." Armonk touches his shell necklace and lifts the twine over his head, lowers it over Thorn's head and adjusts it. "It's a tradition. This little man is now officially a big man."

Thorn laughs, loudly and freely. I've never seen his face so joyful.

We work for another hour, and as we do, the surviving plants thrum in thanks. We're filling in the charred patches and I can see the first baby fronds of Fireseed arc up from the ashes. My lord, this incredible plant grows fast.

The Reds flicker by our sides, and join the thrum. *Beauty, beauty, beauty!*

There's only an hour of sun left. The sky drifts to that magic place where violet and orange blend in candy swirls over the horizon line.

Out, out, out to the dunes we say to each other without saying. We throw off our burnsuits and masks. Our feet carry us out of the field and to the crescents of sand.

Rise up, up, up, beauties, stretch out, out, out, beauties.

Yes, we are beautiful, and yes, when we raise our arm-branches skyward they course with sap and blood and every single astounding lesson we learned this year.

If you enjoyed this novel, please consider writing an honest review on Amazon, Goodreads or your favorite online book spot. Thanks!

Subscribe to Catherine's newsletter to hear about new releases and appearances at www.catherinestine.com
Free downloadable study guide also available.

ABOUT THE AUTHOR

Catherine Stine's YA novels span the range from science fiction to dark fantasy to contemporary fiction. Her futuristic thriller, *Fireseed One* was a finalist in YA and SF in the USA News International Book Awards and is an Indie Reader Approved notable. Its companion novel, *Ruby's Fire* was a finalist in the Next Generation Indie Awards. Her YA paranormal/horror Dorianna, from Evernight Teen won Best Horror Book in the Kindle Hub Awards. She also writes new adult fiction as Kitsy Clare. Catherine suspects her love of dark fantasy came from her father reading Edgar Allen Poe to her when she was a child. She was also passionate about science fiction as a teen.

Visit her at
www.catherinestine.com and
www.catherinestine.blogspot.com.

ACKNOWLEDGEMENTS

Thanks to my insightful editor, Elizabeth Law, who was over in Paris eating croissants and sipping café au lait, and to Skype who made it possible to chat across the 'pond' with her; to my savvy writing group ladies: Holly Kowitt, Jan Carr, Susan Amesse and Emily Damron who walked along every step of the way with Ruby on her perilous journey; to my family, my sister, Kanta, sister-in-law, Ellen and my friends Tate and Helen, who all discussed plot, character, hybrid beasts and the future of the planet with me; to the ladies at Paragraph Writing Space, Joy Parisi and Lila Cecil, who supplied my literary cocoon and dozens of cups of tea from the electric pot.

And finally, but very importantly, to my wonderful online community of like-minded writers, bloggers and sovereign thinkers—you know who you are. Hugs to you all, your support is so very much appreciated!

QUESTIONS FOR DISCUSSION

Who is Ruby at the beginning of the novel and who is she by the end? What weaknesses and strengths does she have and how do those change?

How would you make your escape from the compound if you were Ruby? What skills (and even weaknesses) does she use to her advantage?

What does each student at the Greening bring to the table? How did their own difficult pasts shape their personalities?

What might you invent from the Fireseed plants, in considering their very special properties?

What other types of hybrid blends might be useful in the future? You can open up this concept to tools, people, animals, and even foods. Have fun with this one!

What are the major themes in Ruby's Fire, and what does the author seem to be saying about each theme as the novel progresses?

What is the author saying through the character of Nevada Pilgrim?

Through Blane?

Through Thorn?

What is your prediction for Ruby and Thorn? Do you see her ever being able to make her "blue fantasy house" a reality? What would you like to see happen in a future companion book?

***

Free, downloadable study guide with projects available on www.catherinestine.com

The adventure began in Fireseed One, the companion novel to Ruby's Fire, which takes place ten years earlier. But the Fireseed novels can be read in any order.

44016488R00162

Made in the USA
Charleston, SC
15 July 2015